THE HOUSE OF RAJANI

Alon Hilu

The House of Rajani

TRANSLATED
FROM THE HEBREW
BY

Evan Fallenberg

Harvill *Secker*
LONDON

Published by Harvill Secker, 2010

2 4 6 8 10 9 7 5 3 1

© Alon Hilu, 2008
English translation © Evan Fallenberg, 2010

First published in 2008 by Yedioth Sfarim, Israel

First published in Great Britain in 2010 by
HARVILL SECKER
Random House
20 Vauxhall Bridge Road
London SW1 2SA

Addresses for companies within The Random House Group Limited can be found at:
www.randomhouse.co.uk/offices.htm

The Random House Group Limited Reg. No. 954009
www.randomhouse.co.uk

A CIP catalogue record for this book is available from the British Library

This book was published with the financial assistance of the
Institute for the Translation of Hebrew Literature

ISBN 9781846552991

Typeset in Adobe Jenson
by SX Composing DTP, Rayleigh, Essex
Printed and bound in Great Britain by
the MPG Books Group

Dedicated to the memory of my classmate
Vered Csillag (1971–96)

'We destroyed them and their people . . . So those are their houses fallen down because they were unjust . . .'

The Holy Qur'án, Chapter 27 (The Ant), verses 51–2

PREFACE

This book is based on the letters and diaries of Isaac Luminsky, agronomist and member of the First Aliya.

The language of Luminsky's diary, written in the authentic Hebrew of the late nineteenth century, has been retained. Undated and unsigned pages in Arabic were found appended to the black-bound diary that proved to be journal entries and short stories written at the same time as Luminsky's (1895–6) by a young man named Salah, scion of the celebrated Rajani family of Jaffa. The publisher has taken the liberty of translating Salah Rajani's diary and stories into modern Hebrew and publishing them now, more than a hundred years after they were written, along with Luminsky's diary.

Late summer/autumn, 1895

The eighteenth day of the month of Av in the year 5655 – 8 August 1895 – aboard a ship bound for Jaffa

I have resolved to record my words in this diary for fear, otherwise, of taking leave of my senses. Our small and narrow cabin in the depths of this ship imprisons my thoughts; if I do not share them post-haste I should best jump herewith into the sea.

The root of all my troubles and complaints is Her Ladyship, known legally and familiarly as Esther, like the Biblical queen – and regal she is. More beautiful than beauty itself: thin, tall and erect, high-cheekboned. Were I Esther's King Ahasuerus, I would certainly offer half my kingdom for a mere glimpse of those limpid eyes bluer than the sea.

The first I heard of her, she was a student of dentistry in Warsaw. I sought her out, caught the splendour of her countenance, and at once my heart was pricked by love's needle. This maiden would be the object of my affections for ever, my beloved spouse unto eternity, a member of God's heavenly choir. The timbre of her voice was like the fluttering of dew over a garden bed of spices, her gowns layers of the finest gauze, her hair shiny and golden. Any man who did not fall for her charms had no right to call himself a man.

It was not long before I procured her agreement, then that of her parents, and we were joined in holy matrimony. My joy knew no bounds. And yet scarcely a few hours had passed from our time under the wedding canopy before the first hint of Her Ladyship's true nature became apparent. We were standing in the bridal chamber, our first moments alone as man and wife, when I unbuttoned my waistcoat and placed my top hat on the bureau while Her Ladyship remained immobile in her white wedding gown.

'Come, let man rejoice with his wife,' I said to her.

'Now is not the hour,' said she.

'Do you feel nothing?' I queried.

'I wish to rest awhile,' came her response.

She had scarcely finished speaking when, without waiting for the lantern to be extinguished, she began removing her clothing until every last stitch was gone, and then she walked about in her nakedness, her ivory breasts and soft pink nipples taunting my impatient eyes. Her Ladyship prostrated herself on the bed, turned her back to me and fell asleep at once.

On the morrow I drew near her with words of seduction and love, but yet again she was not of a mind to take part in the intimate relations I had intended. True, she was no longer tired or fatigued; rather, the cause was in the psyche. To hear her tell it she was sunk in the despondency of a new bride faced with an act of contrariness and change, with this shift from the impetuous recklessness of life in the singular to that of the conjugal, to be husbanded by a husbanding husband.

In order to avoid causing her grief or, heaven forfend, the famed melancholy of those who place themselves in the stocks of marriage, I suppressed my desire and left her in peace. Silently I told myself that I would wait to see when Her Ladyship's loving passion would awaken and she would come to my bed with reddened cheeks and flaming nipples, her body sweet and dripping juicily.

To my great misfortune, Her Ladyship stayed her course on the nights to come as well. On those evenings, before we made preparations to retire, she removed her clothing and moved about as a lady might among her eunuchs, her alabaster thighs succulent, her breasts two pomegranates full to the bursting. But if I made it clear to her that I wished to fulfil the pleasant obligation of a husband, she would dismiss me with all manner of excuses and fits of ill humour.

I began to entertain thoughts I shared with myself alone: perhaps Her Ladyship had given up her virginity to some other man in a fit of youthful frivolity and she was full of shame at the indiscretion, or perhaps she had fallen prey to the seduction of one of her fellow students of dentistry, whose desire was strong upon them. Otherwise why would they enjoy mangling the flesh of their peers?

Three days had passed since our nuptials and she was still unknown territory to me. I hinted to Her Ladyship that it made no matter to me whether she be a virgin or not and that I wished she would permit me to enter her gates at last. Her Ladyship issued a brief and nervous laugh and said that a modern girl like herself would certainly be well versed in the ways of the world and the ways of a man with a woman.

'Well, then,' I told her, 'show me these ways.'

And she said, 'Not at this moment.'

'And why not?' I answered, visibly angered.

I determined that, as far as her mind was concerned, she was fit and ready for the act, even desirous and wholly wishful that it should take place, but with regard to the mechanics of it her organs constricted and puckered and she was plunged into a state of great pain and asked to postpone it by two days, or three at the very latest.

I squelched my fury and said, 'My beauty, I will therefore come unto you on the morrow, Friday, be what may.'

Her Ladyship held her tongue.

To myself, I pondered and wondered at these ways of hers. Perhaps the male sex held no interest for Her Ladyship, only the female. Indeed, this matter, for generations considered the realm of the perverse and the insane, had begun to take root among the women of Europe. I have even heard that in Berlin and in Vienna women roam the streets crop-haired, holding hands in public view, their tongues engaged one with the other. While I was thinking these thoughts, Her Ladyship slipped the garments off her body in preparation for bathing and sleep, and at the sight of this purity – the sweet body of woman inviting acts of love – I banished these evil thoughts. Perhaps it was just bad luck: on the first day she had been fatigued from the nuptials, on the second she had been saddened by her new state of marriage, and now, a week later, her muscles had conspired to rout all desire.

On Friday, towards nightfall, I left Her Ladyship in our bed and went to the pantry to fetch a bottle of brandy, which I opened for the purpose of bringing human joy to her and to remove all obstacles to our love and conjugality. When I returned to the bedroom I found Her Ladyship lying prone and naked across the bedclothes.

'My dove,' I cooed mellifluously.

To which she responded, in a cold and measured voice, 'Do with me as you will.'

I drew near, kissed her mouth. Her Ladyship parted her lips ever so slightly. I inserted my tongue and found her own blocking mine, as if to say, 'Thou shall not proceed.'

Kissing a beloved to the depths of her moist mouth is one of the most beautiful gifts given to man. What a pity it would be to lose such a precious gift, but I told myself that not every woman is expert in the mechanics of kissing and, in fact, it had already happened in the annals of history that the worst of kisses had turned into the best. All it took was a husband to instruct his woman and guide her in this most pleasant of tasks.

I began to prepare for intercourse. Now Her Ladyship was pursed and clenched in her entirety: not only her lips, but her thighs, too, clung to one another like a besieged city guarding itself against an army of invading marauders. I touched my fingers to her hair and caressed her face, wishing to bring her to the path of desire. The body of a woman is created from a strange and different mould that one must learn intimately. It must be completely subjugated and only then speared. Subjugation must be brought about slowly, never in haste, first only in words, then in flirtatious enticements, then in sweet whispers, and only after that in hints of lovemaking, followed by kisses and embraces and, at last, a long while later, the act itself, to its completion.

Her Ladyship, however, sealed her ears to my kind words and pressed upon me to carry out the act, then leave her in peace. Neither did she warm to my caresses due to her excessive ticklishness. So, I went directly to her aperture, but here I did not derive any pleasure. And why was that? Because the land that awaited me between her pursed thighs was desolate, a desert with no oasis, sevenfold more parched than the Sahara and the Negev together. So cleaved and recalcitrant was it that there would be no furrowing there without great effort.

As I lay atop her nakedness, attempting to know her, Her Ladyship moaned loudly. 'Are these moans of love?' I asked her.

'No. Of pain,' she replied.

In the month that passed from the day of our wedding, that was the one and only time that we conjoined. As each passing day pummelled me, my wrath grew. For her part, Her Ladyship behaved as was her wont each evening: she peeled off her clothing, exposing her curvaceous body, but permitted no touching, reciting one among a number of excuses. Once she claimed to be unfit for the act because she felt anxious and tumultuous in light of bad tidings of anti-Semites making life hard for Jews; another time she had grown sad due to grey clouds in the sky; on a third occasion she was entirely ready but her pubis was attacked by a worm of some persistence, or a rare redness, or a creeping fungus, and she ordered me to squelch my desire forthwith.

At present, we are sailing towards a new life in the Land of Zion, where we shall live by our ideals among farmers and vine-growers on our ancient land, that of the Jewish people. If ever a man hoped that a sea breeze would cause a woman to weaken and become submissive to him, her soul receptive and desirous, he was deceived and deceiving. Her Ladyship has been completely preoccupied with her seasickness; thus, it has been nigh impossible to approach her on any matter. Even a request for the slightest smile is out of the question as she is nauseous and convulsive.

We are housed in a small cabin on board this ship, and Her Ladyship can observe every movement made by her husband. She does not find fitting those acts committed on himself by himself, so he must abstain from engaging in them.

And what is it that motivates my days and energises my nights? The golden hope that once we reach Jaffa the warm clime of Asia will exert a positive influence on Her Ladyship. I have heard tell of the exceedingly juicy oranges there and of bathing in the sea in the month of August, and how good these are for awakening passion and bringing moisture to the most arid of dry patches.

There are few women on board, and no beauties at all in the

manner of Her Ladyship. Today, in the afternoon hours, I committed an impropriety. A cook, no longer young, even aunt-like, with wispy but pleasant hair, was serving food to the passengers. As she leaned forward to ladle potatoes onto the plates, it was possible to glimpse that pale slit between ample, overflowing breasts. Once I had viewed them I could not remove them from my mind. I went to her, kissed her hand and dispatched my fingers to her breasts. All at once my cheeks reddened and my gullet and palate were filled with a disgusting reflux at this sickening act. As for the cook, she gazed at me with calf eyes full of astonishment.

Thus I understood that I was going mad. I took up my pen and paper and began to write.

Today, when Mother took to her bed early and a lazy summer breeze spread jasmine petals at the entrance to our house and the frogs sounded their full-throated croak among the densely leafed green trees of the orchard, I laid down the stories I am writing and went to Amina's narrow room to find a living person to whom I could unload my searing, soul-consuming secrets, and I found our servant in her chambers, and she seated me in her lap and kissed my cheeks and asked in a sweet whisper, as if sharing a secret, whether my mother had told me about the true goings-on of our estate.

I informed her that Mother never reveals a thing to me so as not to awaken my anxiety, since she is always hugely afraid and fearful for my health, which makes her forbid me all manner of things like riding a mare or a bicycle, which might lead me to fall and break a leg or be attacked by Bedouin bandits or harassed by evil-minded children, and our old maidservant Amina regarded me all the while attentively, wrinkles furrowing her puckered face, and she leaned towards me and asked in a hoarse, hushed voice if I knew about the pleasant *biara*, the orchard pool on our estate, whose well-water is cool and from which run many culverts that travel the length and breadth of the estate, bringing water to the orchards and groves and deep, rounded tree beds, and I told her that I knew nothing about all these, so then, in the light of a lantern that cast long, dark shadows on her face, she revealed to my ears a secret that my mother and father had been keeping from me, namely that in the pool, in the deepest depths, among the reeds and beneath the flower stems, the water-lilies, the frogs' eggs, there lives a green-eyed genie with smooth black skin who draws down to his lair the souls of the dead and tempts every small, innocent child wishing to enjoy the cool water to slip between the tiny waves, so that it behooved me to stay far away from the pool, never to approach its seductive waters, and when she had finished her story she planted a venomous kiss upon me and dispatched me to sail off to my room and dock in my bed, an old woman's laugh lines of bewitchment etched on her face.

I did not, however, ascend the stairs to my room to sink into sweet sleep but, rather, I gathered my courage and took the trail marked by white stones to the hidden footpath, which was, at night, more difficult than ever to find, and barn owls screeched in my ears and ravens cawed noisily from afar, and I drew near the pool in a state of juddering screams, telling myself that Amina was sporting with me, that her words were nothing but fiction, stories, a fable for frightened, gullible children, and how would I ever succeed in wrapping myself in a mantle of manliness if I did not know to govern my spirit in trifling matters such as these?, and I approached the edge of the *biara*, and every small lapping noise from the rippling water sounded to me like the shrieks of a thousand witches, and every sparkle from the reflection of mute stars seemed to me to be the gleaming gaze of the green-eyed genie.

And, lo, my breathing returned to normal, calm, and a smile rose upon my lips, and I even dared to dip my fingers into the darkened waters, and the feeling was pleasant and curative, and I picked up a small, slightly sharpened stone and tossed it into the depths of the pool for the purpose of provoking the genie and blinding his eyes, and I stood to my full height and filled my lungs with the cool night air, and then, when I turned my back to the pool and made my mincing way from there I froze at once in my place, for a low, hushed noise caused the water to tremble and my nightshirt to quiver, and it was the muffled sound of an evil genie feasting on the bodies of small children and lapping at their blood, reviving his devilish soul, and I dared not avert my gaze, but the evil, quivering sound continued to throb inside me, and in spite of the petrification that had taken hold of me and welded my feet to the ground, my gaze slowly drifted in the direction of the black pool crowded with water-lilies and tadpoles and the eggs with tadpoles floating there, and various reptiles and strange beasts in residence, and I was at once a mass of shivering and quivering, for a pair of smouldering, spark-shooting green eyes glared at me, and a low, muffled whisper reached my ears, Salah, Salah, your demise will come from this pool.

12 August 1895, Hotel Kaminitz, Jaffa, twenty minutes before the hour of five in the afternoon
I write these lines from the Land of Israel, Zion, on an oakwood desk in the lobby of a hotel in the German Colony near Jaffa. From the open door one can glimpse the dense green orchards of Jaffa. Sea smells waft through the air. A light breeze brings with

it the chirping of happy crickets. My mood, however, is turbid with the quarrel and squabble that broke out this evening between Her Ladyship and myself. Perhaps writing these words will bring peace and serenity to my heart.

The start of the day was lovelier and more beautiful than any other when our ship anchored off the Jaffa port in the early-morning hours. I was seized with a delirious joy. Like all people of my generation gripped by idealism, I, too, have longed from the days of my adolescence to ascend to the Holy Land, to till the soil and watch over it. Not long ago I completed my studies in the Faculty of Agronomy in Montpellier and I am knowledge-able about the fruits and grains of Palestine. Even Her Ladyship has for ever longed to set foot on this corner of the earth. From the dawn of her girlhood in Warsaw she was an enthusiastic member of the Hovevei Zion movement, active in promoting *aliya* to Israel and settling the land, our desirable piece of earth that pines for us as we pine for it.

This morning we stood on the deck of the ship and watched the pleasant buildings of Jaffa draw closer over the waves. Exhilarated, I clenched Her Ladyship's hand and moved to kiss her mouth, but she wriggled from my grasp. I turned my face toward hers and, lo, her expression was sour, angry. Under interrogation, even she could not explain the cause of her wrath. I pointed to the beautiful land of our dreams but she dropped her gaze and grimaced. Her hands were cold as ice, in contrast to the great heat enveloping us.

Just then a number of quick-armed, black-skinned oarsmen rowed towards us from the port in flimsy boats, their language a cackling like African parakeets, their customs lacking even the most basic elements of culture. I asked the deckhands who these men were.

'Arabs,' they told me.

Until this very morning I had never in my life met an Arab. Only a rumour, slight and feeble, had ever reached me, that a handful of this nation, the descendants of Shem, could be found among the settlers of Canaan, and that these people sell their land to the colonists. I was very eager to cast my eyes upon them. The Arabs drew their narrow boats alongside the ship and our deckhands tossed thick, coiled ropes to them, which the Arabs ascended rapidly in the manner of monkeys, their long, dark arms grasping them with rapid expertise. When they were nigh upon us one could see the ebony hue of their eyes, which sparkled like the skin of a moist black reptile.

Because I could sense that Her Ladyship was close to tears of disgust and revulsion I gathered her into my arms and whispered to her. 'My love, my fair one, my dove, in no time at all you will sample oranges from the Land of Israel and a clean, dry breeze will ruffle your hair and your soul will be restored and refreshed.'

But before I could finish whispering these words of love in her ear, one of the Arabs had reached the deck and was hurling the passengers' belongings into his boat in a cackling, grunting, chaotic manner, for there was little time and he wished to bring them all to shore quickly.

Now during our whole long journey to Zion, from Warsaw to Odessa and later on the ship traversing the waves, Her Ladyship had managed to stand vigilant guard over her square valise, the apple of her eye, in which were amassed her prized gowns from Russia, such as her wedding gown, and a spring dress, and a chiffon gown, and many other dresses and scarves about which men understand nothing – not their beauty or the differences between them or their importance to women – nor will they ever, even if given all the time in the world to investigate.

When the Arab came to relieve her of her valise, Her

Ladyship screamed and waved him off with her hand. She waved him off with her hand and he waved her off in return.

Not a minute had passed before he hurled her belongings onto the boat. However, since he was engaged in battle with her, the valise opened while sailing through the air and the entirety of its contents fell out and floated atop the salty seawater. In just another moment all Her Ladyship's beautiful gowns were fanned out over the waves, the latest fashions from Paris and Warsaw to be worn by the fish splashing about there.

Her Ladyship screamed and protested and raged and grew red in the heat of the argument and Asian sun, and she announced that she would not disembark from the ship by way of the Arab boats. However, there is no other way of reaching the shore, for the port is shallow and steamships cannot approach it. Only after I pleaded and begged with her profusely did she consent to leave the ship, her eyes flowing with tears at the sight of her precious clothing filling with seawater and growing heavy and drifting downwards, all manner of shells and seaweed and green algae clinging to it and bringing it to its demise.

I would have laboured to console Her Ladyship and reassure her of whatever recompense she might require. However, she wanted nothing but to arrive at our destination, at the address given to us and cry upon the pillow in our hotel.

While making our way to the port, our bones trembled at the sight of boulders jutting up between the waves. On the wharf we found hundreds more members of that same race of people called Arabs. Dressed in long and filthy cotton garments with tall red-fringed hats, many carried wooden clubs that they used to rap one another from time to time on the head. At some distance stood two muscled Arabs, one against the other in hot dispute, and I took Her Ladyship by the forearm so that she might not view the impure sight of one bashing the other's head, and the man falling to the ground, blood flowing from his cracked skull and fluid from his brain seeping into the blazing earth.

We hastened, therefore, to depart from Jaffa to the place about which we had heard already, back in Odessa, called the German Colony, a place constructed by Germans and therefore, to our great good fortune, done in the European fashion. The paths are broad, the buildings of wood or hewn stone, and rubbish heaps and sewage are not visible at every corner. At the centre of the colony stands a pleasant inn called the Hotel Kaminitz staffed by excellent servants who speak the German language.

From the moment we reached the colony, Her Ladyship regained some of her spirit. She sampled the figs and dates placed before her, washed herself in a tub of hot water and combed out her hair, whose scent was that of the Garden of Eden, and the air was steaming hot and sea-sodden and a caged bird whistled to its partner and it seemed that everything had been set in place for the sole purpose of the love and desire I had wished for through an entire month of days, from the time of our nuptials.

I came to her and lowered my fingers to her bare shoulders.

Her face darkened.

I brought a date to her lips.

She spat out the pit.

I grasped her arm and said, 'It is only right that this act be carried out.'

She said, 'Not now, for I am distraught on account of the Arabs.'

I held her tighter and said, 'Now. No later than this very hour.'

She burst into hysterical sobbing and called me a villain for coming to her with demands and complaints.

Said I, 'Villainous is she who disobeys her husband.'

'Sex fiend!' she cried. 'Pimp, procurer, panderer, philanderer!'
I slapped her slandering face and left the room.

❦

12 August 1895, Hotel Kaminitz, Jaffa, a few hours later
This very moment I returned from Jaffa to record events with joy and glee.

After nightfall, I rose and left the German Colony, impatient to return to a place in the town of Jaffa about which I had heard the deckhands speak favourably. I walked about searching in vain, coming upon dense groves filled with the noisy buzzing of bees and wasps, then the shuttered doors of shops with signs written in the Hebrew language, until all at once the street opened on to a great square, noisy at this late hour and teeming with many Arabs, some with lips plunged into slices of juicy watermelon, some smoking through long pipes attached to glass bottles filled with smoke, and others roasting the carcasses of calves over open fires and chewing a kind of flat, round pocket bread.

A panderer caught my errant gaze and my tipsy gait and at once fathomed, in his cunning way, the meaning of my meandering, and he signalled to me to follow after him, not far, to a place behind the square, close by the seashore, where there were small houses and cabins painted pink and piled one atop another like a patchwork stitched by a crippled seamstress.

I placed a few *bishliks* in his hand and the squat, squash-nosed panderer whistled roughly and at once a madam stepped from one of the buildings and summoned me inside to some narrow, dimly lit rooms covered with red carpets, which were nothing more than cubicles of iniquity perfect for pleasure and love, the very acts in which Her Ladyship, lying like a carcass in the Hotel

Kaminitz, had shown no interest from the first day of our marriage.

In order not to awaken her greed, I told the Arab madam that I had reached this place without intending to, innocently, but she laughed, jiggling her bejewelled pelvis enticingly, and told me I could tour the cubicles or depart. I announced I would leave at once, but I consented to glance fleetingly at the women performing their holy labour of inserting and removing and, lo, the cubicles were full of life to the last, thick with sweat and moans, and with regard to the harlots there, well, they stirred desire for intercourse with their enormous, quivering breasts dripping with milk and honey, the scents with which they perfumed themselves, the swarthy soles of their feet, their painted nails and, above all else, the submissive positions in which they were posed, on all fours, their moist, puffed pudenda exposed between ample buttocks as if to say to a man, 'Do with me what you will.'

And a man told to do, does.

Afterwards, I returned my slightly rumpled hat to my head. The madam, who trades in the flesh of the daughters of Eve, jumped up and demanded the harlot's price. I asked how much. She told me five francs. I told her that five francs was the sum earned by a colonist for a month of work, while the labours of a harlot lasted no longer than half an hour.

'That,' she said, 'is a whore's wage, and no other.'

Against my will I placed the sum in her hand and went my way. At least my desire had been quenched and my spirit was gay, my body relaxed and depleted and grateful.

Mother says that next year I shall not return to the *madrassa* but rather she shall tutor me in my French and algebra studies at home, for the children at school are evil criminals who raise their hands to me and look to start fights, and they sear my soul in burning flames, scorching my flesh with a fire that will stay with me always.

These are the waning days of summer and the air is not inflamed as it was recently, and I walk for hours on clumps of soil and mounds and furrows, then sit atop the chalky cliffs that lead down to the sea, and there I ponder and weep at my strange fate that is spattered with humiliation, for Allah created me not in the image or fashion of other children in my city, who parade about in groups and gangs while I scuttle about on my own, who beat one another with bars and bats while I pen poems and stories from the depth of my heart, who despise me with a fierce animosity while I myself hate no one – only deep sadness, the woefulness of the salty sea and the dolefulness of the fading summer nibble at me with a greedy appetite.

Across the placid water my future spreads before me, like merchant ships sailing from sea to sea, and I watch as the children of my age sprout and grow tall, and from inside their bodies grow men in the image of men, strong men with deep voices and pot-bellies, and they gallop as one man, as light-footed horses feverish with speed, raising great clouds of dust with their hoofs while I remain alone in their wake.

Mother comes to my room and asks what will become of me, my future, what sort of person will be born from this body of mine, this life, for I have no courage or daring spirit, no powerful body or stamina, so how will I one day overpower my enemies, and how will I earn my daily bread, for I am all the time alone among my books and notepads, and no children are interested in being in my company? and I leave my room and distance myself from her and her bewitchery and I race to the dense orchards of our estate where I frighten a gaggle of chickens and earn astonished glances from the simple-minded tenant farmers who toil in our fields day in and day out, and there I climb with bare hands one tree-trunk that I have chosen at random, scraping my skin against the rough bark until I drip blood in my desire to suffuse my body with the very same lash marks and gruff manners of other boys, and the branches snap under my feet and the trickle of blood on my arms and legs brings me the pleasure of pain, and when I return home I ask Mother for the bathing tub, and she and Amina hasten to carry out my wishes, and I rinse the dust from my body and the water blackens and muddies and changes from pure to impure, and Mother comes to me and soaps my back and sings me lullabies and whispers her schemes into my ears, telling me that at the conclusion of this summer I will no longer leave the estate but, rather, will sit with her and with Amina in the dappled sunlight, far away from the evil and distress of the dark and depraved world.

1 *September 1895, Mishmar Hayarden*

For a period of three weeks I wrote nothing in my diary, and for what reason? For the journey I am conducting through the Land of Israel, from south to north and from east to west. Two letters I have written to Her Ladyship, who remained behind in Jaffa, though I have received none yet in reply via *poste restante*. Our parting prior to my journey was chilly; Her Ladyship failed even to proffer a single kiss on my cheek. We are still deeply embroiled in our quarrel.

For an entire month I am passing from one colony to the next in order to assess the nature of the lives of the farmers and vine-growers, the Hovevei Zion in the Land of Israel.

Many are the rumours that have reached my ears with regard

to the colonists. In the broadsheet *HaMelitz*, the choice land and excellent vines it produces are praised and glorified, and I wished to see these with my own eyes. Alongside the colonists there are also colonists of the fairer sex. I had heard tell of these Jewesses, less restrained than their European counterparts, and of the glorious sun in these lands, which has turned their skin to a lovely shade that awakens one sexually. I was enticed and excited to see all these wonders for myself. Sadly, however, everything I had heard proved to be lies and deceit.

Agronomically speaking, the lands tilled by the Hovevei Zion colonists are so inferior that nothing will grow from them in the next thousand years. Many are the good, fertile, choice lands of the Levant, but upon all of these sit Arabs, who till and guard them. Not a single beautiful garden is there not settled by Arabs. All that is left to the colonists is the worst of the badlands, lands filled with desert sands or swamps, lands malarial or dysenterial.

Another misfortune is a warped custom of the colonists; they are in receipt of monies from the Baron de Rothschild and the head office of Hovevei Zion in Odessa and thus see no value in their insignificant labours. Truth be told, the colonists are lazier than the red-buttocked monkeys that lie cradled in African tree branches. Even the presence of oppressive overseers does nothing to change their evil ways.

No fields or orchards have they cultivated, for that demands toil. Thus, the colonists purchase all of their winter needs – wheat, grains, legumes, lentils – from their Arab neighbours. Even summer fruit, cotton, sesame, sorghum, melons, marrows and all manner of gourds they buy from nearby Arab villages.

Neither was I favourably impressed by the female colonists in the colony I visited. With regard to the beauty of these farmers and vine-growers, well, in the eight or ten years they have lived in the Land of our Forefathers they have grown shrewish and contentious, their faces lined with creases and their forlorn, slothful gaze reminiscent of the Asian water-buffalo that roams the swamps.

In spite of my revulsion towards these females, I tried my luck none the less with several husbandless colonists, who seemed free in their ways. I experienced no great success in this matter, except at Mishmar Hayarden, where I am currently in residence.

This evening, an hour or two ago, I gazed upon one colonist, shorn and turbaned as is their wont, who, I was told, was alone and in hope of meeting a man to plough her furrow. She returned my gaze and smiled ever so slightly in my direction. I said, 'Show me the room in which you live.'

She said, 'Follow me.'

As soon as she had shut the door behind us I encircled her waist with my hand and kissed her lips.

Her eyes were brown and sad, her body lean and weedy, but suited to any act I indicated of the oral nature. Further, her aperture grew thick and ready, and she knew how to move her pelvis fittingly. In short, she brought me to gratification.

Now the shorn colonist is lying sprawled in her room, a cigarette between her lips. But because I was overwhelmed by my revolting behaviour, I escaped from the room to a small hut from which one can observe the valley in order to write a bit in my diary.

Far better than these colonists are the Arab women of Jaffa. They are versed in the act of love and anoint their bodies with fine oil, raising a wondrous scent. Still, those harlots are quite expensive, since the Germanic and Armenian and Russian seamen pay them visits and spend all their silver. Therefore, I have no choice now but with Her Ladyship.

21 September 1895, en route to Jaffa

I am at the end of my journey. In short order I shall reach the city of Jaffa.

Now I know that I will not be able to be an agronomist at any of the colonies currently in existence in the Land of our Forefathers: not in the poisonous swamps at Hadera, not in Wadi Khanin and its terrible sandy earth, not in Mishmar Hayarden or Rosh Pina, not in Zichron Yaacov (Zamarin) and not in Petah Tikva. New and better lands must be purchased from the Arabs, perhaps in the vicinity of Jaffa where the earth is quite fertile. Upon my return to Jaffa I shall pay a visit to the executive committee of Hovevei Zion to speak frankly with them about providing me with money to find choice lands. That is our only hope.

I shall be home and reunited with Her Ladyship. I will write about our encounter immediately after it occurs. If she does not greet me favourably and fittingly it will be upon me to think anew about this marriage.

Father is dead, he is no longer among the living and all the men of our tribe are mourning his death while the women shriek and torment their bodies with tree-branch lashings, and Mother tears at her hair and demands to be buried alive under the desert sands, for Father has been murdered, fallen in battle, and woe to those who took his life, for Father was first and foremost among our tribe, admired by all, a model and paragon for all the boys and young men alike, the quintessence of murawa, that noble masculinity we all wish to attain, and his own burial was presided over by elsha'er, the bard, whose mournful lamentations brought tears even to the beasts – the camels, the horse, the she-asses – as he described the courageous battles in which Father fought the rival tribes, how he showed

no hesitation in slitting the throats of those who sought to slay him, and beheaded and behanded and befooted them, and in days of peace, when warm winds caressed the tops of the date palms and the fruit was a ripe golden brown and the young men surrounded him, ready to serve us the best of the desert fruits, on that manner of days, Father would sit with the women and the children and laugh with them in their gaiety and join the bard with joyful rhymes, and if some passer-by arrived at our black tents, held high with poles erect, Father would slaughter with his own hands a camel cow or bull and serve the good roasted meat as an offering to the guest and would hasten to satiate this man's hunger and wash his feet and shower upon him all manner of honours and delights, and throughout his life, to the very day of his death in battle – the death of a warmongering hero on camelback – his repute was never tainted with humiliation, his every raiment the most splendid among splendid.

Squelched rage, flames of fire and roiling, boiling, bubbling water surge inside me at the mention of our despicable enemies, those sons of Satan known as the Hazraj, for it is these tribesmen – come from who knows where in the east – who chopped down our date palms and abducted our women, attacked our tents and our possessions and helped themselves to what they willed, and when it was upon us, according to the stringency of law and justice, to take back what rightfully belonged to our tribe, and we rode swiftly on double-humped, light-footed camels to kill with swords and spears those evil-mongers, there rose among them, upon a stallion, one most dastardly, leering, who lanced our father's throat and cut him down in one swift blood-drenched motion, and Father is no longer: he is dead, buried beneath hillocks of calamitous sands.

The laws of the desert require me to carry out the noble task of avenging his death, but Mother has been repeating her pleas that I do no such thing, for no wisps of moustache have yet appeared on my lip and I have not yet reached the age of thirteen and my grasp of a sword is feeble and my mastery of camel-riding is unimpressive, and she is joined by all the other women who tell me, Rashid, cease and desist, for revenge will be *achieved by those stronger and more robust than you, by men of our tribe trained for this purpose, and already a scheme was being plotted by the brave-hearted warriors of our tribe, how they would infiltrate, one hot, dry night, the impure tents of the Hazraj encampment and shoot them with our poisoned arrows, leaving no person among the living, attacking the men and rending their flesh, and even I welcome the impending death of my enemies, envisaging with my mind's eye the spear held erect in my hands as I cleave their brows, and how good and precious will be my days once I have taken their bodies piled one atop the next, clusters of trampled, murdered men whom I have eviscerated with my dagger, each and every one of them to the last, and I dispense with their innards on hills of shifting sands, where Father himself died and is buried, interred for all time, and I will enucleate their eyeballs and feed them to wild dogs so that they may lick the warm, viscous liquid that drips from them, and I will present their livers to my mother and aunts so they may prepare delicacies of revenge from which the Hazraj tribesmen will know the depth of our handiwork.*

22 September 1895, Neve Shalom

My return home at first seemed to pass favourably. From afar I spied Her Ladyship leaning against the doorpost, gazing into the distance. I descended from the wagon and encircled her in my arms. She kissed my cheek. Her Ladyship is more beautiful than beauty itself and she awakens my love for her in spite of her shortcomings. For a whole month she had been alone, without her man, and had passed the Rosh Hashanah new-year holiday on her own, so that now the time spent apart from her husband was quite apparent in her countenance. That is not to say she was touched with the hysteria of a lonely woman but that longing and regret had eaten away at her. Without any overt suggestions on my part she hinted that I should join her in the bedroom, the dust from my journey still clinging to my clothing.

I had already grown accustomed to the odd ways of Her Ladyship, who had no desire for words of love or caresses or other pleasures; even the lick of a tongue was filthy and impure in her eyes. Instead, she wished me to come unto her without tarrying unnecessarily. And although Her Ladyship was parched dry, this was man's fate in marriage. At least she did not cast her eyes upon other men, her cool beauty preserved for her husband alone. With time and patience he could certainly teach her all that she was lacking in the sexual sciences.

Hope and a spirit of optimism settled into my soul, but in no time a new dispute infiltrated our household when I requested my meal: not only did I discover that Her Ladyship had not bothered to prepare one, but she chose this occasion to announce that she was of the modern sort of women and would not cook for her husband. Her Ladyship sat cross-legged in her room: she was not impassioned to carry out her duties in the bedroom and now she had no desire to find herself among pots and pans. Disobedient women like this are like wild horses in the desert plains. With no rider, no horseman, their ways become ruinous and they provoke the ire of every suitor and lover.

I lorded my authority over Her Ladyship and commanded her to prepare me a meal.

Her expression grew belligerent and she said, 'Go to the *shuk* of the Arabs and buy your own food there.'

'A rebellious wife you are,' I said.

Once again she called me a villain.

Before I could respond in kind she had closed herself in the bedroom with a slam of the door.

23

Mother has forbidden me to set forth to Jaffa for fear and anxiety that some evil will befall me, and indeed even a light sea breeze, the mere tail of a gust, is enough to send a *grippe* through my body and riddle me with sickness, and even a lone evil gaze or slight threat of being jostled or jabbed is enough to plunge my soul into despair and dejection, and I am confined, on Mother's orders, to my small quarters, whence I may observe a canopied carob, and until the days of summer have ended and Mother will teach me my French tenses or algebraic equations, I shall occupy myself with writing my stories of Rashid, son of the desert, and Leila, daughter of Baghdad, constructing them sentence by sentence, scene by scene, blowing life into those no longer living, who perhaps were never really of this world.

She orders me, too, to sleep much and eat much, but these commands I do not obey, for my night hours are crazed and troubled and the food does not please my palate, and sadness, the sadness of summer's end, has grown and taken root inside me, like prickled ivy on a wall under siege, my disconsolate, fragile image, loathed and shunned, reflected in the ripples of the *biara* in the courtyard of our estate, and I lean over the water to learn the depth of the pool, and how little it would take to submerge myself, to put an end to my abysmal grief, merely a few stones in my pockets and the opening of a throat that wishes to breathe, and many rivers of gushing water coursing inward to my thin body and my strange, flawed soul, and later my bloated, white body in clothing soaked through, and Mother gazing upon it floating in the centre of the pool, her eyes hollow and empty.

Unaccompanied and forlorn, I walk about our estate, kicking the flesh of its earth and wandering among the trees, and the tenant farmers look askance at me from their straw and stubble huts, used as temporary dwellings these many long days, smouldering under a scorching sun, and there are those among them who tell of a green-eyed genie who has taken residence in my soul and rattled it, and Mother sequesters me with threats and pleas and serves me many delicacies drenched in oil for the purpose of strengthening and enriching my blood and body, and she entreats me to drink water and goat's milk and she does not let up her guard over me until she is satisfied that all the labour of chewing and swallowing has been completed, and now she has even forbidden me to step too far from the house itself for fear of summer snakes hidden beneath rocks and boulders, lying in wait to strike my blood and poison it, claiming my life, and so she interrogates me at all hours of the day to learn what evil it is that has brought this sadness and nihilistic spirit to my soul, and I regard her and kiss her cheeks and say, It is the sadness of waning summer, Mother, the days of freedom come to an end, a conclusion, a death.

Each evening I sit with Mother and Amina on low wicker stools in the dark kitchen near shut-lid pots and bubbling casseroles, and Amina shares gossip about a man from Jaffa who attacked his wife, and the wife used a Gypsy knife to dismember his member from his body, and Mother, red-faced, orders her to desist from telling stories unfit for a boy, but I listen to neither of them, wishing only to join the migrating birds passing overhead, the long black Palestine Babbler, with his short beak and eyes brimming with charm and intelligence, to accompany them on their long journey to another land, and my head and scalp become a sleek black beak, and tiny feathers soft as a plume sprout across my body, and my throat issues a chirp of reveille and my image flies to the window, which is ajar, and departs, on its way, and my wings flutter and carry me among the branches of the carob tree and through its foliage, and I am a beautiful-winged bird rising and soaring, higher and higher, high above the estate and the wadi and the sea and the few clouds drifting across the summer-morning sky, and I join the great migration, travelling to and fro, and the city of Jaffa is slowly awakening, her souks filling with merchants and customers, and fresh fruits are amassed on the stands, and bunches of mint and coriander, and copper trays with tea dot my bird's-eye view of the city, and this bird who is I releases its bowels and out fall its fears and strange dreams and end-of-days prophecies, and they are as a weight departing from the body, and the bird now hovers freely on high, and the lids judder and hiss atop the casserole dishes.

23 September 1895, Neve Shalom
Her Ladyship lay supine with a new excuse for not carrying out her conjugal duties: she was in the grip of a terrible frailty and confined to her bed. I went to the Hotel Kaminitz for help in finding a doctor and was told one would be sent round forthwith.

After two hours passed, or three, our saviour appeared in the form of an Arab named Dr Al-Bittar, a blunt-faced man who constantly rolled a string of blue beads, called *masbakha*, between his stubby fingers, and his teeth were yellow from smoking the *narghile*, that bottle-and-pipe contraption I first spied in the square. The Arab's expression gave no indication that he had ever been party to any wisdom; none the less, it was still possible that he had some knowledge and experience with medical issues. The swarthy man answered my question about his professional expertise by telling me that he specialised in sexual diseases, such as syphilis, gonorrhea and nocturnal emissions, as well as impotence, scrotal hernias and haemorrhoids.

I said, 'And what of influenza and malaria and dysentery and other maladies of the body? Do you know how to treat these?'

He rolled the *masbakha* between his fat fingers and whispered, 'With Allah's help.'

With seriousness of purpose he felt for Her Ladyship's pulse, prodded her temples, inspected her tongue, then scribbled a number of notes to himself in the Arabic language in letters that appeared as flea droppings spotted here and there, above and beneath, with dots and dashes, and all the while he muttered in a worrisome manner, his brow furrowed, and he bit his meaty brown lips, and, finally, provided this diagnosis: 'Madame's body has not yet adjusted to the Asian heat. The remedy that will cure her is a porridge of millet and quinine.' He hastened to demand his fee of one rouble and departed post-haste.

Mother placed me on the wagon she had hired in advance and led me to the famous doctor in Jaffa in order to decipher the meaning of my strange malady, and all the while, as we journeyed southwards, at first close to the buildings of Sarona and then beside the winding Wadi Musrara, its gushing water flowing in the direction opposite to our own, she interrogated me as to the reason for the black days that had descended upon me, intent upon my revealing why it was that I awakened night after night, my body drenched in sweat, my throat clogged with phlegm, and she ordered me to sit up straight and grasp the sides of the wagon that I might not fall as it jolted to the left and right, and I gazed upwards at the migrating birds, and the winds of autumn throbbed inside me, and perhaps with the death of summer the evil thoughts would be carried off on a breeze, and within the half-hour the wagon had jangled its way to the outskirts of Jaffa, the dense green orchards and groves now replaced by Gypsy tents and the wooden homes of the Germans come to settle our land, and then by the light-stepping multitudes in their tarbooshes, and with them cattle and mules and camels all assembling in the colourful souks.

However, our path was not taking us there but, rather, our wagon driver let us off at the entrance to the city, near the remains of the city walls and the deep moat that had meanwhile filled with dirt and debris, and Mother was in a hurry to bring me to the gate of the city, and she swaddled my head and body under the wing of her cloak so that the evil eye could not take notice of me, for many were those who whispered of her son possessed by a genie, who goes forth as one of the moonstruck poets of Jahilya, causing strife among the tribes, and Mother's stride was swift as we wound our way through throngs of people, the merchants and the pedlars, the passers-by and the loiterers, and I peered down the twisting alleyways of Jaffa, which I recalled from days not long past when Mother still allowed me out on a bicycle, passing through the orchards and climbing the hills of the city, and it was here, in these very streets, that the prophet Yunis was plagued and stupefied by the spirit of Allah, it was here that he took refuge from the prophecies of wrath, here, among the orange pedlars and tradesmen, that he sought peace of mind from all the horrors he envisaged taking place in the soon-to-be destroyed Nineveh, whose many citizens would all be dead, smitten, trampled and annihilated by the fury of the Omnipotent One who sits on high and flogs them with his whips and lashes.

And my gait is plodding and I nearly fall upon the cracked paving-stones awash in sewage and dung, my body withering like the leaves of the castor-oil plant, and I wish to descend the narrow steps, many in number, to the port and the sea, that I might hurl my body into the raging, treacherous waters, into the gaping mouth of *el-gula*, the sea monster that lies in wait for sailors and deckhands, and be devoured by the whale there, swallowed into its bowels, that it may silence and lock away all traces of a lost soul gone astray a long time hence.

The venerable Dr Al-Bittar Elkhakim fills me with fear and dread the moment we enter his chambers in El-Sarafin Street, for not only is his estimable medical wisdom discernible in him and in his gaze and in his thick escritoire, but his thick black brows and his long thick fingers and his deep thick voice all assault me with some primeval loathing, admonishing me for my strange and varied habits like some heinous stain on our family raiment, for the doctor is well acquainted with my father and my father's father and never witnessed among them some ugly and piteous nestling like myself, and he stares intently at me with his sharp, vexing gaze and commands me to tell him the purpose of my visit, and at once Mother becomes my mouth and my tongue and she recounts in one breath all my sins and transgressions, how for a month of days already I have awakened from my sleep with piercing cries, pulling the entire startled household from sleep along with me, how my sleep wanders and my soul withers and victuals will not enter my lips nor a smile rise in my lips, how more than once I have stood at the edge of the *biara* to douse myself in it and drown my soul, how she watches me with seventy-seven eyes in case I find an opportunity to slip from her guard to do myself harm, and the doctor's voice thunders and he asks, 'Are these things true?' to which I remain silent, averting my gaze, and the room rotates round me on a hinge.

The doctor asks me again about the meaning of these matters and I answer that my sadness is apropos of all that appears before me in my dreams, to which he queries the nature of these dreams and I tell him that, to my distress, they are forgotten to me, all but one of an all-encompassing war and pillars of smoke and boats that jump over the sea, and the doctor examines my tongue and my temples and the veins of my arms to see that the blood is thrumming there, and he pronounces my body fit and says I suffer neither from malaria nor from intestinal maladies, neither from a bodily fever nor from jaundiced, rheumy phlegm, and then he suggests, with a twitch of his black brows, that I step out of the room and wait beside the closed door, and once positioned there I hear Mother's stifled sobbing and scraps of words – 'desperate', 'losing hope', 'losing my mind' – along with his muffled responses – 'porridge of millet and quinine', 'enema', 'castor oil' – and her tears resume anew like a torrent of vomit frothing from the mouth when he uses, pointedly, the word 'madness', and mentions the names of several places of refuge for those whose minds have gone astray, even in Al-Quds – Jerusalem – he tells her, in a building crouched behind a mosque so that the prattlers will know nothing of it, and when her weeping turns to lowing I walk out into the corridor and from there peer anxiously into the street, fearful of viewing that which appears to me night after night in my dreams, and a feebleness threatens to overpower my body for my accusers were right: my soul has been eaten away by a malevolent worm, by the leaves of a castor-oil plant, by lice that nibble away a man's intellect until he becomes mad as a rabid dog, and therefore there is no choice but to go to the sea, a short distance away, to put an end to this strange story of my life, and all the genies will drown with me in the waters of Jaffa and the sea will roil and pull us down to the darkest depths, the site of the eternal graves of the crusaders escaping from the city and of all those who erred in steering their boats and plunged downwards to become food for the fish under a mantle of green seaweed.

The entire week I wandered among Arab panderers asking if they had heard about the land I was searching for and hoping to purchase, and I showed them the promissory note from the Hovevei Zion group for one thousand francs as a down-payment, but I was unable to find that which I desired. My spirit deflated. Even those sublime confections stuffed with crushed nuts and covered with jellied sugar could not raise my spirits and I went from bad to worse with no suitable land and no purpose for the studies in agronomy that I had carried out abroad.

However, alongside the bad something good happened today in the form of an adventure.

In the afternoon I was standing in one of the alleyways close to the *shuk* of the money-changers (El-Sarafin in the language of the Arabs), very near by the northern gate of the city, long and wide strips of coloured cloth draped above my head as protection for passers-by from the burning Asiatic sun. I was there to meet a pair of Arabs, Saleem and Salaam, two procurers of every thing and every matter, whom I wished to find me these two items: Arab land and an Arab woman, so that I might come into this one and come into that one. I had no high hopes for this pair of panderers but was left with little choice.

While I was still leaning against the wall of the alleyway, my hand in my pocket, I felt a pair of eyes scrutinising me. I cast my own in the direction of the open door of the building facing me, stone archways above it and sandstone boulders beside, and there stood a black-haired youth of ten or twelve staring at me, a slight blush rising in his pale, worried cheeks. It was clear from the clumsy movement of his hands that he was not quite right in his mind. At that moment a young Arab woman with green eyes, apparently his mother, placed her hand upon him and joined him in the archway. On the one hand she was not beautiful, as her thick brows were ugly and her head, which was covered with a black veil, did not stand straight and proud on a swanlike neck like that of Her Ladyship; but on the other hand, her skin was creamy brown and enticing, and the curve of a pair of handsome breasts, twin gazelles, could be glimpsed through her dark robe.

From where I stood I raised my hat to the child's mother in greeting. At first the woman tittered seductively, and I made to cross the lane to approach her, but at that very moment, all at once, there came into the alleyway a Turkish official who proclaimed the arrival of a convoy, and after that came a cloven-lipped camel and a pot-bellied mule followed by a parade of defecating mares ridden by a pair of black-skinned drivers, and the whole lot raised dust and a terrible din so that by the time the clouds and noise dissipated and dispersed, the door had closed and the woman and child had disappeared along with her smile and her lips and her infantile tittering.

As I stand regaining my composure in the entrance to Dr Al-Bittar's clinic, Mother approaches and remains at my side for a moment or two and I cling to her, swallowing my tears, and suddenly something strange occurs, for a man, a foreigner not of the Arab peoples, is standing in the alleyway gazing at me and smiling with gaiety, and I bow my head, gripped with shame, but all the while he keeps his eyes upon me, then he removes his hat and bows humorously, and points to me as if to say, You, boy, you, and I waggle my own finger slightly in response as if to ask, Who–me? for what could this tall man and I have in common? and he indicates that it is indeed I to whom he is referring, and I ask, And who might kind sir be? and he says, Do you not know? I am an angel, and he sports gossamer wings on his back and his beautiful golden curls sway gently in the late-afternoon breeze, and the angel smiles serenely, capaciously, and spreads his wings and rises high in the air and as he rises he utters my name, sweetly – Salah, Salah – and tells me, Have no fear, many angels guard you from on high, and a scuffle at my back takes me by surprise and, lo, a pair of woolly white virgin wings flutter there, and clouds of dust from the hoofs of camels and mules and a train of mares from the lane just arrived, in haste, choke the air, and the angel and I hover above it all, the beating of our wings mixing with the dervish dancing of the Jamiya El-Bakhar, the sea mosque, and Jaffa overflows with rivers and rivers of water – saltwater, seawater – and her cliffs and boulders grow more precise and pointed from a distance and her monsters stretch themselves, shaking off thousands and thousands of drops, but I pay no attention to all these things, for I am my good friend's and he is mine.

25 September 1895, Neve Shalom
It is night-time. Her Ladyship is deep in sleep, still ill and feeble. Before going to bed she did not bid me goodnight, nor did she so much as look upon me.

My own sleep is troubled, not by Her Ladyship but by the Arab woman I glimpsed yesterday afternoon.

Her lips were parted, and very handsome. Her skin was bronzed by the goodness of the sun. Her eyes were mischievous, summoning a man to lightheadedness and debauchery. Perhaps she was a harlot looking to earn her wage for her unfortunate son, touched in the head as he is and clinging to her robes. She would have needs in raising him as she is clearly without husband or father.

Tomorrow I will ask Saleem and Salaam about her. Best of friends are they, those stout, gossiping little men. They embrace as they walk along, and even in sleep they are inseparable. There is nothing in the city of Jaffa that escapes their attention. Saleem and Salaam do not demand a wage or salary but, rather, *baksheesh* (a word favoured by the Arab peoples) of twenty per cent of each and every sale. There is nothing they will not do; for a thousand francs they will even dispose of any man who does not find favour in my eyes. I have told them that such behaviour is not my custom.

Baghdad is full of all the finest and most beautiful – pot-bellied, double-chinned merchants load her stands with bricks of gold and silver and troves of spices from the lands of China and India, precious coloured silks and Damascene tapestries, and many are the poets in Baghdad, Abu Nuvas and Abu El-Atahiyyah, and famed singers of international repute, and all these walk long corridors covered with marble, and all around golden fountains spew water into cloudless skies and people sit under arbours of grapevines and palms and sing songs of praise to the wise and judicious caliph Haroun El-Rashid, beloved of Allah, and the canals of Baghdad flow with clear waters, and between her rivers, which straddle a lovely valley, all is fruitful and full of colour, and among these I, Leila, walk alone, my days black and my heart sad, for my father wishes to marry me to a man I loathe, an aged merchant with a harem of twelve women, each angry with the next, their teeth gold, their eyes flashing fire, and even the canaries do not sing in that house and the green-tailed red-breasted toucans do not build nests among the apricot trees in the garden, and I am gnawed away with longing for the love of my life, so handsome

is he, blue-eyed, this man to whom my love flows, not a wealthy merchant or landowner, not a Christian or Muslim, but a man alone, wandering, with no name or home, and his looks are pleasant, his tongue drips finery, speaking many languages, he is tall, and laughter is etched upon his face, his eyes wiser than wisdom itself, and I am overcome with love for him.

But my love has gone out from the walls of the city, his evil enemies have driven him away, my father's emissaries caused him to flee for his life, but through which of the four gates leading to distant lands he departed I shall never know, and to where his life and his soul will be led I shall never fathom, and night after night I slip silently from under the watchful eyes of the servants and eunuchs and I ascend the walls of Baghdad, and there, on high, my eye catches all, searching and seeking my beloved, and I wonder – can he hear the rhyming songs I sing for him, can he see my fingers curling and twirling in a bewitching, silent dance, and am I able to draw him with the dense magic of my city to its rivers and douse him with many waters? – and in my imagination I ride his tall, proud horse, escaping with him to an unknown land, the horseman of the jilted elderly groom hot on our trail, hoping to overtake us, but we gallop and gallop, clouds of dust billowing upwards behind us, and my beloved kisses my lips, and how sweet is his tongue, how limpid his eyes, I shall cling to him at night and sleep across his broad chest as it rises and falls in slumber, I shall kiss his gingery beard and sniff his sweetly pungent sweat redolent of almond and lemon trees, but no man answers my cries, only the guardsmen of Father's house have found me and point and call in the darkness, and I wish only to die, to meet my death plunging from these very high walls, the abyss spread out below them, and blind, I lean backwards, allowing my body to fall down and down to the cold, hard stone floors of the city, between the walls, and on my plunge downwards a sweet smile forms on my face, the memory of my golden-haired beloved bubbling inside me like a poison, and the guardsmen raise a hand and stop me in flight and, like a newborn butterfly, I am trapped in their nets, and they carry lovesick Leila, whose madness is known throughout Baghdad, *all the way to the caliph himself, back to Father's house to marry the grey-haired old groom only to die again night after night.*

26 September 1895, Neve Shalom

Saleem and Salaam brought no news on their wings, neither did they know anything about an Arab woman with green eyes and parted lips with a feeble-minded boy in tow. Instead, they led me to the Gypsy camps close by the seashore for the purpose of buying knives and daggers and swords studded with rhinestones. They themselves are laden with many rings and chains, while above their feet, which sport wooden clogs, each wears a golden anklet.

On their advice I purchased a high-quality dagger with a sharp-edged blade, for which I paid them their twenty per cent. While I was still positioned beside the Gypsy stands a quarrel began to brew between the two about some trifling matter and, to the din of a noisy, excited crowd, they grabbed hold of one another and rolled about on the ground, first Salaam atop Saleem, his hands at his throat, then Saleem atop Salaam, until it was no longer possible to discern which was Salaam and which was Saleem as the two mixed with the sound of cheers from the gathered crowd. The Arabs are extremely fond of brawls, imbroglios and blood.

I distanced myself and walked away from them, alone and reclusive, and I came upon a young Gypsy girl of nine or ten years of age who called to me to buy from her wares, all manner of the most wretched chains imaginable hanging from a burned and battered wooden board, and when she saw the look of indifference on my face she began to plead with me: 'For your wife,' she cried, 'for your wife.' My pity for this impoverished

Gypsy girl was aroused and suddenly my heart constricted for Her Ladyship, unloved by her husband. I produced ten *bishliks* and, to the girl's astonishment, I purchased every last item from her. As I was handing the money to her Saleem and Salaam appeared from nowhere, shirtless and panting from their wrestling match, and as one they made vociferous demands for their share. I produced several more coins for them.

Upon my return to our home in Neve Shalom, my pockets filled with the chains and beads of Gypsy handiwork as gifts for my wife, I found Her Ladyship risen from slumber and looking somewhat refreshed, but she failed to greet me and her expression was sour. I grew angry at this manner of hers in estranging me and took all that worthless jewellery and hurled it into the street.

Amina came to my room to ask why it is that I do not descend to her kitchen as I was once wont to do, and why it is that I have been sequestering myself from her and from Mother without uttering a word, and at once she took note of the abundance of drawings covering my bed and my writing-table and my chair, all in the image of the handsome foreigner, some depicting his height and others his muscles, like firm, round apples, and others his curly golden hair and still others his blue eyes, those repositories of goodness and wisdom, and how esteemed was this angel of mine, his smallest finger more precious to me than my own body, and Amina grew alarmed and she pressed me to reveal the meaning of these many drawings that had emerged from my brushes, and she poked at my ears and nose and declared that my eyes had grown dreamy and that there was a flicker of hope in them, and I affirmed to her that my drawings and my poems and my stories had flowed from me of their own accord, good and pleasant, and my nightmares had desisted and my sleep was no longer fitful but restorative; however, I did not reveal who this new friend of mine was, this large, golden-curled man I had met in front of Dr Al-Bittar's home, and I hastened to conceal the drawings and turn them right-side down, one atop the next, so that her prying, gossiping eyes would not defile them.

28 September 1895, Neve Shalom

In honour of this holy Day of Atonement the Street of the Jews – called Bustrus Street – was very nearly devoid of people, desolate, and no one in all of Neve Shalom and Neve Tzedek did any manner of labour, a spirit of awe and reverence having descended upon the buildings.

In our home the heat was suffocating. Her Ladyship has not spoken a word to me in the past week or two as she runs hither and thither, always preoccupied with establishing her dental clinic in a room of our home. This afternoon she stood in the kitchen, which was bereft of even a bread crust, and began tearing the hair from her head in a most neurotic fashion.

'Esther,' I said.

She glanced at me attentively.

I approached her from behind and encircled her, my arms around her waist. I spoke softly into her ear: 'I hereby beg your pardon for my estrangement.'

Her Ladyship sobbed copiously. She said this was not what she had expected from conjugal life. Dejected she was, disconsolate. In her parents' home her every whim was catered to, and she was especially pampered by her father. It was not the beautiful gowns that the cursed Arab had drowned in the Jaffa port that she pined for, nor did she demand to live in a fine house with cool air as was her home in Warsaw, only the love of the man who had placed a ring on her finger.

I said, 'Your love is the very same thing I ask of you.'

'It is not love you ask of me,' she said, 'but rather your way is to satisfy your desire in the manner of a bandit preying upon an innocent passer-by.'

'Then I shall change my manner,' I told her.

'You are away from home for long days and hours,' she said.

I said, 'I tour about in search of land for the colony, for Jews.'

'The colonists have plenty of land,' she said. 'Let them work the land they already have.'

'This, too, I shall change,' I said.

'Earning our keep has fallen completely to my clinic,' she noted.

'I will, one day soon, provide for all your needs.'

She remained silent.

I said, 'Are there any more sins from the list of misdeeds that I have committed?'

She said, 'At the moment there are none.'

'Will you, then, forgive me my sins?' I asked.

Her eyes filled with tears once again as she said, 'I shall grant my forgiveness.'

I grasped her fingers, poised to kiss them, but she removed them from my grasp. 'It is Yom Kippur today,' she said.

I left her alone.

It could be that Her Ladyship is not evil as she seems. Her behaviour does not stem from a foul nature, but rather from the narrowness of her brain, for a woman's brain is as small as that of a bird that will never see or understand anything beyond its own small wings and tiny beak.

Amina did not give up and continued to interrogate me, and in the end she wheedled me into reading to her from my newest story about Leila, daughter of Baghdad, who had been married off to an old man but loved another, a stranger not of the city's residents, and after listening attentively Amina asked me who this foreign man was for whom Leila pined, whether this was the very same man in these new drawings of mine, and I stuttered and mumbled and reddened and failed to conceal this one last thing from her, and I asked her, Do you swear never to speak a word of this to another human being, most especially my mother? And Amina said, I swear upon my right hand and my tongue and my life, and I told her, Amina, the cause of my happiness is a good-hearted man who wishes to be my friend and comrade, like an older brother, and she asked who this man was and I told her that I had met him three days earlier in a Jaffa alleyway and he had smiled broadly at me as no man had hitherto smiled at me, and had asked for my friendship and promised he would return soon to visit me, and Amina wondered at these strange visions of mine and asked that I describe him, and what language he spoke, and once she had heard and had learned that he moved about in the company of the twin procurers Saleem and Salaam, she proclaimed that this man was none other than a procurer of Jewish persuasion, a member of that strange people that breeds like lice and fleas in every corner, no honour or dignity to them in their tattered clothing and bleary eyes, their only occupation being unnaturally long prayer, and there are those among them who are money-lenders at interest so as to suck the blood of good people, and many of their kind have come to Jaffa for commerce, and to exploit the people of Jaffa in accordance with their level of malfeasance.

I told her that although the Jews are evil my large friend is kind, and he is stronger and more handsome than the most illustrious of our own people, and his comportment is excellent, and I told her how on the day we met he wished to embrace me warmly, lovingly, but that at that very moment the doctor had summoned me inside to his chambers and given me bitter, foul potions and the Jew, if that is indeed what he is, vanished, spread his wings and flew skywards into the blue heavens, and at once Amina suspected that this was nothing but a fanciful story of my own imagination, but I told her, No, this is not merely a story but the absolute truth, and Amina wiped her hands on her apron and waggled her fingers at me and commanded me to desist from thinking about this man, this foreigner, and I whispered to her in an unheard voice that this man would restore my health, and after she departed from the room I remained alone to draw the foreigner again and to write stories about him and rhyming odes, and I used my quill pen to draw the contours of his face, and in my head I sang the pleasant words he had imparted to me on the streets of Jaffa, and I seemed to see his wings stretched forth across the entire heavens, and in my heart I told myself that if he never returns to see me I will go to the genie and drown myself in his watery arms.

28 September 1895, Neve Shalom, two hours later
When the Day of Atonement ended Saleem and Salaam together paid me a visit and not because they wished to join the meal at the end of the fast but because of a note that had come into their possession and was addressed to me. First, however, it was necessary for me to pay them their *baksheesh*, so I provided them with a few *bishliks* found by chance in Her Ladyship's

pockets. These, then, are the contents of the note, written in the French language, which I record verbatim into my diary:

Dear Sir,
We encountered *le monsieur* perchance in the money-changers' market several days ago. My son is quite ill and asks after you, wishing to meet you at our estate. Please be kind enough to respond by return post as to whether you will be able to join us tomorrow evening.

Madame Rajani

This was a strange and unexpected note to receive. No temptress or harlot was she, heaven forfend, but the mistress of an estate, a married woman by the name of Madame Rajani who wrote in a flawless French.

At once I reddened, embarrassed at my misperception of *la madame* as a woman of low culture, but at least with regard to the boy it seemed I had not been mistaken. He was ill, this young man, and in need of treatment for his feeble body, that of a retarded child touched in the mind.

I sat at my desk and penned the following letter in response for Saleem and Salaam to deliver:

Dear Madame,
It will be my pleasure to meet your young son as you have requested, and I stand prepared to be at his service – and yours as well – in whatever matter you may see fit.

Respectfully,
Isaac (Jacques) Luminsky

The tops of the carob and cypress and acacia trees sway at me, the genies gaze greenly into my eyes and the gates of the estate creak noisily, for the world scorns and taunts me, and a hoarse and thunderous laughter moves from cloud to cloud, and all of them mock this haughty child, this dupe, for being so proud as to believe in the love of this angel, for being seduced by his golden curls, for erroneously thinking that such an exalted, heavenly creature like him would go out of his way to bestow friendship upon him, for Salah is wretched, the most dejected among the dejected, loathed by all, even his father and his mother, while this angel stands in proximity to the Creator of the world and floats between holy temples on high, so what possibly could the one have to do with the other, the contemptible and downtrodden with the most wondrous?

Alone and forlorn I sequester myself in my room, filled as it is with drawings and drawings and more drawings of the handsome one, but the fruits of my brushes' labours seem different to me now, crackling with primeval enmity, for thick, black, heavy lines have infiltrated the beauty of this angel – whose name I do not know – and I despise my feeble image, whose clothes are ragged and stained and tattered and smeared with excrement, and with heart grief shall I take up my notebooks and rip them to shreds, and I will cast them into the steaming rain and soak them in the water of rivulets and rivers until they reach perdition, the underworld, and the inky words will disappear, and when I look at the pages of my notebooks ripped to pieces and borne aloft by the wind there arises in me a sharp grief that batters my innards and froths upwards to poison my throat and my tears, for the angel upon whom I shall no longer gaze – his good-hearted smile never again to be beamed in my direction, his blue eyes never to watch over me, his fingers that shall not interlace with my own – and I call upon Leila so that I may fold myself in her embrace, that we may sob together in our mutual misery, but even she has estranged herself from me, her words are not rinsed away by the water, her descriptions are lacking, her plots dead-ends, and when Mother calls me to dine I lock the door and shut the blinds and do not respond to her cries, for it is better that not even a morsel of food pass my lips and that my life reach its last page here and that I write not even one single line more in the pages of my life's diary.

30 September 1895, Neve Shalom

All night and all day I have been turning in my bed, restless with passion for the green-eyed Madame Rajani who writes me love letters and invites me to enter – in the name of her imbecile son. Her bronzed skin and rosy lips have stirred my desire and there is a scent of adventure in my nostrils.

I asked Saleem and Salaam to shed light on Madame Rajani and her note and her son, and they informed me that the family lives on a remote and secluded estate which all fear to visit.

At the time, Saleem and Salaam were entwined, kissing and petting one another mischievously, a bottle of liquor in their hands.

They said, 'If you wish us to bring you more information, you will provide an advance of two and a half francs.'

I told them, 'Find out, first and foremost, why all fear to visit the estate.' In unison they told me of rumours passed along by mule- and horse-drivers that the evil eye had descended upon it and that all manner of genies and spirits roamed among its trees, but more than that they would only divulge with *baksheesh*. I said that this was the idle chatter and mean-spirited nature of Arab simpletons and that I had no intention paying either heed or a fee.

I took my leave of them.

30 *September 1895, Neve Shalom*
My heart is still burning and throbbing from the events that took place during my visit to the estate today. Now it is very late. I shall continue writing my report on the morrow.

1 *October 1895, Neve Shalom*
This is the order of the events that happened to me last night at the Rajani estate from the first to the last. I will attempt not to leave out or conceal even the slightest detail. I am thereby writing them down before they can disappear from my memory or be swallowed into the abyss of oblivion.

Yesterday at the appointed hour I set out to meet the Arab woman and the sick child who requested my presence. In our home Her Ladyship was preoccupied with the extraction of a rotten tooth from an Arab man of prominence (known in the local language as an *effendi*) in the clinic she had set up for herself, so I put a hat on my head and was able to slip away with ease into the lane.

From Neve Shalom I walked to the railway station near our home, then continued up the Street of the Jews to the square, and at the crossroads leading to Jerusalem I entered a wayfarer's inn favoured by Hovevei Zion members called the Khan Manouli.

The innkeeper – a coarse peasant woman named Srorika with stubby fingers, a red kerchief tied round her head and eyes shining with a greed greater than that even of Saleem and Salaam – rented me a lame and scrawny horse for an exorbitant fee, and I mounted him quickly, pressed my shoes to his belly to coax him northwards and off we went towards the estate.

I took the twisting road that runs parallel to Wadi Musrara, close to the shacks at Sarona, where one encounters the dwellings of the German colonists. I was riding the lame horse in high spirits, imagining the Arab woman with the parted lips lying naked upon her bed, my own head buried between her bronzed breasts as I know her.

As I glided along on Srorika's sorry Arabian stallion the groves and orchards grew thicker, denser, greener, and began to climb the sandstone hillocks forming on the western bank of the wadi. I guided the horse, according to the instructions provided by Saleem and Salaam, along a narrow path that encircled one of the hillocks just north of the homes of the Germans and found myself facing a thorny hedge, a most unattractive and unpleasant plant known by the Arabs as *sabras*, and beside this was a closed gate with a sign upon it written in both the Arabic and French languages: 'La Maison Rajani'.

On my earlier journeys to the colonies of Hadera and Kfar Saba and to the colonies situated in the Galilee, I had no doubt passed along this lane more than once but had never taken notice or paused. Now, I tied up the horse with its reins and went to open the gate. As I drew the bolt the horse began to neigh and snort loudly, and stamp its hoofs. I tightened the reins and moved towards the entrance.

A pleasant dimness, a mistiness, gathered in my eyes as I passed through the gate. Very slowly I began to discern the features of the estate, enshrouded in that same mistiness, and with it came a sense of sweet sorrow like that of an old man contemplating a life of missed opportunities.

The grounds of the estate were densely populated with fruit trees too closely congregated, and tall weeds grew beside them. Juicy fruit hung from the trees, shiny with colour, but much was rotten and still more had fallen and lay rotting in muddy puddles, prey for hordes of fruit flies. I knelt down to take up a handful of earth in order to assess its quality. I passed a clod through my fingers, sifting it, then sniffed.

My heart clenched with envy.

The earth of La Maison Rajani was lush and fertile, the finest, choicest land I had come across in all the Land of Israel. Even the worms there I found to be pot-bellied and lazy, lolling in pleasure.

I rose, heartened, to tour the estate. Among the trees I found many water canals, some obstructed, others mildewed, but fresh and revitalising water flowed in a number of them. I searched out their source until I came upon an ancient well, built of pale, well-worn stones, next to which stood a deep collecting pool covered with thick green algae, lilies and other agreeable plant life. A sad-faced aged mule stood harnessed to a hoist meant to draw water from the well, but at that particular moment she was resting, busy chewing clover and fanning the flies congregating round her tail and her dung.

The path I had been walking along twisted and turned and led to a capacious Arab home one hundred or even two hundred years old. The magnificence of its past was clearly discernible in the elegant, rounded veranda decorated with tiles festooned with Arab lettering. Most of the tiles were faded and worn down with age, but their beautiful colours still displayed a measure of graciousness. From the veranda, three marble steps led up to the engraved and embossed front door, on which the cracks of time

47

had sprouted greenish lichen. A wide sandstone arch had been affixed above the doorway, and atop that stood the second floor, filled with high, broad European windows covered from within by thick curtains.

Over everything hung a pall of mystery and sorrow, as though the estate had been left behind in the race against time and its fine trees and orchards had grown wild, and this impression was very different from the vivid one I had formed upon glimpsing the young and seductive woman of the estate, whose green eyes had swallowed my body that afternoon in the money-changers' market in Jaffa.

As I approached the mansion an evil-eyed old woman crossed my path and called to me in hushed Arabic. Her hissed garbling led me to understand that I was to follow her as she rounded the house from the right, until we reached a back entrance, hidden from view, that led to a tiny, gloomy bedroom whose door I opened in search of the green-eyed woman.

The old woman slipped away into the house through a low, small wooden door while I waited as instructed in the stuffy little room, which, by the look of the furnishings, was the maid-servant's. It contained a large wooden chest for dresses and blouses, and a straw mat for sleeping and a shelf set with a toothed comb and a basin for washing the face, and a tub standing on a wooden pallet, and over it all hung the mouldy odour of a room whose windows have never been opened, and the gloom encircled and encompassed everything.

I waited there some ten minutes, then twenty, but no one came to this small room where I had been left alone. Before another five minutes could pass I went to the low door that led into the rest of the house, and when I opened it I found myself in a long and narrow corridor lined with dusty old red drapes and all manner of daggers and lances and spears affixed to the walls, no sunlight or candlelight on hand to dissipate the thick, silent darkness.

The corridor ended at another wooden door, taller than the first, and when I opened it I found myself standing in a spacious foyer, its floor piled with ancient, thick, embroidered carpets in many hues, one atop the next, each with a layer of dust and dirt accumulated over the years. The windows were covered with double curtains hung heavily one behind the other, and there were stools and low tables and straw mats scattered about in a charmless and inglorious fashion. I sniffed about there and my soul wondered who the owners of this estate were and how it had come to pass that they had been so negligent in their care, and why it was that the fruit trees were stuck in mire, their leaves dropping to the ground and their fruit rotting, and why it was that such a grand house should be stifling and gloomy, as if all love of mankind and vitality had been sucked from it.

And while I was standing there, thinking these thoughts, the feeble-minded child appeared before me, descending the stairway slowly, silently, from the second storey to the first, all the while staring at me, his sad eyes fixed upon me in the same manner as at our first meeting in the money-changers' market, and now, just as then, a reddish blush bloomed on his cheeks like that of a nervous virgin facing her suitor.

When he drew near me he lowered his eyes and whispered, 'You are the Jew.'

His voice was as quiet and reedy as that of a studious girl, though from the way he enunciated his words in the French language it seemed to me that I had been mistaken about his feeble-mindedness.

'I am he,' I answered.

He said, 'I have waited long days for your arrival,' and, to my great astonishment, he crossed the one step separating us and embraced me long and hard, first round the neck, then at the waist. As I allowed this embrace, tears flowed from his eyes, and I was overcome with consternation at the child's odd behaviour. Perhaps he was not feeble-minded, but he was certainly disturbed, and perhaps this was the reason that my horse had snorted and whinnied at the gate, and why everyone maligned the estate.

Her Ladyship is calling for my assistance from the next room. I shall take up my pen again later.

Now I know the name of the good man, the angel, and, lo, he is the angel Gabriel, and I know this because it was revealed to me not in a dream or vision but because he appeared in my home as a wondrous miracle in the form of a man, a flesh-and-blood man whose foot trod on the floor of my house, whose spirit mingled with the air of the estate, whose sweat wafted among the leafy branches of the carob trees; here he stood, here he spoke, here he turned his back, and so lengthy was our meeting, while at the same time so short, that from now and for ever after I shall sit in my bedroom day and night like a nesting bird over many waters and I shall raise in my memory each and every detail about him, how he appeared suddenly here like a ray of sunlight splitting the darkness of an abandoned cave, how he spoke plainly – 'Here you are, Salah, why did you hide from me?' – and I regarded him with the greatest wonderment and awe and exaltation, and he looked at me and said, 'For many long days I have sought you out, Salah,' and I asked him how that could be, but he merely smiled his dimpled smile.

Never before has a man so large and handsome and admired been present in my home, never before has the soul of a man shared with me its secrets, and I plunged to the depths of a deep and embarrassed silence, cursing myself for this tongue that cleaved to the roof of my mouth, but the angel Gabriel did not recoil at my touch – in fact, he put forward his shaven cheek and the sharp contours of his jaw and his eyes, with their piercing look, and asked at once to know everything about me, and I shared nothing with him of my bouts of insanity, my madness, nor of my strange dreams or fevered prophecies; instead, I pretended innocence, and told him of the bicycle I ride when Mother does not forbid it, and in a roundabout manner he asked several questions about her as well, such as where her room might be found and where her husband is and what her life is like and her character, and then he returned to me and wanted to know more and more – about who my friends are and which school I attend and what sort of schoolwork I am belaboured with during the long summer holidays, and I admitted in a weak voice that I had not a single, solitary friend and that the other children loathed me and kept me from the circle of their friendship, and he looked deeply into my eyes, true wonder shining there, and he asked if I would be interested in sharing a bond of friendship with him, and heat throbbed in my face and I told him sincerely and humbly that never had I had a friend or cohort, not even a brother, and he said, 'Salah, good Salah, this is precisely how good friends act towards one another, by sharing sorrows one with the other, and I hope and pray you will agree to be mine.'

And from that moment a covenant was formed between us, that we shall embark upon the path of true friendship together, and my new friend will visit me weekly in my room at the estate, and I shall share all my thoughts with him and impart my torments, and this angel and friend, Gabriel, may remain among the pleasant orchards of our estate for as long as he pleases, and he may quench his thirst in the fountains and canals and rivulets, and walk among the rooms and beat his wings in the hallways, and this covenant we sealed with a hearty embrace of true friendship, and this large friend, a man, this man embraced my body and, lo, this was the first time that a good older brother had enclosed me in his arms, and without thinking, my eyes filled with tears that I wiped away without him seeing, that he might not catch a glimpse of a single one, and all at once the image of a woman burst into my imagination, a beautiful but angry woman all coldness and chill, and I understood that she was making this angel's life a misery, and he did not love her, and fled from her presence and even the sight of her, but I said nothing of any of this to my new friend so as not to sadden his soul, and his embrace is still imprinted upon my tunic.

1 October 1895, Neve Shalom, a few hours later
Her Ladyship demanded my help in procuring medicines for her dental clinic from the Arab market, including a powder applied to perforated teeth, and juices and other liquids used for soothing bleeding gums. I accepted the task – and her authority – without question, for she was uncharacteristically pleasant and I had no desire to darken her mood. She seems to enjoy her profession immensely and the act of mangling the gums of the Arabs who visit her.

Now I shall return to the events of last night at the estate.

As the deranged Arab boy stood embracing me for several long minutes, the angry old maidservant came rushing up and pulled his hands from my waist and commanded him to return to his room on the second floor. She was clearly furious with me and made it abundantly clear that she did not appreciate my disobeying her by leaving the tiny room and she banished me back to that narrow, crowded place.

I did as told. In the tiny room I sat on a stool until the low door to the room opened and, to my delight, the Arab woman with the parted lips and the tinkling laugh and the mirthful eyes entered. She had left the maidservant and the boy elsewhere in the large house.

In French she said, 'Good evening, Mr Luminsky.'

I said, 'Please call me Jacques.'

She said, 'Welcome to our estate. I am Mrs Afifa Rajani.' She twirled a lock of hair in her fingers. 'I am terribly embarrassed by the behaviour of my peasant servant.'

In jest I responded, 'I am accustomed to such treatment from women.'

She regarded me questioningly but I did not explain. I had never before been so near a woman of Muslim Arab extraction, a married one at that, and at her estate, no less. I was surprised at the open and liberal behaviour she was exhibiting towards a foreign male she had met in a Jaffa market. As if she had been reading my thoughts Afifa hastened to ask, 'Did any strangers glimpse your approach?'

'No,' I answered.

'Not even a farmer or a hired labourer?' she asked.

'No.'

'You must watch after yourself,' she said. 'My husband is a very jealous man, and easy to anger. At the moment he is abroad, but if he were to find out about the presence of a man in his house he would rise up and slit your throat. I would never have thought to invite you here were it not for the grief that has visited us.'

A choking fear clogged my throat but I said nothing. The woman began to speak in a cheery manner and with a sharp and intelligent tongue. It seemed she was not a loose woman at all. Only slightly younger than I – perhaps twenty-five or twenty-six years of age – she had probably been snatched away from her dolls as a child of twelve or so and handed over to this tyrannical and malevolent husband of hers, to whom she had then borne a son. Such things were unheard of in Europe and other modern countries, only in the most barbaric lands.

I told her, 'The slip of paper you sent to me piqued my curiosity.'

'It was the child who requested it, and I answered his pleas,' she said.

'And what is the boy's name?' I asked.

'Salah.'

Knowing that every woman loves to hear praise and exaggeration where her son is concerned, I said, 'He is a clever and handsome boy.'

She smiled broadly and laughed that tinkling laugh of hers. 'Your words convey not even an eighth of his wisdom or beauty. But he is ill, and that is the source of our sorrow.'

'This saddens me terribly,' I told her. 'Would it be a bodily disease, like dysentery or cholera?'

Her cheerful visage and bronze skin and green eyes now took on a sheen of sadness and woe. She began to recount the events of her life, and through her words it became clear to me slowly that she was marooned on the estate with her son and her maid-servant, for her husband, Mustafa Abu-Salah, sailed from port to port and sea to sea, conducting his many and varied business affairs. During the long days when he was abroad, it was left to her to subjugate the band of labourers who toiled to pick the fruit from her trees and send them in large wooden crates to the port in Jaffa. This was a big job, a man's job, for which she was not trained or equipped. The assistance of her maidservant was therefore a necessity, for all were subject to the old woman's authority and lived in fear of her sharp, jangling tongue, and she was still strong enough to look after all the needs of the household – the sweeping of the floors, the preparation of the meals, the darning of the socks.

Madame Rajani prattled on and on while I listened and did not listen, for my eyes were fixed upon the long, thin fingers resting upon her thighs, and I was thinking thoughts about how I would raise those fingers between the palms of my hands and then I would kiss them and douse them with my love, for we were two in this narrow little room and her husband was away and the maidservant had departed and the boy was confined to his room on the second floor; the unpleasant old woman's bedclothes would serve us well and we could kiss our kisses and conduct ourselves in the act of love, and I could lick Afifa's nipples and her various apertures and this tongue of hers that was spewing a litany of ancient troubles and tribulations.

The Arab woman asked me, 'Are you listening?'

'I am,' said I.

And so she continued. All would have been well and beautiful with the affairs of the estate but during the last year a terrible malady had befallen her only son, Salah, and he was a sensitive boy and quick to cry, one who loved to sit facing the sea and tell his tales to the waves.

I could sense the exceptional closeness she felt for the boy and that she wished only for his well-being and would do anything to ensure it. I asked, 'What is the nature of this malady?'

'The boy wishes to die,' she said.

This news was unexpected, and very odd. It is the way of children to love life and to play many games and enjoy themselves. They never ponder the one wretched fate of all humankind.

She was silent for a while, then said, 'This malady comes and goes. At times he is gripped with the will to die in the middle of the night, as he sleeps his nightmarish slumber, and at times as he walks along in the middle of the day. Thus, on his father's orders, he is confined to the estate so that he will not bring shame and disgrace upon our family. On the morning we met you he was burning with fever and talking nonsense about some strange war and disaster and destruction, so that in spite of the prohibition set by my husband, the boy's father, I rushed him to a well-known doctor in Jaffa who provided us with a porridge of millet and quinine. When we emerged from the doctor's clinic, Salah's spirits were terribly low and he was feeling morose and contemplating his demise. The moment he spied you, he said, "That man will cure me."'

Surprised, I said, 'And how did he reach this conclusion?'

'I myself will never know,' she said, 'but as Salah prophesies, so do I carry out his wishes.'

I said, 'And how will I bring about his cure?'

'That we shall know only once he has spent time in your presence,' she said, then fell silent. She settled her sharp green gaze on me and her lips parted in a small, seductive smile and she leaned slowly in my direction and asked, 'Is this seemly in your eyes?'

And I told her, 'I will come and be a friend and brother to him and I will help in any way possible to save your son, Salah.' And with that I placed my fingers on her thigh.

She did not remove them.

The ill-tempered maidservant's footsteps resounded outside the door. Before anything could be said I took my hat and left the small room and the estate.

❧

Saleem and Salaam, after bathing in the sea and returning more bronzed and brown than usual, came today to ask my impression of the estate and of the young woman whom I met there yesterday. Sand clung to their dark bodies and the smell of the sea rose from their chiselled faces. I said nothing about either the estate or the woman in order to prevent them from demanding a fee, the twenty per cent *baksheesh* they love so well.

In the afternoon I walked the alleyways of Jaffa, whistling lightly to myself and causing the Arabs to look askance at me. Truth be told, a spirit of optimism had taken hold of me, and it was like a dream that I had not dared share with a living soul, only with the pages of this diary.

One worry I had was that the ways of women are furtive and filled with ruses. He who wishes to beat a path to their door must also behave furtively and proceed with caution. There is no way of understanding women absolutely, for their minds are as fickle and fraudulent as those of cats, creatures who cannot be governed or bridled and are subject to their own whims and caprices, who will learn your desire and do precisely the opposite.

Such are cats and such are women. One may not approach a woman directly but via twisted, winding paths. A man who comes to fornicate without foreplay will find her devoid of all sweetness. It is necessary, therefore, to feign disinterest in the act and distract her with stories and visions; only then can the flame of desire be kindled.

In short, the words of Afifa Rajani caused me to decide to send no note to the young Arab woman, nor to visit the estate or pass along any hints of any nature. I would simply let the touch of my fingers seep into her thigh and allow her womanly instincts to absorb what had happened in that tiny room, and her female desire would slowly ignite so that eventually she would come to me of her own volition and she would place her love and her land before me.

Thus, I will wait for the period of one week and I will see how these matters develop.

9 October 1895, Neve Shalom
Exactly one week has passed since my visit to the Rajani estate. As yet I have heard nothing from Madame Afifa. My nerves are frayed. My passion is aflame. Why has she sent no additional notes or entreated me to come to her? Or perhaps I have erred? These women are as wily as snakes lying in wait among dense undergrowth. Their patience and cunning would astonish any living creature.

Ten days have passed, ten long days, and the angel Gabriel has failed to return to the skies of our estate, has failed to bring all the goodness and grace that lie in his fluttering wings, and Mother pays me no heed, is preoccupied with walking among the tenant farmers and filling crates with oranges to be sent by sea to the ports of the world, and Amina is busy with her pots in the kitchen and with cleaning this large house in which we live, and even the stories that occupy my mind in less turbulent times have turned their backs on me and refuse to be told, the characters fleeing from my presence, burying themselves under blankets of lies, and they are lifeless, untrue, mere verbosity and wind with no beginning or end.

10 October 1895, Neve Shalom

Still no word or even a peep from that temptress. I shall remain stoic a fortnight longer. After all, man's strength is far greater than that of woman.

11 October 1895, Neve Shalom

Man is weak, his urges stronger than he. My heart would not allow me to wait until the end of time, or even a single week longer. So today I took my hat with the intention of leaving the city. But before I could even cross the threshold of our home, Her Ladyship had espied me and demanded my presence that whole evening. I improvised all manner of responses, telling her that the Hovevei Zion group wished to meet urgently with me at their headquarters. And where might that be? she enquired. In the Nabulsi building, I told her, at the end of Bustrus Street. Then I shall wait for you there, she told me, and we shall go to the perfume and flower market. Suddenly this vexed and vexing woman had changed her tune and was playing the role of the romantic lover wishing to remain at my side like a tick on a lion's fur. I plied her with excuses and angry words until she desisted and I was free to depart.

Only the genie residing at the bottom of the *biara* listens to me in silence, for he is pleased with my offer to slip between his watery arms and die there beneath the ripples and water-lilies, and in his husky whisper he reveals a secret to me – that death is nothing but the start of a different life, pleasant and cool, deep inside the well, a place of whole worlds, lustrous and radiant, of genies-in-arms making the rounds of parties and swallowing live fish and sipping the nectar of lilies, and I stand poised on the edge of the *biara*, my pockets heavy with plump stones, but I do not jump into the water to meet his embrace: instead, I gaze upwards to the woeful autumn skies, to the grey and pregnant clouds moving in from the sea, and the genie mocks me with poisoned laughter – Salah, Salah, he calls, there is no true thing to keep you on earth, for even the stories and characters you create no longer desire you.

And among the wavelets of the *biara* I foresee the vision of the future that keeps me awake at night, and among the scenes of war and pillars of smoke I see our Arab brethren fleeing for their lives towards thin-skinned skiffs and citrus groves while behind them pots are left bubbling and simmering on hot coals, and an overwhelming sadness weighs heavily upon my shoulders at the disaster and destruction that bring about this stampede, and it is better that I console myself in those watery arms of the genie in the pool, and I stretch my legs and descend slowly into the water, and my legs do not falter, for quite miraculously there is a hidden ladder I have not hitherto discerned, and little rings form in the water, and they grow and spread as if bringing good tidings at Salah's arrival in the watery kingdom, and the water of the *biara* is warm and pleasant and it pools around my body while good-natured ogres bearing tridents stand guard for me and send fleeting smiles my way, and in just another moment my entire body will be immersed, only my nostrils above the surface, still breathing the air of stiff-necked land-dwellers, and the genie winks at me with his green eyes and cajoles me to descend to the lowest rung of the hidden ladder, and to pique my interest he tells me the water is good, teeming with aspirating life, and in just another moment my head shall dip beneath the surface of the *biara* and I will depart for ever from the few people who granted me love in this world, until suddenly a word, a single word, calls out to me in a large and reckless voice: Salah!

§

12 October 1895, Neve Shalom

While I certainly had pleasant memories of the Rajani estate, my second visit there only fortified the impression of splendour and grace. True, the tenant farmers do not care for it as they should, and their knowledge of fertilisation and irrigation and pruning with secateurs is sorely lacking, but the land itself is excellent, lovely; pools and springs abound and a charming river flows alongside it, and a handsome woman reigns supreme there – what else could an agronomist wish for, and what else could a man desire?

I told myself I would go and speak with the disturbed young man and I would find a path to his heart and bind his soul to mine, thereby bringing his mother's love in tow, and from there I would gain power over her through flattery and sweetness, allowing me to have my way.

As I walked along my spirit was uplifted.

I approached him in silence and whispered, 'Salah.'

He raised his eyes in surprise. The moment he saw me a virginal blush bloomed on his cheeks. He was clearly delighted.

I drew near him at the edge of the pool. The mule hauling buckets from deep within caused the water to eddy into small whirlpools. I picked up a stick and moved aside the algae and weeds to discover clear water bubbling from beneath. The boy was silent, his gaze serious and contemplative. I, too, remained silent. A pleasant autumn breeze passed through the trees. Rueful clouds traversed the sky. After a while, Salah said, 'You see this pool?'

'What of it?' I asked.

'From it will come my demise,' said he.

'Is that what you wish?' I asked.

'Whether I do or do not is of no import.'

I submerged the stick in the dirty water. The boy is strange, that much is clear to me. His speech is hushed, and soaked in melancholy, as if the grief of the world rests on his tiny shoulders. His facial expressions are chimerical: at times he appears dim-witted, at others wise and wizened. His body, too, is odd. His limbs are graceless, his black hair thin and wispy, bereft of that Asian sheen. He did not inherit the green eyes of his mother, nor her gracious comportment, or the laugh that brings magic to the hearts of all men.

Still, this boy is the sole pipeline to the Arab woman's heart and to her splendid estate, more beautiful than beauty itself. An idea blossomed in my mind. I said, 'Are you versed in the skill of swimming, either in the sea or the river?'

'No,' he said.

'Your father has not taught you?' I asked.

He said nothing.

'Remove your tunic,' I told him.

At first he seemed embarrassed at the idea of undressing, but after I stripped off my shirt and trousers and stood before him nearly naked and jumped into the pool, he did the same. His arms are scrawny and fragile, as if not a scrap of bread has crossed his lips in some time. All his timid mannerisms made it clear to me that he has spent too much time in the company of women and that he has no experience of spending time with his father or any other man.

After removing his clothing he stood conflicted, weighing the possibilities, as he tickled the water with his toe, and glancing to and fro. I saw no other way but to pull him into the water. He plunged downwards, thrashing about and trembling with fear, then rose up out of the water, bluish and flailing but alive and breathing, his eyes shut and sparkling with droplets. An astonished gasp of laughter escaped from his mouth.

When we were clothed once again the boy seemed revived and happy and a bit more joyful. His mother and the maidservant had heard sounds of laughter and came to us, disbelieving. The old woman's wrath was tempered, and she stood gazing in astonishment at the boy as he frolicked and laughed. She embraced Salah firmly and led him to the capacious house in order to dry him off.

Afifa and I remained alone. She was quick to thank me for the kindness I had shown her son, Salah.

I said, 'The boy is in need of a male presence in his life.'

She laughed her tinkling laugh and said, 'His mother, too.'

'May I come visit the two of you again?' I asked.

She ran her fingers through her hair, parted her lips and said, 'With pleasure.'

I kissed her lips and departed.

After the angel Gabriel had saved me and saved my life and removed his clothing and jumped into the pool and waged a brave and courageous war with the green-eyed genie, and his naked body struck my detractors mercilessly until the genie and the other sea monsters retreated in defeat to their deep and hidden dens, and after he had departed from me with a kiss and an embrace and a promise to return to me soon, without tarrying as before, as one friend does with another – after all of these, a terrific row broke out between my mother and me.

That day Mother entered my room and slammed the door

behind her, and told me that my carrying on – the communal dips in the *biara*, the stories and poems I compose in his honour – with this strange and foreign man, a Jew who comes and goes like an estate-owner or a husband, must cease on this very day, and she informed me that she would forbid him to enter the estate again.

This outburst astonished me: after all, it had been the angel Gabriel who had bestowed his grace and all manner of pleasures upon me, and I let Mother know that he was my saviour, and my close friend, my ally, and I revealed to her this secret covenant we have formed between us, and informed her about our activities in the *biara*, but she took back not a word of what she had said. On the contrary, she explained that she had already told the tenant farmers to be on the lookout for the foreigner and that if they saw him within the grounds of the estate they should turn him over at once to the local Turkish governor for the purpose of incarcerating him and torturing him, and far better: let them judge and punish him as they see fit.

I croaked a short, dry laugh and announced to Mother in no uncertain terms that whether she would allow me or not I would continue my friendship with the man I admired so much and, if necessary I would disobey all her other orders as well, and I would fish out my bicycle and escape from the estate, which had already become loathsome to me, and I would venture to Jaffa or to the Jewish quarter where he lived, and that was where I would live out my days.

Mother reddened in anger and commanded me to apologise, but I refrained from responding, and she made it clear, in the language of a threat, that one day my father would return from his worldwide travels and when he heard of my impudence towards my mother, my parent, my life-giver, he would punish me in such a way that would cause even the cruellest of the

Turkish pasha's soldiers to pale in horror and revulsion.

It was then that I released all manner of things from my heart, for this woman known as my mother wished only the worst for me by routing my few and only friends and dispatching me to a contemptible and perverse loneliness, for she passes her days in doling out prohibitions and limitations against me in such great numbers that my life loses its very flavour, and all those horrible nightmares and visions that come to me in the evening and which I forget by morning are the result of her tyranny, and I wish that these days under her sovereignty would come to an end and I could escape from her, and her plotting intrigues, for she is an evil woman, worse than evil itself, and her sole purpose is to keep me in her shadow, in her image – that of a bitter hag – and Mother planted two slaps on each of my cheeks and told me that from that moment and until the end of time I would be imprisoned in my chamber and that I was not to descend to the foyer or the kitchen even to pass water or bring a morsel of food to my mouth, and after these things she locked the door and clattered her way quickly down the stairs to the first floor.

As for me, no worries entered my heart, for I knew the angel Gabriel would fly through the window of my home and keep me company and rescue me from Mother's malice, and until that time came my old friends Leila and Rashid would keep me company on the page and through their stories, in my diary and on my easel, and now they were once again in good spirits, and grateful for their very lives, and many characters are born each day from the stump of a thought, from flickers of ideas, and I bring them to the page at once and breathe souls into them, am happy at their joys and sad at their miseries, just as I am bringing these very words to the page with my pen.

In the end, Mother's ire cooled and only a few hours had passed from the onset of our ferocious battle when she ascended to my room and rescinded her prohibition, and she had thought, after consulting with Amina, that she should allow me to meet again with the foreigner in my room as long as no other soul caught sight of us, for there were many tongue-waggers and gossips among us, and in any case when the day came for her husband and my father to return from distant seas I must swear an oath never to mention even a single word of this new friend of mine, for the wrath and envy of this husband and father are incendiary and could lead quickly to destruction and loss.

I promised what she asked and we stood in my room embracing one another. She asked if I would like to step out into the autumnal air, to breathe into my lungs the sea air and the breezes that would soon turn stormy and wild, and she suggested that I come to sit with her in the small shed covered with grapevines where she was embroidering rosebuds and roses on tablecloths, as she was always wont to do, but I hastily refused her entreaties, preferring instead to remain in my room for the purpose of continuing to work on my stories and poems.

19 November 1895, Neve Shalom

My diary will have to forgive me for neglecting it. It is the way of the world that when days of happiness arrive, writing is pushed aside. How can I sit pondering the ruminations of my heart when the very essence of life itself, frothing and foaming, waits stormily outside the door to be sampled?

The past month has been perfectly simple in nature as I have come and gone at the estate and taken great pleasure in such. It has become my custom to whistle upon my arrival at the gate, whereupon Salah appears, like a faithful dog wagging his tail, and welcomes me each time with a blush and lowered gaze. It is quite clear that he enjoys my presence very much. I, too, enjoy the time I spend there.

Bit by bit I have come to know this boy and his life and deeds. He cannot be called to task for his timid ways, for he has spent his entire youth uniquely in the presence of women, with his mother and the wrathful maidservant, and has no knowledge of the ways of men. He was not sent to school due to his inability to find favour among his peers, and his mother has instead taken it upon herself to instruct him in the French language and algebra while the maidservant serves as his nanny.

The lack of a man in his life is so apparent that it screams to high heaven. His every action is conducted in the shadow and image of the female. Instead of heading out to enjoy the beauty of the estate, to till its land, to swim in its pools, to run to the hot, wave-swept seashore, to roll and tumble with other children, to fight them for his land and heritage, to toss stones at wagtails and chase after cats' tails – instead of all these, he shuts himself in his room on the second floor day after day after day to write poems and stories.

I went with him to his room, which faces the sea, and even there heavy curtains conceal the view, and books lie piled high, and above it all the boy's papers reign supreme with their handwritten stories and poems. Salah writes in Arabic, so I cannot read what he has penned, and he evades my requests for translation. Only this has he agreed to reveal: that it is his intention to write a broad-canvas tale of the Bedouins with which his mind is preoccupied so that he toils through long days and nights.

All the while that Salah and I spend time with one another, his mother observes us with satisfaction and prepares sumptuous meals for us. Imagine, first, the meals prepared by Her Ladyship, who is always angry, coiled like a web of nerves: she sends her husband to the Arab market to buy their produce so that she will not – heaven forfend! – be required to lift a cleaver to a cut of meat or prepare a porridge or dice parsley and onions and tomatoes. And now, contrarily, picture the meals prepared by Afifa as she stands in the cavernous kitchen of her Arabian house and trims the unwanted bits from vegetables and laughs her many laughs, and all that she does is accomplished with a light-hearted spirit and a love of life and frivolity, and she sears strips of aubergine over an open flame and bakes steaming pocket bread that she smears with a strange paste made of sesame seeds, called *tehina* by the locals. And she fills vegetables, like marrows and gourds and tomatoes, with all sorts of delicacies, such as mince with rice and carrots and raisins; further, if Salah and I are seated at the low table and the boy is, as usual, a bit melancholic but nevertheless has a healthy appetite – from our frolics – and finishes his meal, his mother brings us sweetmeats in the form of semolina biscuits with nuts and dates, served with the pungent *qahwah* drunk by Arabs, and I recline against the curtained wall, embroidered pillows stuffed with feathers and straw beneath me, the dessert dishes in front of me, and I drum my fingers on my sated belly and think, It could not get any better than this.

The Land of Israel boasts a marvellous feature: during the months of autumn the Levantine weather is unusually pleasant; the wind is calm and does not freeze the blood in one's veins; the sea is stormy at times and at others not. How good it is to sit on a sandstone cliff and look up at the clouds as they gather in clumps over your head and you take in the excellent air of the Rajani estate.

At first I would come to them for an hour or two at twilight, then after a while I started coming at midday and staying for hours on end, walking about with Salah among the trees and the orchards in an attempt at coaxing the boy, whose voice has not yet changed and whose lip remains hairless, to speak with me about his odd and mirthless malady. But Salah shares nothing of it with me, only informing me that when I am with him and when he is with me his spirits lift and are merry. Even the ruminations of his own death, and the nightmares that plague his sleep, have passed from the world, and it seems that he is growing stronger and healthier just as he prophesied to his mother.

One day this week, as we were walking through the village of tenant farmers on the grounds of the estate and observing the wretched labourers as they toiled like donkeys, my bladder felt full and I said to Salah, 'Come let us pass our water.' He was flustered and flummoxed; none the less, I led him behind the trees where I pushed aside my clothing and proceeded to urinate on the wall. Salah stood watching me, gripped with wonder and stupefaction. It turns out that he carries out the act of urinating by crouching, like his mother; no alternative had ever heretofore entered his mind. He regarded me with a gaze of sheer admiration, pushed aside his clothing and emulated me, a burst of excited laughter pealing from his tongue as he grasped his trickling member.

On another morning I asked him about his father, trying to fish from him the information necessary to me with regard to the estate. His face grew angry and he told me that his father is always abroad, sailing the seas, and during his rare and truncated stays at home he makes the lives of everyone a misery. His mother bawls, the grumbling maidservant grumbles more than ever and Salah himself returns to his evil thoughts and envisages himself with laden pockets and waterlogged clothing that will pull him down and down to the depths of the turbid pool to choke and die and drown there.

I asked him, 'When will this father of yours return?'

'I do not know,' he told me, his lips trembling as one poised to burst out in tears.

I wished to help him forget this terrible vision and so, the next day, I brought him a gift that I had purchased in the Gypsy market, a sort of felt-covered ball used for tossing and kicking by children at play. Salah regarded me like one who had never seen a ball in his life, and in the end he went to be alone in his room with his writings.

Every day of this month I have gone to be with the boy and play with him and enjoy myself in his company without asking any recompense from the laughing Arab woman. I pondered this business of giving something and being reimbursed for it, and determined that I should not press the issue. In fact, the longer it goes on, the higher the price should rise; not only that, but it seems preferable to wait and see what Afifa will offer me. I have observed her watching us, a beatific smile on her face as she takes pleasure in the change occurring in her son, and I have noticed that when I take my leave of Salah she finds ways and obstacles to prolong my departure so that we spend long moments alone together, just she and I, no other person from the estate anywhere near us, just we two side by side.

Today, before parting, as once again she fiddled with her dark hair, she coyly mentioned a secret hut at the western edge of the estate, very near the sycamore trees. It is surrounded by spindly grapevines and roofed with date fronds. When the moon is full the Arab woman goes there alone, the estate's jasmine blossoms a path for her small bare feet.

Something that has never before happened to me is actually taking shape and becoming real and true, and it is that I now have a friend, a flesh-and-blood friend, who comes and goes from my house and shares secrets with me and plays games, and this friend is not some runny-nosed boy with a bitter soul like those who roam in flocks and loathe me and call me strange and terrible names, and this is no character created from words, trapped for all eternity between the pages of my cloistered diary, inside the obscurity of my drawer in the shadows of my dark and gloomy room, but a man, a real man, whose laughter thunders and whose bristles prickle and whose feet are wide and large and whose curly locks skim and bounce like swallows at dawn, and he spends his days with me and knows the very nature of my character and is familiar with my stories, and his voice resounds in my ear and his scent lingers on my face and hands, and his eyes encircle my head and heart and he is present in everything, poured into every goblet, trickling onto every tongue: it is he, my beloved friend.

On occasion, when the onset of winter gives way to a sudden flame of fleeting summer heat and the air turns sweaty and steamy all at once, the angel Gabriel and I flout Mother's orders and we leave the estate, and I take him to a place for which I have great affection, a walk of an hour or two but well worth it, towards the great cliff overlooking the sea near the ancient graveyard where my ancestors are interred, and there we sit one next to the other facing the hot winds, Jaffa's teeming port winking at us from the south and steamships passing from horizon to horizon, and the angel Gabriel removes his clothing and urges me, with his thunderous laughter and white-toothed smile, to do the same, to allow this late sun to bronze our skin in preparation for the encroaching winter chill, and I steal glances at his body, a body into the likes of which I, too, shall grow, and like the seashore I am set awash in the waves and I am filled with admiration for the thin, invisible line of his clipped whiskers, and the thick neck, hard as a tree-trunk, and the wide shoulders carried on high like a trek through a large and goodly land, and the shoulder-blades drawn like muscled hills, and from there I lower my gaze to the long, thick fingers brimming with crafts-manship, to the tapered legs covered with a fine plume of golden hair, and the angel Gabriel smiles from ear to ear, and as he drums on his belly he says, 'Salah, my friend, it could not get any better than this.'

Only Mother tries to tear our friendship asunder: each time after he departs she pours lies and fabrications about him into my ear, such as that he is a Jew, a Jew as dastardly as they all are, and that his eyes are ploughing evil and his heart is sowing mischief, and one time she ascended to my room to whisper goodnight and told me, as if it barely bore mentioning, that the angel Gabriel had uttered my name in her ear, and I asked, in a trembling voice, what he had told her, and she answered, in an absentminded fashion, that it was nothing, and I said, Why did he mention my name? and she said, But a single word about you was spoken, a single word and no more, and the word was *odd*, that you are an odd child, odd or strange, and I was overcome at once with a blurred saltiness of tears, tears that stand in front of my eyes and swallow whole the prattling vision before me, and I answered her with a shout, A liar you are, a liar! and she repeated his words with a stab of her tongue, An odd child, she said, and she left my room, and I retrieved the portraits I had drawn of the angel Gabriel, and the pages of the story that I have been writing in which the angel Gabriel is the hero, the saviour, and I began to speak to him, to encourage him to respond, and he laughed his pleasant, familiar laugh and reassured me that this was the way of women, that they are filled with jealousy and eager to provoke quibbles and quarrels and I should not listen to their chatter; instead I must remain fast and true to my friendship with this good man, the angel Gabriel.

And it happened that three or four days after I spoke in that vexed and infuriated manner, and refused to answer even her most trifling questions, she was overcome with remorse at her evil deeds, and in order to appease me she toiled to prepare a sumptuous meal for me and for him, but her malevolent spirit and her fuming, sickly jealousy contaminated the food, so that the aubergines lay on the plate like the bodies of dead soldiers and the marrows grew limp and feeble, and over everything wafted the taste and scent of tainted, spoiled meat, foul as bad breath or the carcass of a fly-infested cat, and I pushed away the plate with both hands and brought no food to my mouth.

2 December 1895, the Rajani Estate
I am lying in a hut on the Rajani estate under a full moon. I have just lain with the Arab woman.

Her comportment in bed is good, if slightly lacking. On the one hand her passion is ardent: her kisses are wet and watery, her sex is damp and deep and invites a man to drown wholly in it. On the other hand, the influence of the wrathful, ageing, malevolent husband who snatched her from her dolls at a tender age is all too apparent. She knows nothing of bringing pleasure to herself. She had neither heard nor dreamed of orgasm for women.

The thrusting of my tongue into that comely pearl hidden among many folds, that oral act absolutely forbidden by my wife, Her Ladyship, was met with wonder and astonishment by Madame Rajani. When I moved those folds aside with my fingers and planted passionate kisses on her point of pleasure (which in Hebrew has no name but is called 'clitoris' in the cultured languages), then wiggled and jiggled and jiggered and joggled it, the Arab woman croaked a surprised cackle and began shaking and quaking, her hips roiling wildly, her thighs heaving like a ship in stormy seas. I thrust an anchor inside her until she sank.

Like me, the angel Gabriel does not love Mother and shrinks from her presence; this is what he told me himself, and he prefers to be alone with me, only me, and he whittles sticks for me and presents me with knives, and balls for games, and it is enough for him to spy her from afar to turn his back and take me to another place, and he snorts with derision, for he has grown accustomed to her unpleasant character and her aberrant ways.

The tenant farmers are now used to seeing him walk about the estate with me and they find nothing odd in this – *au contraire*: they, like me, are filled with admiration and gratitude towards the angel Gabriel since he has studied all there is to know about soil in kingdoms across the sea, and at times he points out their errors and shows them a better irrigation method or how to graft citrus trees, and once they even handed him a large leaf, pointed at both ends and overrun with grey aphids and he handed them a remedy for disinfecting the plants, thereby bringing peace and prosperity to our estate, and immediately a rumour circulated among them that he, the angel Gabriel, could overcome genies and strike fear into them, and the farmers brought before him a rheumy-eyed, feverish infant and he banished all her demons and restored her to life, and this is the handiwork of an angel, my friend the good angel Gabriel.

Every hour of twilight and evening, of day and night, I spend at the Rajani estate, where Afifa attends to my every need with delights and pleasures. There is no manner of Arab sweetmeat or delicacy that she did not serve me today, much as a bride prepares for her groom or a fiancée for her betrothed, such as the sweet noodle dish called *kadaif*, or the orange-coloured dough filled with goat cheese and sprinkled with sugar, called *kanafeh*, all proffered with the dark and bitter coffee drunk by Arabs, many grains of which stick to the sides of the glass and can be used, by knowledgeable Gypsy women, to predict a man's fate.

The boy, too, adores me and follows close by me at all times, desirous of my company. I have begun to show affection for him, the sole purpose being the opportunity to find myself in the arms of Afifa Rajani, his mother. The long hours he has spent with me have slightly altered his ways. He has already learned to stand up to an adversary and face him without acquiescing. When I instructed him in the skill of selecting a stone and throwing it at the head and body of one who wishes evil upon him, the boy regarded me with astonishment, picked up the stone and tossed it slowly into the air. I removed a thick chunk of wood from a tree-trunk and whittled it down with a penknife until it had turned into a bar good for clubbing. The boy took part in the game at first but after a while he asked to be excused to his room so that he could write a bit in his diary. I permitted him to leave me.

When at last Afifa and I were alone, night having fallen early and the stars and crickets buzzing above the damp earth, I took her hand in mine and we walked to our hut, kissing deeply and lushly and caring not a whit even when the skies opened up and poured vast quantities of rainwater on us in an attempt at extinguishing our love. But, in fact, our love cannot be quenched.

My sleep wanders again at night, not from soul-disturbing dreams but because of the angel Gabriel, and I revisit in my imagination all that has transpired between us throughout the day – there he is, handing me a ball made of knotted clothing; there he is, laughing with me as he leans against the doorpost of the house; there he is, instructing me in how to hurl rocks in order to slay my enemies; there we are, riding invisible horses as we kill loathsome children; there he is, tossing me high into an orange tree to hide among its branches; there he is, ascending to my bedroom and chuckling at the sight of my many stories and poems; and as I lie back on my pillows – night descending, the broad window facing my bed framing a darkened tree in whose branches the wind whistles, announcing the onslaught of winter – my door creaks on its hinges like an old crone praying for her own death, and in this hour of black gloom it is clear to me that these wondrous days will not last for ever and, lo, they are already waning, passing from this world and vanishing as if they had never existed, and what is left now, as night encroaches, of the sunshine and light of day – what is left but these few sparse words in my diary, and these thoughts and memories in my head, for the thoughts will be forgotten quickly and the words perhaps will last a bit longer than I, but how few and paltry they are, and who will ever make the effort to read them, and if he does read them, will he understand them, will he be able to picture that which was written by a tortured, loving, hopeful soul? Thus it was: there they are, the boy and the man, and this is how they laughed, this is how they hoped, and this is how all became silent, and ended.

Bad tidings. The man known as Mustafa Abu-Salah has returned unexpectedly to the Rajani estate after lengthy travels to Alexandria and Algeria. He sent no telegram announcing his impending arrival, and at the very hour of the afternoon that his impressive entourage reached the port – masses of luggage along with a convoy of camels, mules, horses and other beasts of burden glorifying the presence of this dignitary, this personage – I was entwined in lovemaking with his wife, Afifa, in that excellent vine-covered hut.

Were it not for the startled cries of the maidservant Amina, Afifa would never have managed to return to her capacious house at that last minute to greet her husband on the wide veranda, as loving wives are expected by custom to do. As for me, I dressed myself and disappeared into the thick orchard surrounding the house, then came round to the front to catch a glimpse of a fat and bloated man with a swarthy, sun-baked face, a carpet of thick black hair covering his body.

I was eventually able to slip away from the estate but cannot return so long as the *effendi* squats there. Five days have passed since then and I yearn to see the Arab woman and the estate, though for the time being that is not possible. Back and forth I pace our home in Neve Shalom, waiting for a note or letter or some sign of life from Afifa, but nothing comes.

As for Her Ladyship, instead of assisting her husband who is in the throes of a very bad spell, she has become even more difficult, as if to enrage me. She trails after me, wishing to make plans for the future, pressing me to engage new accommodations, larger ones, since her clinic is too small and narrow to contain her Arab clientele. On occasion she even seduces me to join her in lovemaking, tempting me with that most arid sex of hers. But I am wholly taken with the Arab woman; she, and no other.

Father, who has for the time being returned from his journeys before setting out once again, is occupied all day long in quarrelling with Mother, while I of the wilting soul stand panting, like a dog, at the gate of the estate, waiting in vain for he who comes not, and so I took action and went to the ground floor of our home, near Amina's tiny room, careful not to attract her inquisitive stares, and Amina was searching for something in her trunk, so I waited until she bent over to thrash about in her clothing and then, her stooped back to me, her enormous buttocks covered with the black cloth of her dress, faded with age, blocking the doorway, I stole away to the hiding-place of my bicycle, the very bicycle that had been relegated to a hidden corner the entire summer as a result of Mother's prohibition, and now, with a scraping, screeching sound of surprise, it responded to the forgotten touch of my fingers, and I grasped the handle-bars with my right hand and wiped away the rain spots from the seat with my left, and I noted with great pleasure that the tyres were not completely worn away, and all at once there was a crashing sound from Amina's room, the shattering of a china plate or a glass, and the old maidservant let out a stream of curses and straightened herself as if to leave the room and I knew she would at any second catch sight of me, so I took hold of the bicycle, jumped onto it and rode hither and thither towards the closed front gate that stands among the prickly-pear bushes, from which I would escape as I had been planning for three long days, the days during which the angel Gabriel had been absent, and I would find him and revel in his embraces.

The bicycle under me was wild and hard to handle – the front wheel wreaked havoc, threatening to collide with sharp stones or career out of control on a downward slope – but my hands held true, for my purpose was high and noble: to save the angel Gabriel from whatever misfortune had befallen him, and through these three long days and nights gruesome and disturbing visions had visited me of the many forces who desired the angel Gabriel, such as the evil demons and genies, those who dwell in trees and those who dwell in the depths of the sea, the black-eyed spirits and the green-eyed spirits, all nourished by envy and avarice, by greetings of death and curses from hell, and perhaps some had even banded together and set traps for him, and this thought shivered through my brain, as if some genie at the bottom of the *biara* had avenged him. I rode my bicycle past the sad-faced mule harnessed to the water-hoist, and the wavelets in the *biara* stirred something in me, the dense, mildewed foliage a snare before my eyes, and I pushed all thoughts of evil from my mind: I would ride to the place the angel Gabriel had described to me many times, his house at the edge of Jaffa, in the Jewish Quarter, for his soul was pining for mine and mine for his.

To my great surprise I found the gate to the estate open, and a flock of seagulls was flying to my right like an arrow pointing towards my path to success, behind me the cries of Amina, who had alerted my mother, now standing at the doorpost of the house, speechless and motionless, while Amina shouted again and again, Salah, Salah, return at once! But I rode away from them, onwards and forwards, on the track that leads to the paved road that runs alongside Wadi Musrara, towards my good friend, the angel who saved me from watery death, so that I may return the favour and rescue him at once from the grasping genies, their hands around his neck, those lovers of evil and war who had united for the purpose of bringing about his demise.

I had never before left home alone, never disobeyed Mother, never stolen or lied, but now I understood that my actions, which seemed wrong-headed, were in fact good, for a winter breeze flooded my cheeks with wet kisses and a light, warm drizzle tamped the path ahead, and my legs pumped harder and faster on the pedals and the tyres carried me along the river and then the sea, and suddenly I could see the minarets of the muezzins in Jaffa above the dense orchards and the pomegranate trees and the wild herb bushes, and to the east of the city as I pedalled southwards I caught sight of the homes of the Jews, and their style was strange, unlike the buildings of Jaffa, and how would I find that of the man for whom my soul pined, the house described to me absentmindedly by the angel Gabriel as being adjacent to the railway station built for us by the sultan, which was where I dismounted from my bicycle, which I tied to a stone pillar, and stood bewildered and bedazzled.

I had never before stood alone among Jews, had not so much as observed their customs or been familiar with their actions. Their skin was white, clear, they walked erect, spoke in loud voices, their language a stammering, jammering gibberish like the cackling of cranes, and near the railway station they had set up shops and cafés, not the kind of *maqha* popular in Jaffa, where the uncles and grandfathers sit fingering worry beads as they listen to soulful tunes on the violin and suck the smoke from their *narghile* pipes, but a place where crude and chattering bare-armed women lick ice-cream in spite of the winter chill, and they argued vociferously with the men while the men, dressed in strange, long-sleeved garments and black hats, some with papers spread before them, read just as I do in the privacy of my small room, and one woman touched my arm and asked my name, and I told her in the French language that my name was Salah and I asked where I could find the angel, and where I could see his wings, and she waggled a finger at me as if to tell me no, and then all was drowned by the horn and smoke of a careening steam engine.

A bevy of passengers from Al-Quds, that is Jerusalem, alighted on the platform, among them fellow Arabs travelling to Jaffa-town and Christians bound for the southern neighbourhoods, and I followed the Jews in order to learn their ways and, lo, here was that blond hair and those curls bobbing like a swallow on the water, and I shouted, Gabriel, Gabriel! but he continued in a hurry, absorbed in the chatter of a group of fellow passengers, and they walked as one, their faces turned towards the houses set near the station. I took up my bicycle and began to chase after them, and Gabriel's golden hair appeared and vanished from one moment to the next, and then he took leave of his comrades and removed his hat as a way of saying goodbye, and I wished to call to him but my throat clenched and fell dumb, for what if no evil had befallen him and the angel Gabriel simply no longer desired to see me?, and the angel entered his home, a small, crowded place of two storeys, and the sound of a dentist's drill rose from it, and a lone, wretched tree unlike the ones on our estate stood in the garden, and I hid in its thin foliage and peered in through the window, and a woman with beautiful eyes dressed in a white smock, her hair gathered in a bun atop her head, like the bulb of an onion, greeted him warmly, and he returned the greeting and kissed her lovingly and removed his jacket and placed his hat on a rack and stretched his arms, and in another second he would draw near the window and catch my peeping gaze, and silence gripped my throat as if all my words, these words written fluidly here, many lines of them without punctuation or cessation, had suddenly died, expired, for the angel Gabriel sprawled out across a high-backed sofa, his face tranquil, and from one of the interior rooms of the house an Arab dignitary suddenly emerged, his face and jaw dressed in bloodied bandages, and the white-skinned woman escorted him out of the house, in a hurry to be rid of him, and then she locked the door and unknotted her long, golden hair, which flowed past her neck, and she curled up to the angel Gabriel and removed his shoes and then her own, and they were barefoot, barefoot for all to see, and they tickled one another, his plump toes encircled hers and the pleasant fragrance wafted all the way to me, through the glass windows, and she was telling him something, whispering it into his ear, and they laughed, together sipping wine from crystal goblets, and a low, pleasant fire crackled in the hearth, and thunder pealed in the heavens – soon there would be lightning and bones would rattle and become soaked to the marrow – and there I stood in the shadow of the single tree, wind rasping through the leaves, its trunk thin and young, and in another moment everything would break apart and collapse from this raging wind.

The way back to the estate was wet with the water flowing from the skies and streaming down my cheeks. The bicycle became mired in muddy earth and the wagon drivers and horsemen I met along the way shouted warnings to me – Boy, where are you going? The river is about to flood its banks! – but I continued riding, at times fighting the ferocious, terrifying winds that skirled in my ears, at times relaxing my grip on the bicycle so that I might be caught in the fangs of the roiling river and swallowed into its deep, wet mouth, and my thoughts were confused and they clashed against one another: the angel Gabriel no longer desires me, he is busy making mirth in his warm home in the arms of a golden-haired woman and every memory of his friendship and camaraderie with Salah has long since been forgotten, and what could this handsome man want with such a boy, whom everyone loathes? and I reproached myself for such pride that had taken hold of me and led me to believe that I would ever walk the road of such a beautiful friendship, to hope truly and wholeheartedly that beauty could ever bind itself to ugliness, purity to ignobility, courage to fear, and once again I envisaged the angel Gabriel safe in his home with his adoring wife, and they kiss and embrace, their world is closed and conjoined, and they have no use for Salah or his drawings or his stories, but then a new and consoling thought rose in my mind, that perhaps the man I saw was not the angel Gabriel but another Jew, for the Jews look so alike that among ten you will not find a single difference, and all the more so among thirty or forty Jewish passengers who have alighted from a train. I raced home, and in the darkening night I lost my way and no longer knew where the estate was, or my home, or my notebooks and poems and drawings filled with my only friends, until I caught sight of Mother standing beside a rusted gate swinging on its hinges, her robes fluttering in the wind.

She pulled me to her bosom and embraced me, pulled me from the bicycle, and in the house she stripped the wet clothes off me, replacing them with dry ones, and placed a bowl in front of me, and she did not leave my side until I had finished the last drop of hot soup, and after these things had come to pass I wished to kiss her cheek, but she whispered sweetly, Salah, the punishment for your rebellious mouth has not yet passed, I will speak with your father; for now, ascend to your room before the great storm ahead.

17 *December 1895, Neve Shalom*
Today, in the afternoon, the opportunity to meet Afifa arose since her husband the *effendi* had travelled by train to Jerusalem to attend to his affairs there. Afifa, since I had last seen her, had changed immeasurably. Her face was veiled, by command of her husband, and her great fear of him was etched onto her pale face

and in the various wrinkles now creasing the skin around her lips. Afifa had missed me terribly as I had her: she had pulled out her hair, was wringing her hands, her heart was shattered, and when at last we were together she planted her lips on mine, her eyes trickling with tears.

It turned out that her husband had returned from his journeys abroad because he was not in the best of health. He had been having some sort of convulsions, and strange sensations in his body, and he wished to receive the counsel of the best doctors in the Holy Land, or at least the chance to rest in his homeland until the malady would depart from his body. I began to preach to her about the commandment to love one's husband and to care for him in his hour of need, but she had no use whatsoever for these words of sweetness and consolation that I was imparting to her. Instead, she repeated again and again that it was only I whom she desired, I alone, and not merely for the blazing love she felt for me but also for the boy, the boy, and that was when she began recounting the changes and transformations taking place in Salah since his father had returned and I had ceased to come to the Rajani estate. She said he was back to his old ways, having nightmares every evening, speaking hallucinatory nonsense about the end of days and about Judgement Day, when the heavens will cleave and the graves will crumble, and about a war that will visit them, and how the unyielding vanquishers will slaughter the Arabs by sword and will strip them of their homes and raze their villages and throw salt on the wounded earth, and Afifa was utterly distraught because Salah was once again prophesying his own death, pointing to the pool from which would come his demise, and all the rosiness of joy that had reddened his cheeks and all his exuberance and gaiety of recent days had dissipated and was gone.

While she continued to jabber on hysterically in the manner

of mothers worried for their offspring, an idea was forming in my mind: that on the morrow I would pay a visit to Mustafa Abu-Salah, face to face, and I would offer to purchase lands from his estate. Surely now, at this time of the man's infirmity and fragility, and the fact that this estate was an enormous and expensive burden, he would see fit to sell parcels of it to the Jews as a means of helping him maintain the place.

24 December 1895, Neve Shalom
Today I paid a visit to the estate. The first person I met was the grumpy old maidservant, who was busy running a tunic over a washboard. Her face gave no clue whatsoever – not even the slightest hint of a smile, the tiniest grimace – that she recognised me. She invited me into the house, which was, as always, steeped in gloom and a mouldy smell of great old age and of standing water, and I pondered the presence of Afifa and Salah in that house at that very hour, so near and so distant all at once. We entered a large reception room filled with red and orange lounging pillows faded by sunlight, and it was there that I met, for the first time face to face, body to body, soul to soul, the celebrated and illustrious husband and father, none other than his lordship the *effendi* Mustafa Abu-Salah Rajani.

For three months I have been spending time with members of the Rajani family and its employees, coming and going, learning their natures and ways, for three months I have been listening to their tales of this man of honour and importance and my curiosity was sorely piqued to look upon the face of the husband and father, proprietor of these fruitful and bounteous lands, yet when the maidservant with the malevolent gaze opened the door to his chambers, a snigger escaped my mouth, for the man before me did not look like a man at all, but like a woman: his expression was feminine and feeble, his eyes watery as a mad dog's, his fingers bejewelled and his neck bedecked with gold, and on his head sat a ridiculous tarboosh covered with red felt and fringed with gold. Had I not been certain my legs were standing on Arab lands I would have thought I was in the presence of a whoring ballerina in a Viennese street theatre.

The *effendi* placed his wide, padded bottom on the velvet lounging pillows, folded the sleeves of his glittering, foppish gown, and waved to me weakly, with limp fingers, to join him on the pillows and to help myself to a tray filled with biscuits and dried fruit.

Following a lengthy and wearying exchange of greetings and other formalities customarily performed in Asia, the *effendi* listened to my generous offer to purchase his estate for an outrageous sum of money never before offered in these parts, some fifteen bona-fide francs for every *dulam* of land. He pretended to be thinking – perhaps about the golden fringe on his tarboosh, or Lord knows what else – and then he looked out of the window, took a dried chickpea from the tray and said, in his feeble voice, that for less than forty francs a *dulam* he would not sell the estate.

I am well acquainted with the bargaining customs of these people, and so I offered him all manner of options, and I thought about the various ways I could obtain such a sum for the wondrous estate, but the beefy *effendi*, covered with jewels like some handmaiden in the sultan's harem, simply repeated his unheard of price – forty francs per *dulam* – and curtly showed me the door.

I have not seen Father for ages and ages, always occupied, as he is, with business overseas, never available, and today Mother angered him with all manner of chatter – for example, she recounted to him my absence from the estate a week ago, and the bicycle journey I took without her consent – and this evening, when I was seated on the lounging pillows, a glass of water half drunk and a white saucer with a pool of soup floating in it upon the table in front of me, he entered, and I lowered my eyes to avoid his gaze, but from the corner of my eye I could see his tall height, his black hair, the fire in his eyes, for Father is strong and frightening, able to move mountains and hurl boulders, and his slaps are sharp and stinging, and every word he emits from his mouth, blasting from his throat, casts fear into the hearts of the entire household, and Mother follows him as a shadow, a black veil covering her face, her silence heavy and foreboding, and Father asked me, Where were you on the days I was away from home? And Mother whispered, He disobeyed your orders and took his bicycle and left the estate, and Father said, Answer my question at once! and my gaze lowered even further, and he raised his voice, spittle spewing from his mouth: Answer my question at once! And Mother whispered, Stay yourself, do not strike the child, to which Father replied, Shut your mouth! And I said, in a thin and birdlike voice, Father, I went to the angel Gabriel, and Mother regarded me with astonishment and at once I told him the story from beginning to end, about this good and handsome man with golden curls who visits our estate every day and walks the groves like the owner and proprietor, and Mother hushed me and said, with a startled laugh, that I was speaking from my imagination, and I told him, Father, the angel Gabriel is a flesh-and-blood man who lives and breathes, and the tenant farmers have seen him sitting with me on the chalky cliffs by the graveyard where together we gazed out at the sea, and he has fixed their tools and walked among their flimsy huts, and Father said to me, Go up to your room and do not come down from there, and as I ascended the stairs I heard her laughter turn to tearful shrieks, then there was thunderous shouting and there were reproaches and the sound of a glass of water and a saucer of soup shattering on the floor.

25 December 1895, Neve Shalom
Drenched with rain, I went to ask the advice of Saleem and Salaam. I found the two in a heated room in Jaffa, a bonfire of coals glowing in the belly of the room, smoke rising up and up until it reached a round window near the ceiling, and the two men were massaging one another's bare bronzed backs, at first Saleem standing and Salaam sitting, then Salaam standing and Saleem sitting. Slowly I have come to realise that love between men is a known phenomenon among Arab men. That is because this nation, at one time among the most fearless on earth, has grown weaker from generation to generation, entrapped in the flimsy, poisonous webs woven by its spidery women so that now its sons have lost all semblance of manliness, for the marrow of life has been sucked wholly from their bodies.

Saleem and Salaam listened to the tale of my meeting with Mustafa Abu-Salah and laughed scornfully. They told me that the man would never sell his estate. Five or six years earlier the Jews had approached him, led by the illustrious Zev Tyomkin, and they had handed Mustafa Abu-Salah a handsome down-payment, but the man never sold the estate and never returned the money.

I took leave of them in low spirits.

31 December

With great effort I was able to steal my way into the Rajani estate today. My soul was yearning for the place. All my sweet memories of the time I spent there have become more dear than ever to me of late, and my longing was so evident upon my face that even Her Ladyship noticed my sadness and ceased her labours on the teeth of her Arab clients and offered me tea with honey, the act of a wife taking pity on her husband, and she even asked several times what had befallen me, worry and anxiety present on her face.

In the afternoon hours I left home, took a donkey and some planks of wood and brought them to the northern edge of the Rajani estate, where the prickly-pear bushes do not grow too tall and the tenant farmers who sow evil and other tongue-waggers would not be, and there I built a ladder from the planks and I ascended it, and I jumped and rolled and fell to the other side, into the Rajani estate, onto the fertile land, damp from rainwater and covered with low green weeds.

I walked among the orchards and groves, Afifa's words of warning, old and new, echoing in my ears, that if I was caught by her husband walking on the estate he would behead me and slit my throat. I laughed to myself for being afraid of this man who is no man, this male who is no male, this father who is no father, as I slipped between the long, narrow irrigation canals, many of them stagnant and clogged with putrescent algae.

I considered walking right up to the spacious house and bribing the grumpy maidservant to dispatch to her mistress a note I had prepared in which I had written words of appeasement to persuade her to meet me in our hut that evening at midnight, for her husband would never dare or venture to raise his rattling bones at such a late hour to go searching the estate, and as I walked along, my footsteps crushing twigs and crunching pebbles, the large house came slowly into view, old and crawling with green vines, enshrouded in its gloomy melancholy as if death itself had wrapped its fingers around it and caused it to fall into eternal slumber.

In the midst of this doleful scene my soul was suddenly startled into wakefulness and bathed in a great light, for I caught sight of the boy Salah sitting in the window of his bedroom and looking past the curtains to the black horizon, and his gaze caught mine and all at once both joy and hope were kindled, and he instructed me, in a whisper, to climb a broad old carob tree with sturdy branches winding in every direction for the purpose of reaching his room, and he signalled me to use extreme caution, for the husband and father was in residence, and I jumped from branch to branch like a monkey, clinging to the bark and scratching my skin, making my way up step by step as if by the rungs of a ladder built especially for this purpose, and once I reached the highest, thinnest limbs, so quick to break, I encountered Salah's face, even sadder than the first time I had laid eyes on him though slightly gladdened at my presence, and he wished for me to leap from the tree and hang from the sill of the window, then pull myself into his room, and I looked downwards to the ground, now two storeys distant from me: if I missed I would fall into the abyss and give my body over to agony and torment even before Mustafa Abu-Salah could slit my throat. Still, in spite of all this, I chose this path of madness and leaped to the window-sill, pulled myself into the room and found myself among the boy's books and scribblings.

Salah ran to me at once and embraced me with warmth and love, all the while muttering strange things, such as he forgives me for my lengthy absence, and I was astonished to discover that the boy's love affected me and I felt love flooding and gushing between us. In the light from the lantern in his small room I could see that the fountain of his tears had been flowing profusely, and I asked him, 'Salah, where is your mother?'

The boy spoke in a whisper, confusion in his eyes. He was trembling, too, and started at every noise from the hallway that lay on the other side of the closed bedroom door. He told me that the angels of death had come down to amble along the paths of the estate and he spoke wildly of genies and demons and spirits that were tormenting his sleep and his soul, and I grabbed hold of his shoulders and shook him, since my time there was short, and once again I asked him, 'Where is Afifa?' and I was overcome with fear and worry lest the boy had gone out of his mind, but Salah took hold of himself and, in his weak and terrified voice, he related to me that his mother was in the room she shared with his father.

Just as he told me this we could hear coarse and heavy footsteps on the stairway, and Salah paled all at once, his eyes bulged, his pupils dilated and even I froze in my place. The footsteps grew louder – clearly they were those of the sick man – and at the very last second Salah jumped up on his short legs and with his tiny arms stopped the door opening. He motioned to me to climb under the bed, and there was banging at his door until all at once – I could see from my hiding-place on the floor – it flew open and there before me were, on one side, Salah's small reddish slippers and on the other, a pair of fat black hairy feet with long toenails painted pink.

The detestable, feminine voice of Salah's father resounded immediately in Arabic, and it seemed he was demanding something from Salah, an answer to some question, a rejoinder to some allegation. Salah stood on wobbling knees, responding in brief, his thin childish voice nearly giving him away by breaking into tears before their short conversation ended and the door slammed.

When Salah's father had departed I came out from under the bed, planted light kisses on the frightened boy's hands and face, and descended the stairway unimpeded in the wake of the husband and father. I held my breath, and my stomach was flattened to my back so no evil eye would notice me. I reached the ground floor of the house at the place I recalled from my first visit to the estate, and this was where Afifa shared a room with her husband the *effendi*. Mustafa Abu-Salah had gone out to the veranda, so I took the opportunity to steal into the room, where I found Afifa, pale and sobbing, her face a patchwork of dried blood. There was little I could say, so I merely kissed her hands and took my leave before my presence could be discerned.

The hour was late and the house teemed with noises large and small – a thousand ravens cawed shrilly from every branch of every tree, the cypresses stood in hot dispute with one another, a myriad waves stormed the distant sea, and the river, Wadi Musrara, snarled strangely – and I rose from my bed in the small hours of the night and walked about with shut eyes, and near the bottom of the staircase, in the thick gloom, I spied Mother and Amina whispering over the burning embers in the stove, one's ear pressed to the other's mouth, their hands exchanging hidden objects, their eyes darting to and fro as if they were odd characters in a poorly written story that ends too abruptly, and Father was there beside them, sleeping soundly on red pillows, his large feet stretched out on a small stool, his massive, muscled arms splayed across the pillows and mats, his grand moustache, black and dense, moving slightly with his snoring.

The creaking of the stairs beneath my feet alerted Mother to my presence, and she gazed up at me, alarm splashed across her pale face, and she whispered loudly to me, Salah! Back to your room at once! And Amina hastened to hide something under her black robe, and I said to Mother, I had nightmares, and I continued to make my way down the stairs, closer to the vision of them in the thick gloom lit only by tongues of fire glowing in the embers, but Mother was at my side in an instant, and she grabbed hold of my arm and led me back up the staircase to my bed, where she laid a trembling hand on my shoulder willing me to fall asleep as quickly as possible, and sleep in fact subdued me and I sank into the sheet, buried in the shroud of the blanket, and the leaves of the carob tree outside my window rattled and whistled with every gust of wind, and Mother left the room, secretly locking the door behind her.

And after all these things came to pass, and I found myself in a long, black sleep, an odd silence fell upon the house: the din of the rain ceased and the gutters no longer flowed and the wind left off its whistling and the clouds stopped thundering in the darkness, and inside my chest there was a huge void, desolate earth and a flying sprig, and the green-eyed genie arose from the depths dripping water for the purpose of heralding strange terrors, and a blind girl, half naked, with black curls and gaunt arms about to break called to me in a shattered voice, Salah, Salah, save us, save our people, and I twisted and turned in my bed, wanting to rid myself of this crazed sleep and these horrible dreams, and I whispered words of consolation to myself, These are nothing but dreams, bad dreams, and nothing worse than that, and I returned to my resting-place to write these words in my diary.

27 December 1895, Neve Shalom

I just now received an urgent missive from Afifa, the strange and astonishing contents of which I copy herewith:

> Mustafa Abu-Salah Rajani died today. He is no longer.
> The Widow R

How and in what manner he took his leave of this world she did not mention. It was clear from her handwriting that her mind was confused and agitated. In any case it has come to my attention – through bearers of tidings and gossip – that the burial will take place this afternoon and Madame Rajani will assume the Muslim customs of mourning as of this evening.

A strange sensation took hold of me with regard to the meaning of this turn of events and my role in it. My odd fate was written in heaven – to pay visits to land owned by Arabs and to their women. It could be that now the paths to conquering both have opened up before me, so that I may become lord and master of the estate I so wish to possess. But what is the meaning and purpose of this story being formed and written in my diary? That is unclear to me. If only I could turn the pages, skipping forward and back, to learn what is tucked into them and still to come, to decipher the intentions of the great writer in his labours.

This morning Mother shook me awake. Salah, a black day! A black day has arrived! Father is dead! He died in the middle of the night on the red pillows, his heart deceived him suddenly, his days on earth drained away, his brows sank; and all the while I was still in the clutches of sleep, the remnants of my disturbing dreams mixing with her horrible cries, and without dressing myself properly I climbed from my bed and descended to the first floor of the house where everyone was already gathered – Mother and Amina and the tenant farmers and their children – all steeped in mourning and lamentations, and the women cried out in sobs and flailed themselves with branches, and Mother was pulling the hair from her head, and only Father was not with them – and to where had the glory of his musculature disappeared, and his grand, thick moustache? – and I was suddenly struck by this wilderness, and a billowing wind and a flying branch awakened me to the fact that Father is dead, he will rise no more, will never again return from abroad, or raise his voice or his hand, and these tidings are exceedingly strange in my eyes, for how could Father have died so suddenly, how is it that he breathed his last? and I filled the house with my wailing, but no one came to console me, they simply fell silent, that very same odd silence of the angel of death as he rides about on his cart collecting souls with his pitchfork.

27 December 1895, Neve Shalom, a short while later
Without knowing what I was doing I opened the door to the clinic, where Her Ladyship was welding pieces of gold together for the teeth of rich Arab women, one of whom lay prone in the chair beneath her.

I asked the Arab woman's pardon and approached my wife to embrace her waist and shoulders. Her Ladyship was quite taken aback by this unaccustomed behaviour, but she left the room with me and kissed my face. I told her she was very dear to me and that I wished to grovel in mortification before her that she might forgive me all my evil deeds. Her Ladyship laughed lightly and told me I could atone for my sins by joining her for Arab coffee one afternoon. I acquiesced.

I wish, at this critical hour, to seek counsel with the angel Gabriel, to set down before him all my delusive contemplations, to hear the pleasant, calming voice that fills me with serenity and lucidity, but the angel Gabriel has not yet returned to my bedroom the way he did that night, and even the flickering of the candle has ceased, the lamp of the lantern has gone out, and only you, my diary, my sole true and unique friend on the face of the earth, will be safe-keeper of this final testimony to the madness of a lost and erring soul branded by heaven from the very day of its birth with a single word, one word and one fate, that of death, for not all souls are destined to live out their full allotment of days, and many are the babies born dead, and the lives of those not born dead are cut short by pneumonia in the cold of winter, or intestinal maladies in the heat of summer, and others will drown in water or be murdered or contract a deadly disease so that only a small number will continue to live, and not all souls are destined to long lives – most especially that of Salah.

27 December 1895, Neve Shalom, a short while later
These are the news and announcements borne to me by Saleem and Salaam: this morning, near daybreak, the maidservant Amina found Mustafa Abu-Salah seated in the reception room of his home, his skin and clothing exuding a pungent odour of sweat, and when she brought him his morning repast and the

narghile pipe he loved so dearly she saw that his eyes were bulging and his lips were blue and she examined his chest as well as a wretched human being like herself is capable, and she discerned that he was dead, absolutely and irrefutably and incontrovertibly.

In the manner of all simple Arab women in such circumstances she began shrieking and ululating, which caused all members of the household to gather round her post-haste, the delicate, melancholic lad among them, and they began their lamentations, soon joined by the tenant farmers from the fields and orchards.

Not one among them thought to call for the doctor. Instead they summoned the witches sitting in the farmers' tents, and these women mumbled verses from the Koran for purifying the body and for bringing the soul in peace to its proper destination. As soon as these simple women arrived they began to covet the clothes of the deceased, so each witch who approached the body for the purpose of praising it took something for herself – one helped herself to his tarboosh, another to pieces of his fancy costume, others removed his earrings, his rings, his ankle bracelets, and then they fell to quarrelling among themselves over the dead man's inheritance. Meanwhile, Afifa and Salah stood to the side holding one another and crying, and no one tried to make sense or order in the midst of the muddle; on the contrary, the farmers, feeling the absence of their master, eyed the handsome drapery and the woven carpets and started to remove them at will, and it was only the shouts and ranting of the maidservant, Amina, along with the ladle she fetched from the kitchen and was swinging in their faces, that caused them to leave off their plundering.

Now they are all deep in mourning, and deep in preparations for the funeral ceremony and burial. The deceased will be interred and gathered to his ancestors in the small graveyard overlooking the sea on the sandstone ridge that lies just a few miles from the western edge of the Rajani estate.

The moon continued to shine this morning as well, but its light was sombre and chimeric, and strange winds jostled the objects in the room, and I moved about the walls that run from corner to corner, and the floors called out to me to hurl my life at them, and from the rasping breaths rising from my chest are Mother's words of mourning and lamentation, her dress blacker than black, her eyes filled with tears, and she is speaking of her wretchedness without Father, raising dear and distant memories of how he took her from her dolls and made her his wife and the mother of his son, and because she mentioned me she gave orders to confine me to my room, to keep me from the grave-diggers and the grave, for my soul is too young and delicate for matters of death, and I should not make the trip to the funeral, and Mother began explaining to the tenant farmers and all who entered that Father had been gravely ill, physically and mentally exhausted, and she was joined by her faithful companion Amina, who was pulling her hair out and wringing her hands, and I stood by the window-sill in my room facing the full black moon rising at midday and my soul wished to hurl itself two storeys down, to hover in the air a while with my invisible virginal wings before being dashed to the depths of a dark and gloomy pit to sleep the sleep of eternity there.

This afternoon I grabbed the branches of the carob tree outside my window and descended to the ground, for although Father was never a friend or companion to me, and never rumpled my hair or shared his love with me, I am none the less overcome with grief and a sense of emptiness at the dog's death he endured and at the gaggle of peasant women come to despoil and denude him, and I slipped away from the house, skulking from tree to tree and among the wild bushes with Father's white shroud a beacon to me, a pillar of fire, and I did not set my eyes upon the mullahs and imams or my many cousins arrived from Jaffa and Nablus and Acre on swift horses, only on Mother and her strange behaviour, for her gait was that of a fool, a drunkard, her grief so deep that she was filled to the brim with waves of putrid laughter that she dammed with her hand so they would not escape her mouth and flood the shore.

An hour or two later, when the dignified convoy reached the small cemetery on this cold winter day of skies garbed in black and grey clouds so heavy with rain that even Jaffa had shut itself in out of fear and respect, Mother's strange laughter began to cause her body to convulse in waves and she danced the dance of the inebriated and chortled more and more, and the Turkish officials and judges who had come to pay their respects to Father, the deceased, were vexed and angered by this behaviour while Mother continued to whirl about, thumping invisible drums, blowing kisses to the aged, doleful trees whose branches overhang the cemetery.

The grave-diggers had already lowered the body into the mouth of that gaping pit, Father's new place of residence, his enormous body with its swarthy muscles and black moustache doomed to concealment beneath sand and soil, and the peasant women startled the heavens like a flock of ravens with their shrieked lamentations, and the sea sulked and all was silent and still, and Mother's lunacy seemed to be that of widowed women, which cures itself miraculously, but then, to everyone's horror, she began her crazed laughter again, this time accompanied by a merry song sung for festivals and joyous occasions, and she hurled herself into the pit as if asking to be interred along with

Father, and suddenly she grasped a corner of the shroud and was about to pull it free of the body, and all the gathered mourners called to her to desist from this impure, forbidden act, and Mother fell onto Father's chest, her soul tittering and her eyes gleeful, and when I returned to my room the door was still locked so I climbed the branches of the carob tree to enter, and now I sit alone in my room in front of my notebook filled with densely written lines and I write and write all about her, and my fury is tempered by tears, how the grave-diggers pulled her off Father's body by force and distanced her from the fresh grave, how she struggled against them with renewed vigour and wild strength not befitting a widow such as she, and I add in the margins of the page a drawing in blacks and greys of the giant cypress and acacia trees and two lines of a poem join together on their own in a strange manner, damaged and incomplete.

28 December 1895, Neve Shalom

All morning long I was in the throes of stormy emotions because of what had transpired at the estate. I tried to rest but my soul could find no peace. Even the moon had changed its habits and was appearing in the afternoon sky, full and violet in colour.

I counted the hours one after another until the sun fell into its grave at the western side of the sea, and I rode off to the estate. A hushed stillness stood among the many trees, the hushed stillness of the angel of death himself come to visit his living subjects, plunging his pitchfork into their wet and fertile earth. Tearful sighs could be heard dully from a distance inside the grand house, and I made my way towards them.

I ascended the stairs to the veranda, pushed open the front door and proceeded straight to the gloomy, mildewed reception room, where I found Afifa, her back to me, staring at her pale fingers as they swirled around one another, twirling her ring. At the sound of my voice calling her name, she began to shake violently. She pronounced my own name and sighed grievously, then asked me to sit in an armchair nearby where she joined me, all the while dabbing at her nose with an embroidered handkerchief.

She said, 'It was a terrible funeral. A strong wind began to blow with a vengeance on the mourners. As my husband's body was lowered into the pit that had been dug for him it seemed the wind had abated and I dared to step closer for a last look at the man I had married in my childhood, but just then a crazed wind took hold of my body and plunged me into the hole where I lay prone like a carcass alongside the body still warm from its death, and the grave was cramped and narrow, walls of earth on every side, and my heart shuddered and juddered with fear at the thought of being imprisoned for all eternity, to be buried alive and breathing under the sand and soil as was done by the desert Arabs to their girl-children upon birth, and the qadi and the elders hastened to assist me, to pull me from the pit dug not for me, for my own grave lies beside this one and awaits my eternal repose.'

While she was speaking the wind returned and whistled through the rooms of the house, rattling window-panes and causing the curtains to billow, and Afifa looked about her home and her surroundings sorrowfully, a moan escaping from her breast. I hastened to her and took her hand in my own, but she refused to touch me or my body as she cried bitterly that her husband had left her and died and now she was a lone woman with a large estate and a child, whom she loved, to look after.

I consoled her with kind words until she grew tranquil and her terrible sobbing abated and ceased, and she rubbed her rounded nose and dabbed at her watery green eyes with their thick brows, and when I asked her about Salah she told me he had been locked in his room all day on her orders and that he was sad and dejected, and after the funeral she had come to console him and embrace him but her strength had given out and she was praying now to Allah for Him to remove the sting of the black days that lie ahead so that she may live out her days in peace and serenity.

She wished, then, to repair to her bedroom, and I escorted her there while a sombre, lacerating silence stood between us. I left the estate filled with grief, but I promised myself to return soon for the purpose of meeting the woman and the boy, to stand beside them in their hour of need.

Mother's crazed laughter finally abated at sunset, and her weakened nerves began slowly to return to normal, and she even sent Amina with a pitcher of water and lemons to revive my funereal soul and release me from my locked bedroom, but I chose not to join them downstairs, preferring instead to remain in the depths of my poems and to read through my own writings in my diary, and it seemed to me that lines written in the past conceal secrets not yet revealed to me, codes yet undeciphered, as if my diary were cleverer than its foolish author writing in innocence, or as if the silent words written in a cramped and tiny hand begged to shout wildly to overcome their muteness, but try as I did to find some clue or hint of acrostics or abbreviations or transposed letters waiting for me to rearrange them into some eye-opening pattern, I came up with nothing at all.

Only the insignificant chords of memory were plucked as I read the words written by my own hand, like the wonderment of meeting the angel Gabriel for the first time and the infinite joy of walking together past the tenant farmers, and the deep, inexplicable sadness of the waning days of summer, and each chord vibrated a bit then rested, and I lowered my pen and allowed my thoughts to wander unbridled and masterless to his golden curls and his fine beauty, and I wished he were here with me now in my room, on my bed, to console me in my orphanhood, and I pined for him to be my friend and comrade once again, my fellow and my cohort, and from my window as I gazed at rays of evening sunlight I suddenly understood that the angel Gabriel still loves me, that the memory of our friendship has not abandoned him, that he has stored in his heart our best days, and how beautiful the world is, lit by the late sunlight, since the angel Gabriel walks it as well, his bare feet plodding the soil, his excellent, coarse scent mingling with the smell of rain and wet leaves and citrus fruit.

A new strength flowed through me for my ears did not deceive me – it was Mother and the angel Gabriel I heard below me, chatting quietly in the reception room, and if I was not mistaken my beloved friend had returned to visit me, and I descended in silence to fall into his arms, but the first floor of our home was shrouded in the deceptive darkness of twilight, and the voices were hushed and only shards of words were discernible, words of consolation at Father's strange and rapid demise, and words of purity and goodness about the beautiful virtues of the deceased, and the events at the funeral, and my name was uttered as well, and I found a place to hide myself in the thick double curtains dark as night, a place where I could peer from within between two curtains and *his light is as a niche in which is a lamp, the lamp is in a glass, and the glass is as it were a brightly shining star*, and from the light that glowed I could see his great, sturdy height, the laughing eyes all the same filled with grief and consolation, and Mother thanked him weakly, murmuring, and it was apparent that she did not look kindly upon his presence here with us, and I strained my ears but the words were soft – 'boy', 'Salah', 'alone', 'estate' – and I was unable to form sentences, and I was saddened to watch Mother as she burst into a great wailing, her body trembling and convulsing, and she said, Salah, Salah, and the angel Gabriel was as stunned as I at the sight of this waterfall of tears, and he took her into his arms and kissed her cheeks and her lips, and they went together to the room shared by Mother and Father and closed the door lightly, pleasantly, behind them, and many chords were sounding and resounding inside me now, for I knew nothing of this friendship between the two of them; rather, I thought the opposite was true, that they loathed one another as could be seen in their eyes, and the kiss he planted on her lips seemed to sear my body with its heat, and the green-eyed gruffness of jealousy rose up inside me and I made my way quickly to the far side of the reception room to a small, forgotten side door, a darkened tunnel that led to their bedroom, and I crawled among furniture and other belongings long abandoned, tearing through cobwebs, making my way through dust gathered over generations, dirt from all ages, until I reached a hidden doorway at the very end of the room, and it was there, in the dim light of a late afternoon sun, on the wide bed as white as a dead man's shroud, that I saw this vision, of Mother's bare thighs dripping with sweat, and her deep moans, and above all this, rising and falling, up and down and up and down, with speed and diligence, with temperance and speed, the angel Gabriel's two naked buttocks.

Winter, 1896

1 January 1896, Neve Shalom

Late this afternoon I went to the Arab perfume market and bought beautiful flowers for Her Ladyship and announced that it was my intention to engage her in a romantic promenade through the streets of Jaffa, which is exactly what I had promised to do ages and ages ago.

Her Ladyship was quite pleased with this invitation, and she locked her clinic, drove off her clientele and set out on foot with me, her arm crooked in my own, white gloves on her hands. In spite of all Her Ladyship's failings she is a fine conversationalist, so a man out walking with her for a while will derive much pleasure from her company. We walked through the German Colony and its European-style gardens, with clover and tall trees, beside which stood small yellow Asian flowers, and Her Ladyship spoke to me from the depths of her soul.

She was in a tizzy over her shoes, which were still splendid on one side but worn on the other. She was even more worked up over an Arab seamstress with whom she had nearly come to blows when the latter demanded four *bishliks* for repairing a sleeve that Her Ladyship felt should cost no more than two *bishliks*, and the two women had tussled over the dress, one pulling from the right, the other pulling from the left, each cursing the other.

Her Ladyship continued her prattle as we perambulated,

sharing other feminine pragmatics with me. She asked my advice on the Arab seamstress and shoes, then told me about the telegram that had arrived from her sister Rivka announcing her plan to visit the Holy Land and perhaps even remain here, finding a husband for whom she could bear children; then she moved on to gossip, slander, impudence, idle chatter, riveting matters with no practical importance, suggestions, arguments and disputes about the shells of eggs as yet unhatched, excellent advice on how I can find work as an agronomist in the Land of Israel and another thousand bits of gibberish, nonsense and drivel.

As we walked along I listened and did not listen, for my soul was engaged all the while with what was transpiring back at the Rajani estate during this period of my absence. It is now the season for harvesting oranges and the fruit of the estate is ripe for the picking but no one is there to take charge. I was thinking, too, of the Arab woman and the dilapidated hut of our lovemaking and wondered if she was missing me as I was missing her, and from there my thoughts drifted to that poor boy living out his life on the estate, and his strange, bitter fate, for he is not a boy like other boys: he carries the world's sorrow on his shoulders. He is in some ways a Jew: in the seriousness of his discourse, in the paleness of his face, in his feeble hands incapable even of whittling a twig into a knife or of tossing a ball or sailing a wooden boat in shallow water. And as I was thinking these thoughts, Her Ladyship's sharp, dry voice suddenly split my ear and said, 'Listen to me!'

'I am listening with the utmost attention,' I said.

'And what did I just say?' she demanded.

'You were talking about a telegram from your sister.'

Her face grew angry. 'That telegram is already ancient news. This is meant to be a romantic stroll but your thoughts are elsewhere, not on your wife.'

'Forgive me,' said I.

'Asking forgiveness is not enough,' she said, her eyes stormy with thunder and lightning.

'When we return home I will make you a cup of tea with a biscuit.'

Now she was truly furious. 'One does not offer a Warsaw girl tea and biscuits in her own home. Invite me to a café.'

There are few taverns in Jaffa since the city is a Muslim one. There are, however, quite a number of cafés. The Arab ones are dense with smoke from *narghile* pipes, and bereft of women. The Jewish ones can be found in Neve Tzedek and Neve Shalom and are populated by crowds of gentlemen in black hats and ladies in fine dresses, with musicians playing the clarinet and the violin for the enjoyment of the clientele as they sip their coffee or liqueur.

There are two cafés in Neve Shalom, both near the railway station. To the right is the Café Armon, and to the left, Café Hermon; the two are arch nemeses, the clientele of one never visiting the other. The Armon plays host to the miserable and the wretched, bankrupted colonists and drunkards, while the Hermon is popular among the clerks and the taskmasters who consider themselves privileged.

At Her Ladyship's behest we turned left and seated ourselves at the well-appointed Café Hermon, with its wide veranda and hewn-stone façade, where one could find people in fancy hats and elegant apparel, with the sound of gay conversation and tinkling laughter.

From the moment we stepped into the café, Her Ladyship's expression turned benevolent, and all my sins and erring ways were forgotten. And because she was in high spirits, so, too, was I. She pointed to the table at which she wished to sit and at once ordered a *café au lait*, while I am always happy to partake of one liqueur or another, and so imbibed a little of this and a little of that, each one sweeter and more potent than the last.

Her Ladyship took a sip of my liqueur and began to giggle in a cloying and lustful fashion, then dipped her spoon into the vanilla whipping cream and stirred vigorously, making wavelets in the cup, all the while gesticulating to various friends and passers-by, including Russian *émigrés* swigging hard liquor and ideologists holding forth and all manner of poets and scriveners writing their letters in the Hebrew language.

Many were the gentlemen who approached Her Ladyship's table and bowed courteously and removed their hats in obeisance, and it seemed to me that in the many days of my absence from home she had made a very large number of friends and acquaintances, an endless train of suitors and attendants who aroused my amazement and pride in her beauty, as well as the pinprick of jealousy a man feels for his wife.

One man of my age, wearing a pair of spectacles on his nose, kissed her hand in the manner of a gentleman in the empire of Kaiser Wilhelm II. Her Ladyship hastened to introduce him to me, her voice slightly giddy. His name was David Kumar, the new head of the Hovevei Zion group of Jaffa. He had a wide and handsome brow, his eyes were full of vitality and wisdom and he was as yet unmarried. With him was his friend and colleague Yehoshua Eisenstadt, a tall man with the dreamy look of a person with malaria. He, too, fawned over Her Ladyship and planted two kisses on the back of her hand. A third man, Nathan Kaiserman – short of stature, wrinkled, fat-fingered and portly – joined in the kowtowing. Like me, he had studied agronomy, and was teaching at the Mikveh Israel School south of Jaffa.

I addressed Her Ladyship with an angry frostiness. 'Has the parade of suitors come to an end?'

'For the time being,' she answered.

I went to pass water in a pit to the right of the café, and when I returned to our table I discovered that, in spite of her promise, Her Ladyship had not been sitting idly but was nattering noxiously with some wretched soul, a ragged-looking man who was declaiming some poem written in a black notepad he had removed from his tattered suit, until the chief waiter took hold of his lapels and hurled him into the street.

I asked Her Ladyship, 'Who and what was that?'

Her face reddened. 'A comic poet who was reciting to me from his poems,' she said.

'And what is his name?' I enquired.

'No one knows,' she told me, 'but everyone calls him the Wildebeest,' and with that she let out a giggle.

1 January 1896 (continued)

On the way back to our house Her Ladyship behaved strangely towards me. For example, she pointed out the thin crescent of moon, which would wax and grow large until the middle of the month, and the rain-swollen earth, and the pregnant bellies of passers-by, and all this was unusual for her, out of character, as if she were inebriated, or witless, but though I perceived this I did not understand; though I heard it, I did not comprehend.

When we returned to the four walls of our home, Her Ladyship bolted the door, drew the curtains, extinguished the lantern and said, 'Come to our bedroom.'

From worry and alarm I asked, 'Have you taken ill?'

She said, 'I wish to fall pregnant.'

My chest was aflame. I hastened to disrobe from top to bottom, then entered our room and shut the door behind me. And there was but one word in my heart: Hallelujah.

A black and heavy curtain through which no light passes and which carries the grief of all ages surrounds Mother's bedroom, and I have taken to slipping secretly into it through one of the small passageways just right for a child's size but not for an adult's, and there, behind this curtain, in its folds, I crouch in silence, my ears pricked, my eyes wide open, so as to learn all that the woman known as my mother is engaged in, that very same woman who appears to be a devoted widow, to fathom who she is, this person who gave birth to me against my will, and would that all the pages of my book, which she created, be erased and lost to the world without her ever having written even the very first word of them.

Mother spends most of her time hunched over on her bed and in bad spirits, her hands frozen, a winter wind whipping through the trees outside her window and stealing into the room, but sometimes she rises and sighs heavily, and once she even stood facing the slit in the curtain that serves as my station from which to spy upon her, and my brown eyes peered into her black ones as she regarded me, unaware, and I stopped breathing when she called out, Salah! Salah! again and again, and in just another moment I would step out from behind the folds of the curtain, from among the forgotten quilts and the empty cobwebs abandoned by their owners in desperation, and in just another moment I would return to embracing Mother with love and forgiveness, for perhaps I had been mistaken and all that I had seen with my own eyes was nothing but a dream, or a vision, or a story driven by the imagination of a not-yet-and-may-never-be writer, someone who has not yet grown to be a person, only a young child bewildered by the intrigues and torturous path of the world, but just then Mother turned her head and it was clear that the words she had uttered were to herself and only herself in the absentminded manner of a person in a room alone surrounded by heavy curtains.

It seemed to me that Mother was anticipating the arrival of that angel, and sometimes she would call out his name and crane her neck and let her hair cascade down her back, and it was clear that these two loved one another and a scheme had been hatched by them, and once I watched as she crouched above the bed and removed her dressing-gown and her two despoiled thighs, still glistening with rivulets of salty water, were exposed before me, and then I beheld the strangest sight: from between her legs there fell a wad of many strips of cloth, their dull whiteness stained black with heavy bleeding, and a scream flared at my temples with regard to all the secrets hidden in the chamber of chambers – what was it that took place here, what manner of horrors was concealed beneath the pillows and blankets? – and the blood drained from my legs and soon it seemed I would fall in a dead faint and I would lose consciousness, but my eyes were wide open in astonishment, riveted to her strange and silent actions, for in the misty light of the room I watched her remove her clothing and, below her breasts, and beneath the round navel that protruded slightly, there was a dense, triangular thicket of black hair, and the blood flowed from it like a battered child running for its life, and Mother took the dirtied cloths and dispensed them into a small hidden bin, and the odour was fetid, that of a life cut short by a dagger or sword, and it rose and spread and pounded at my nostrils, and new, dry strips of cloth, whiter than white, were taken up and administered to the hirsute triangle, while behind my curtain and in hushed groans so as not to be overheard or spied or exposed I retched from the bottom of my soul.

6 January 1896, Neve Shalom

At long last the Muslim period of mourning came to an end and so did the period of my banishment from the Rajani estate, as decreed by Madame in no uncertain terms due to her fear of provoking slander and lies and gossip. The truth be told, Arabs set great store by their honour and are liable to behave indecorously if they feel slighted or disrespected.

Now I was free again to visit the Arab woman, to come to her, so that after I had kissed Her Ladyship farewell, as she toiled to save the sole remaining tooth of the aged wife of an *effendi*, I took my leave and set out on my way.

I rode a mare under grey skies while copious quantities of water flowed in Wadi Musrara to my right. The gate to the Rajani estate stood wide open, swinging on its hinges, and the paths inward were overgrown with weeds, and everywhere there were deep, rutted holes filled with water and tadpoles and frogs croaking in the marsh grass.

Dark and heavy rainclouds filled the sky and rain began to fall. Sadness and sorrow hovered over everything.

I entered the spacious house with awe and reverence and found the woman Afifa seated in the same place in the same room as the last time I had paid a visit. Her eyes were swollen, her shoulders hunched, her clothing black and worn, and the curtains hung a dark and sombre pall over the entire scene.

She took notice of me and said, 'Jacques, Jacques,' and her entire being was caught up in weeping and sobbing. I took hold of her hands and kissed her fingers while consoling her with comforting words. She sniffled and dabbed at her eyes, puffy as they were from all that crying. It was quite clear that she had not yet recovered from the well-known *faiblesse* endured by widowed women.

She began telling me all that had transpired in the fortnight that had passed. Black days had befallen the estate, one trouble after the next. First, harsh and bothersome winds had begun to blow from corridor to corridor, from room to room, and in the curtains. A rumour had spread among the tenant farmers that it was a ghost, and they staged a rebellion of sorts, unwilling to work the fields until such time as the angry spirit would fall silent. She had no strength in her to go out and subjugate them. Even the maidservant with the evil expression failed to command their attention.

With these workers striking, the fruit was rotting on the trees and weeds were springing up in every corner and there was no hand to hoe and rake, no one to remove stones or unwanted grasses. And if this were not enough, the driving rains that fell two days ago caused Wadi Musrara to flood its banks, and a tremendous amount of water had reached the orchard.

She continued her litany, adding that because of my abandonment of the estate, the boy's spirits were terribly low. He remained locked inside his room, setting eyes on no one, refusing to answer her questions. Only the maidservant Amina was allowed to pay him visits and bring him morsels of food. She told me that the boy calls my name day and night but I do not answer, and this caused her to begin crying once again, for she is a widow, widowed and alone, and how would she maintain the large estate without a husband, and how would she sell her fruit if it all rotted, and how would she manage the business of raising her son, and how would she pay property and other taxes as a widow, widowed and alone, and I rose to my feet and went to her. I embraced her and wiped her tears, and I whispered into her ear,

'Afifa, do not think of yourself as alone because I am at your side and will remain so whenever you need me.'

She said, in a shaky voice, 'If that is so then why did you come only now?'

And I said, 'For the simple reason that you demanded that I wait until the mourning period was over.' I told her, 'You asked me not to come so as not to awaken slander and gossip and lies.'

Her lowing grew louder. 'I demanded no such thing,' she said.

I levelled my gaze on her since she was becoming addled. I said, 'Forgive me for I have erred.'

She continued to cry.

'How can I make up for my sin?' I asked her.

The tears continued to flow.

'Shall I subjugate the tenant farmers?' I asked.

She said, 'Yes.'

'Have you then forgiven me for all my many misdeeds?' I asked.

'I have,' she said.

The female is an emotional creature, utterly prey to tumultuous feelings, which is why her thought process is not lucid and her speech never well organised. However, there is one consolation in all of this: some time very soon she will have a need for a man's proximity and will open her sweet gates for him

Something transpired today: my good friend until only several days ago, that golden-haired angel, finally arrived at our gate, though this time not walking proud and erect with pomp and stateliness like a dignified *effendi* but, rather, he stole his way onto the grounds of our estate like a cat, stepping quickly and with apprehension, his eyes scanning in every direction trying to discern whether I had caught sight of him, and how wretched had my good friend become, how vile and contemptible in my eyes, and to which room would he proceed, this despicable ally who is beneath all honour? Not to Salah's room, where he would be welcomed as a fellow, nor to the orchards of the estate, where he would be welcomed as a guardian and friend, but straight to the ground floor, to Mother's bedroom, where she fell into his arms and cried out the name she has given him – Jacques! Jacques! – and the scent of vomit from the last time reached my nostrils and clogged them, and the good angel planted a large hand on her buttocks and I prayed that they would not once again contaminate my late father's bed, that they would not grunt their dirty, sweaty grunts and, lo, his fingers that were prodding the contours of Mother's body discovered the blood-soaked strips of cloth, and he left off with his prodding and instead the two sat together at the edge of the bed and conversed, but no matter how I strained my ears and eyes I could not learn what scheme they were concocting, since they were speaking in muffled tones, a whisper, as if they knew that someone was eavesdropping on their skulduggery, and then an idea came to me, that I should leave my hiding-place behind the curtain and crawl on all fours to the far edge of the bed to listen to the two conspirators, and my heart was beating fast and hard at these thoughts and I caged my breath and opened the curtain just a slit and lowered myself to my knees and crawled in utter silence, and the angel and Mother were deep in conversation, though apparently not in agreement – rather, it appeared that a heated argument was taking place between them – and I slithered in silent speed to where I could wrap myself in the blanket that draped down to the floor and hid my body from head to foot, and I returned to normal breathing (albeit shallow), and at last the words were stringing together in my ears, and I could hear her telling him things about me – Salah is sleeping, Salah is shut in his room, Salah this and Salah that – and that wicked man, that prince of malice, said in a sharp and evil tone, Better that he should remain there, and she told him of a great misfortune that had befallen her, that the tenant farmers had broken free of her control and refused to obey her or work the land, and sobs leaped from her throat as she pleaded with him to help her so that the estate would not foreclose and she would not have to forfeit her assets, and the angel said to her, You know my condition for assisting you, and she said, That is a condition I can never agree to, to which he replied, Then we shall wait until such time that the trees have all decayed and their fruit has rotted, and Mother cried and cried and begged, saying, I am a widowed woman, take pity on me, and he said, That is my sole condition, to which he added a warning: If you do not do as I demand, I will leave at once, never to return, and you will be left alone with your strange and disturbed child. And Mother wailed and railed and sank to her knees and pounded on his chest with her small fists, saying, No, Jacques, don't leave me, and he took his hat in hand and told her, Tomorrow, in the afternoon, I shall return here, and at that time I will see that the condition we have discussed time and again has been fulfilled and everything has been attended to, for if not I shall tell the world that you are a whoring adulteress, and a band of avengers will come here to draw your blood, and Mother could no longer stand and had not noticed that her bloodied bandages had fallen from their place in that strange black triangle of hair, and she shrieked, Jacques! Jacques! And he turned away from her, his lips pursed and his fists balled, and in another second he would stumble on my body hidden in the blanket, and at his departure from the room I squirmed back to my spot behind the curtains, back to the realm of darkness and gloom, and from there I climbed the blackened branches to my childhood bedroom where I was met by that odour of stuffiness and mildew mingled together.

❧

7 January 1896, Café Armon
I am writing this at the Café Armon, frequented by the proletariat and its foul-breath drunkards, but the liquor here is bubblier, tastier than that of the competition. A few moments ago I met Mr Wildebeest, and I had the pleasure of becoming acquainted with him. It turns out that he is not a poet but a penniless beggar. He showed me several of his poems, Hebrew stanzas filled with pathos and ill-fitting rhymes. So be it.

He makes his living penning poems for the colonists. Once he received a turnip for a poem he wrote in honour of the colony at Hadera and another time he was lodged at Mishmar Hayarden, in the room of a sad-faced female colonist. I told him that I, too, was familiar with her and we both laughed raucously. I perceived that he was terribly poor so I bought him some vodka and a biscuit, for which he thanked me profusely. We agreed to meet again.

Now I will return to the events of yesterday.

At the request of the Arab woman and in order to calm her troubled soul, I became the agronomist and overseer of the Rajani estate, in charge of subjugating the Egyptian tenant farmers. It is harvest time and the workload is heavy and there is no time to waste. To that end I rushed to the farmers' hovels for the purpose of leading this riff-raff to goodness and efficiency. These farmers are simpletons, their eyes wide open with stupidity. They squatted oddly on the moist earth, their knees pointed outwards, and ate a sort of green legume they call *foulle*, which would cause the intestines of any European to become agitated and rebellious.

The elders among them hastened to greet me warmly for they were familiar with my deeds on the estate. The women lowered their eyes in awe and the youngsters fell silent. At once I ordered all the men to rise to their feet.

They did as I bade them, though it was clear they were uncomfortable, all the while rolling their eyes in search of genies or spirits or ghosts or Lord knows what. I had a club in my hand and I waved it in the air, summoning them to follow me to the orchards to harvest the fruit. They followed without pause: the Arabs love a show of force and obey it to the letter. At every turn it is necessary to maintain an iron fist with them. Otherwise they become insolent and fail to carry out the task at hand.

In the ensuing hours we turned the estate into what it had not been for at least twenty or thirty years. We deepened all the beds, removed weeds one by one, disposed of troublesome stones. Thirty-four trees that were infested with diseases and parasites were set afire and turned to dust and ash so they would not contaminate the others. All the irrigation ditches were cleared of debris gathered over generations and then reinforced, the tenant farmers all the while toiling productively, for, although they are awash in superstition, they are as industrious as the beast of the field, as a threshing ox, and when I gazed into their eyes brimming with stupidity I saw there a glimmer of joy for a day of work well done, and much astonishment at the wonders and miracles that had taken place, under my tutelage, with their own hands.

In the evening I came to the Arab woman's quarters to boast and impress her with my deeds and to show her how lovely the estate was becoming, but she cast me from her room, claiming a terrible throbbing at her temples and an ache in her head.

🦂

12 January 1896, the Rajani Estate

My voice is hoarse and my hands exhausted for I have spent the day overseeing the orange harvest. Much of the fruit was spoiled due to the inept management of the estate, but there were many round specimens dripping their juices from the choicest variety of the fruit. We loaded all of them into heavy wooden crates for shipping to Europe.

The Arab woman agreed to the purchase of a diesel engine from a factory in Manchester, England, that will replace the lazy old mule pulling buckets of water from the well with steam power. This will enable better irrigation of the orchards and groves during the hot Asian summer.

While the tenant farmers indeed obey me, there is still one obstacle to working with them: their strange belief that an evil genie prowls the grounds of the estate, so that whenever the wind moans in the branches they prostrate themselves facing to the south-east, towards Mecca, the city of their prophet, and offer supplications and prayers to Allah to save them. The women then beat the ground with branches from a willow tree or some other wilting plant while the children run to and fro shouting, 'Al-Roch! Al-Roch!', which, in the Arab language, is the name of the spirit of the dead. Little by little my patience for these perverse customs is waning. Perhaps I will approach those Jews who have tired of the colonies and take a few to work with me.

In Jaffa there are many such Jews, disgruntled and dis-illusioned with the colonies and their terrible soil, and they wish to emigrate. Quite a number are men of honour and strength, true craftsmen. Instead of them returning to Russia and suffering the anti-Semitic pogroms there, instead of emigrating to America to become indentured servants in a sweatshop, why not join my legion of farmers and vine-growers?

I must think more on this topic.

A few hours later
Upon my return home I found Her Ladyship awaiting me in her bed. She ordered me to lie with her; according to her calculations, the time was propitious for conceiving.

On the advice of Saleem and Salaam, I had bought a lubricating ointment that they use for their sodomy and which I could use for intercourse.

They demanded their cut. I gave it to them.

13 January 1896, Neve Shalom
Good times have reached the estate. It is flourishing, blossoming; all is roses and pleasantness. As I pass by the greening hillocks and dense foliage and toiling farmers I fantasise and dream, for the abundance and splendour I have brought to the estate in a short time are only the beginning. The exceedingly healthy soil of Rajani can support extensive seeding and planting and it is my intention to add, alongside the citrus trees, ten hectares of almond and olive trees, which, though they produce late, provide a decent income, olives being particularly safe because they are not prone to disease and can produce fruit for hundreds of years. I will replace the prickly-pear bushes at the western edge of the

estate with eucalyptus trees, which will grow quickly and provide all the firewood the entire Rajani household will need.

Even the Arab woman is slightly encouraged, and little by little the blush has returned to her cheeks. Perhaps – Allah willing! – she will soon resume the delights and pleasures she once showered upon me. She is still fearful of loneliness and terribly anxious about the boy's future and talks about him whenever we are together.

The boy.

Whenever I visit the estate and the woman, I take a short break from my many tasks and ascend to the boy's room. I greet him and he returns my greeting with a delicate smile, but still, in spite of the smile, it is abundantly clear that he remains shrouded in mourning for the father who never loved him. His new-found solitude has left him as wilted as petals parted from a lily.

The Arab woman spoke with me today, saying now that the estate matters are on the right track and the oranges have fetched a good price and the tenant farmers have been subdued and subjugated, perhaps I would once again walk with the boy and renew our days of old together, for Salah has eaten little and his gaze meets no one's, and her heart – a mother's heart – tells her to expect the worse from the psychological aspect.

I replied that her wish was my command.

That angel came to visit Mother again today and I hastened to my secret kingdom among the folds of the curtains to spy upon them and their actions, and since sparks from their quarrel were shooting as high as the heavens, I comprehended quickly the source of their disagreement and the condition he was demanding, which was no less than that she give him the *kushan*, the deed to the estate, while she, as tormented as a wounded animal, begged him not to make such a demand, for how could she survive in her widowhood without the sole property that would assure her fortune, our blessed estate, and he stated emphatically once again the *kushan*, the *kushan*, the *kushan*, and then in a rage he overturned her trousseau, which Mother had been keeping from the day of her marriage, and he emptied all of it – the faded wedding gown, the trinkets and baubles, the books from her childhood – and all the while he bellowed in a way I had never imagined possible, Where have you hidden the *kushan?* to which he added a curse – *sharmuta*, whore – and I wrapped myself inside the curtain and cried silently, not for my tormented mother or for the estate falling into the talons of strangers but for the waning days of my youth, which these scenes and visions my eyes have witnessed have taught me are the true, filthy nature of life and humankind, and for Mother's disloyalty and for the evilness of my one good friend, so that there is nothing left for me to do now but grow until my limbs and organs stretch themselves into the very shape of those I loathe.

In the end, the pernicious angel departed without finding the *kushan*, signed as it was according to law by my late father so that any man finding it might claim as his own the Rajani estate and its groves and orchards and pools that flow from the river to the sea and the sea to the river, and he added, in the form of a threat, that she must fulfil the oath she swore to him within a week or at latest two.

A few hours later
I left the Arab woman frightened and worried on the ground floor of the house and ascended the dark and neglected stairs on

my way to Salah's room, all the while making lists for myself of the many things that need doing: remove the ugly, heavy curtains; burn the threadbare carpets, dispose of all the pillows embroidered in tasteless Asian patterns, polish the floor and the staircase.

I knocked at his door, solicitous and fawning, and persuaded Salah to tour the grounds with me. I told myself that when the boy saw how the estate had changed so dramatically, how it was blossoming and blooming, how it was preening and greening, his hardened heart would open and he would return to eating and playing and enjoying himself in the manner of children his age, and our own happier days would return as well, when we were a valiant pair.

I took his hand in my own.

He did not withdraw his fingers from mine. I took this as a good sign.

I led him to the sloping hillocks alongside the capacious house, to the trees now standing tall and proud and trimmed, their fruit plucked one by one so that even the neighbours in the German Colony looked on with envy.

The boy walked about with his eyes downcast and his shoulders sagging like a person ashamed of his evil deeds.

I asked, 'Why do you spend all your time alone in your room?'

'That is my way,' he said.

'You are still grieving for your father?'

'Do not speak of the deceased,' he said.

'Do you wish to play ball with me?' I asked him.

'No.'

'Perhaps we'll sail the wooden ship on the lake.'

'No.'

I said, 'Have you noticed the miraculous changes that have

taken place on the estate?' I pointed out the newly planted eucalyptus trees. 'Look, Salah, what do you see?'

'A war,' he said. 'A huge and bloody war.'

'What?' I said, astonished.

'You are a Jew,' he said.

'Yes, I am.'

'I have just come to realise,' he said, 'that the Jews will one day declare war on the Arabs.'

'What is this you are talking about?'

'A prophecy that came to me in a dream,' he said.

'And what is the purpose of this war?' I asked.

'To expel the Arabs from their homeland,' he told me.

I stopped walking, bent my knees to stand eye to eye with the boy, and said, 'It is because of these imaginings of yours that you despise me?'

'I despise no one,' he said.

'Have you forgotten,' I asked him, 'all the wonderful hours we spent walking here hand in hand?'

'I have not,' he said.

'Salah,' I said, 'I am your friend, your comrade, your mate. All these thoughts and hallucinations in your head are the result of the shock of losing your father, may he rest in peace. In spite of your harsh words I forgive you completely. Only promise me this: that we will go back to better times and that you will cease to speak of such madness again, for you know not how great my love is for you.'

The boy gazed at me, tears flooding his eyes.

I spread my arms. He looked at me like a person giving in to his own sweet destiny and allowed his body to be embraced.

Although I instructed members of the household not to disturb me in my room, the pernicious angel broke every rule today when he ascended the stairway and knocked at my door, and I found myself knowing exactly what I should do, namely, to take up the small knife I had whittled with my own hands from the branch of a trusty tree and plunge it between his eyes, on the downward slope of his forehead, to puncture his brain and cut short the forward thrust of his life, or at the very least to shout wildly at him about his plots and schemes, the depths of whose villainy I have not yet plumbed, but instead, when the door opened and the pernicious angel stood there in his great height and with those laughing blue eyes and curling blond hair, a wave of heat flooded my breast, for how could I feel even a whit of anger towards so beautiful and beloved a creature as this? and the angel took my hands and led me outdoors, from one side of the grounds to the other, for the purpose of sensing the saltiness of the sea in my nostrils and the surging wavelets of Wadi Musrara on my cheeks, and the good-hearted pernicious angel was merry, and in just another moment I would fall, seduced, into his enchanting trap, when suddenly the visions of wars to come returned and rattled my soul, and I recalled the sight of his naked buttocks rising and falling atop Mother, and his threats and his search for the *kushan*, so that only one last conundrum troubled me, and that was whether he dared to commit the act one must never commit: had he sailed into the bay of blood and taken Father's life? I observed him with one eye and then the other, and at one moment he appeared true and virtuous and in another base and vile, and in this vortex of perplexing ruminations a scheme of my own arose, to hurl the pernicious angel onto the rubbish heap of his own words and to cause him to make full confession, among friends, to having committed the very crime that would require me by command of my people to rise up and cut him down, to avenge blood for blood, his soul for my father's.

Owing to the fact that humans tend to lie rather than telling the truth, one must extract confessions in general conversation, by discussing important matters that touch upon them and their lives in a roundabout manner, and owing to the fact that humans give away, in their prattling and idle chatter, all those matters they work so hard to conceal, I began to talk in a general way about the nature of his people, the Jews, and whether the accusations of the peoples of the world were accurate about their tendency towards lies and subterfuge, and the pernicious angel answered that, yes, this was true and the accusers were right in their judgement, for lies and subterfuge are the way of the Jew, so I added another question in an offhand manner as we walked along among prickly-pear bushes and rocky terrain, namely, whether the Jew covets other men's property and wives, to which the pernicious angel replied in the affirmative, even laughing confidently, as if we were exchanging jokes and jests, though as for revealing something of himself he did not, which provoked me to continue asking other accusatory and provocative questions in this vein, and the pernicious angel unwittingly confirmed all my suspicions about his people, the Jews, and I walked alongside him vexing my brain with ploys to vanquish this adversary, whose tongue is so well trained and versed in lies and deceit, and how I could cause him to make full confession and then take his life with my own hands, and yet I came up with not even a single good plan.

14 January 1896, the Rajani Estate
The boy's psychiatric health has improved immeasurably and

today he even agreed to walk about the grounds with me to chat about all manner of things.

I am not ashamed to admit that I have many fantasies about the estate, like bringing colonists and building many towers here, like clearing whole *dulams* of land and planting all manner of trees, and establishing a colony that would be the crowning glory of all colonies in the Land of Israel but, more than all of these, I am preoccupied with worry about the boy and how to restore him to perfect health and *joie de vivre* and the childish mirth of children his age.

I spent the entire day trying to draw his attention away from the fearsome and frightening visions he has of impending war. In order to boost his spirits I allowed him to ride his bicycle through the puddles left by the rain, and I built him three small wooden boats that we sailed on a small, shallow lake.

While we were sailing one of the boats among the reeds, the boy suddenly grasped his head in his hands and began to scream. His body convulsed. His skin turned to gooseflesh. For an hour he sobbed while I tried to calm his nerves. I held him close, feeling completely useless, and as I did so there came to mind a certain Viennese Jew, whose name escapes me, a doctor of the modern sort, who accepts to his clinic all manner of crazed and deranged patients, and these patients lounge on an ottoman while the doctor listens intently to their every word and, without contradicting them, he heals their deformities and restores them to sanity.

I decided, therefore, to educate the child in a way that would suit him.

I said to him, 'About this war you mentioned yesterday . . .'

'What about it?' he said, still trembling.

'Tell me more,' I said.

He said, 'But you told me these thoughts were false and misleading.'

'I was ill-spoken,' I told him.

'No,' he said. 'You were right. My mind was crazed, or immensely stupid.'

He began to veer the conversation into various pathlets, but I encouraged his prattle and entreated him to tell me more, for the express purpose of getting him to discuss this most recent vision and what had caused his body to convulse. Slowly, he came round and began to speak. The visions that had once visited him at night were now visiting him during the daylight hours as well. Nightmares were becoming daymares. He could see them before his eyes as if they were beasts of the field cavorting like insects. Had these been happy visions he would have regarded them with pleasure. But they were vile and terrifying.

He looked up at me with sad round eyes.

I said, 'Carry on.'

He continued to describe his strange visions. One was of a large and terrible war, the cause of which was unknown to him though it lived and breathed before his very eyes. He could picture his fellow Arabs locked inside their besieged homes while the Jews showered them with fire from catapults and other arms. The Jews also had a worm of fire whose purpose was to burrow between the homes and crack them open. Its mouth spewed sparks and the worm took buildings and lives at will. With his own eyes Salah watched as the worm scorched the limbs of a newborn babe and blinded a toddler in one eye.

I wished to put a stop to this flow of words, for the Jews are known among all the nations of the world for their excellent morals. Even if they possessed, or would one day possess, such means of destruction as this so-called worm of fire, they would never, ever dare to go to the Arabs and kill them. But then I remembered the doctor from Vienna and did not open my mouth, and I continued to listen to the boy with rapt attention.

He said, 'As we were walking together I came face to face with a pair of annihilating eyes from that very worm of fire, and twenty Jews were riding it and seeking to kill me. My skin turned to gooseflesh and my soul shivered.'

He fell silent for a moment, then said, 'Am I completely mad?'

'I do not know,' I said.

He said, 'Do you see the great house of the Rajani estate?'

'I do.'

With a burning tongue taken hostage by the delusions of a baffled soul, he said, 'In the big war the Jews will raze the estate and one day in the future will build three towers on its land, all very tall, their heads in the heavens, and one will be square, one triangular, and one round, each tower made of glass from top to bottom. The Jews' children will be fair and golden haired, the mothers will promenade nonchalantly between the towers, scantily dressed. They will crush beneath their feet the dry *biara*, the uprooted orchards and the ruined groves without knowing a thing of Salah or Afifa or Amina or Mustafa Rajani, may his soul rest in peace, all of whom once, at a certain time in history, lived here and loved here and were sealed in their eternal resting-places here.'

15 *January 1896, Neve Shalom*

Good tidings. Saleem and Salaam have investigated and discovered a diesel engine like the one I want in a well near the Arab village of Sheikh Munis. We rode out there today, passing by the El-Ouja river, and came upon the large and agreeable homes of the village built atop a pleasant hill and surrounded by numerous plantings. I have never before seen such an elegant and beautiful settlement. Even the Arab women carrying their loads on their heads walked with the grace and poise of Europeans.

Saleem and Salaam bargained with the owner of the engine for more than an hour before the price of twenty-five francs was agreed upon. Not another hour had passed before we had it assembled in the well at the Rajani estate. The old mule with the stupid expression regarded us, her eyes peeled. I gave her to Saleem and Salaam as a gift, for them to use her hide to make a nice carpet. They demanded their per cent and I paid it.

In other news, Her Ladyship has not, in spite of her hopes, conceived as yet, her body still behaving in the natural way of women. These, too, are good tidings, for it means she will make herself available to me for at least another month.

Mother wishes to visit my room on the second floor of our home but I have locked the door in her face, for her eyes are fouled and the smell of a strange man is upon her, dripping from between her thighs, and the odour of those blood-blackened bandages rises to my nose, and Mother knocks and knocks and a shrill note of insanity creeps into her voice, and after that she dispatches Amina to tempt me into eating a morsel or to entertain me, but I estrange myself from them and their actions, seduced instead by the genie's familiar and consoling melody that wafts to me from the *biara*, for why should I suffer the skulduggery of a man who pretends to be my friend or the deceptions of an adulterous mother, or the rejection of children my age who loathe me, when I can enjoy a place under the water-lilies, a place where heaven meets water and birds fly upside down?, and so I descend to the pool to be greeted by the genie, for my life's journey is too heavy upon me.

But when I reach the *biara* I find that disaster has befallen it, that the good genie's dwelling-place has been destroyed, for evil people have replaced the sweet and loyal mule with a fiery machine that bellows and twists pipes and has upended the ways of the world so that the water-lilies now float on their backs, the rippling waters have shattered into shards of dew and the friendly genie has escaped to the depths, to the unexplored caverns, and I kneel at the edge of the pool in search of him and call him by name, but even this last and final friend of mine, this wondrous creature of water and the abyss, has fled from me, and there is now no other soul upon whom I may cast my mounting agonies.

16 January 1896, Neve Shalom

Today at long last the Arab woman opened her wet and slippery gates to me. However, my great joy quickly changed to burning disappointment, for she had absolutely and completely altered her behaviour towards me.

She no longer wished to visit our hut, for there were cold winds from the sea that would make her hair stand on end, along with a thousand other odd excuses. That left her bridal bed, the very same one in which her deceased husband had lain when it was plundered by a great number of farmers and their cackling wives. And, like her deceased husband, Afifa lay on her bed like a lifeless carcass. She could not bother to issue even the slightest groan of pleasure from between her pursed lips. For the duration of our coupling her ears listened attentively to the walls in case any prying eyes lurked there. Her pupils darted to and fro as if possessed. Before our lovemaking was finished she leaped up as if bitten by a snake and raced to the basin near the bed, where she scrubbed at her hands as though they were impure.

The moment that she began to wash I rose from the bed and paced about the room like a caged lion. As I walked about stark naked, my organ dangling in front of me – pale and plucked from exhaustion, like someone summoned for no good reason to a place far off and difficult to reach – I heard a strange rustling, like the squeaking of a mouse or the dance of a rat or the race of a vole. I leaned my head towards the source of the sound, at the back of the room, under the bed, but I discovered nothing at all.

'Why do you bend down there by the bed?' the Arab woman said, in a high and bitter voice pregnant with agitation.

'No reason,' I answered.

She affixed her black veil and left the room.

My enemies are schemers with plots and intrigues abounding, and I must be clever and swifter than they, must remain a step ahead of them, surprise them and undermine their tranquillity with an unanticipated manoeuvre of my own, and to this end I conceived a scheme to cause Mother to confess, for if she desires to be near me, why should I not grant her this wish with pleasure?, and I will tumble into her arms, all the while maintaining my composure with wordless flattery so that she will fall into the spidery web of her lies.

Her eyes widened and her face shone with pleasure when I entered her bedroom, that very same bedroom into which I have been spying on her from between the curtains, but now I found myself on the stage itself, as one of its principal actors in a play of tumult and terror, and I said, Mother, forgive me for these many days of estrangement from you, for the loss of my father has left me disturbed and distraught, and I request to return to your wings, and she was overcome with mercy and forgiveness, and copious tears moistened her face, and she embraced me as a mother embraces her son, but I could feel her talons between my ribs and I breathed deeply so as not to retch, and then I engaged her in an arbitrary conversation for the purpose of discovering how it is that she has been passing her days, what she has been doing alone in her room all this time, and Mother told me she was contemplating her strange fate, and she was filled with self-pity, but most of all she was worried and anxious about me and my life, for what would she do with no man, no husband, with so many eyes upon the estate, men's heels waiting to trample and humiliate her?, and I told her, Perhaps you should marry the foreign man who is the overseer of our estate, to which she laughed nervously and said, What a strange idea that has come to your mind, and she hastened to the basin and washed her hands, rubbing them vigorously, and I said, Mother, and she turned her startled face towards me and said, What is it? and I said, Do you know that my love is yours for all eternity, and you need not hide or conceal any matter from me for we two are now alone on this estate and will govern it as we see fit? and she said, I do know this, and soon you will grow into a young man and the estate will be yours to lead wisely, and I pray that we may be strong against the coyotes seeking prey, and she dipped the edges of her sleeves into the water that cut like ice, and her hands reddened from the cold.

17 January 1896, Neve Shalom
I had my first big and stormy row with the Arab woman today.

I arrived at the great house with a shining face, a joyful spirit and a large smile only to find her angry and tight-lipped, her thick hair fanning out wildly, her green eyes skittering under her bushy brows, her entire countenance shouting of antipathy and ugliness.

'A very good morning to you,' I said sweetly.

Her reply was a grumble.

'How lovely,' said I. 'I am grateful.'

She glared at me.

This, from generation to generation, is the fate of man with woman. At first she seduces him with laughing eyes and handsome breasts. But the moment he links his future to hers her mask of beauty falls away and she shows her true face, that of the stubbornness of a mule, the stupidity of a sheep and the petulance of a ram. Every man who has ever wedded a woman or bedded a woman who is not a whore has certainly met up with that expression – the eyes spewing terror, the lips crooked with displeasure, the nose raised in such a way as to provoke fury, all those many hideous details that combine to make a single glorious picture, which I have come to refer to (only to myself) as *tuches face*.

This was exactly the expression worn by the Arab woman, which caused me to leave her company in thunderous silence in order to tyrannise the farmers.

Tuches Face followed me, and said, 'The boy.'

I said, 'I am no longer free and available to listen to a single word about the boy.'

She said, 'The boy.'

I told her, 'Dam up your mouth.'

The Arab woman hastened to block my path and she whispered venomously, 'An evil man you are, wicked-hearted and lustful. I hope you find your death in this place.'

I stood still and said, 'I told you on our first meeting that I am accustomed to this sort of treatment by women.'

Sparks flew from her eyes, and she said, 'From the moment you stepped onto my land you swore an oath that you would bring succour and salvation to the boy.'

I said, 'I promised no such thing.'

She raised her voice and shouted, 'Indeed, you have brought no succour to the boy, only sickness. Heart sickness and soul sickness.'

So that she would not descend into complete hysteria I placed heavy hands on her shoulders and gazed deep into her eyes. I whispered in a voice oozing with tranquillity, 'Afifa, beautiful-eyed Afifa. Please calm yourself.'

I walked her back to the house and said, 'I am all ears. I will listen to all you have to say. Tell me everything, from start to finish, and I will do all I can to help you and your son.'

Afifa swallowed and began a litany that had no order and no logic to it, but slowly I came to understand the source of her great anger. Apparently, a terrible argument broke out between the boy and her last night and he had behaved insolently, which caused her to punish him and he had stamped his feet and she had tweaked his ear and in the end he had uttered many unkind words that hinted at all manner of things, mainly that she is a woman gone astray, a whore.

I said, 'Is this what he said?'

'In exactly those words,' she said. 'A woman gone astray. A whore.'

'Who taught him such words?' I asked.

'I do not know what sort of words Amina pours into his ears.'

'With a scheming maidservant such as she,' I said, 'you would be better off dismissing her.'

'"A woman gone astray. A whore." And he repeated those words several times,' she said.

As a form of advice I said, 'Forget the whole matter and return to being quiet and pleasant as ever you were.'

She said, 'Jacques,' and her voice played the chords of insult and guilt all in one melody, 'you understand nothing. I believe the boy spied us in our misconduct.'

I said, 'That is not even a possibility. The boy is shut inside his room most of the day, hunched over his books, and we have taken extreme precautions. Even the maidservant knows nothing of our trysts.'

'The hut of our lovemaking contains many holes,' she said.

'No person would ever think to approach it at night,' I told her.

'Why, then, did he call me such disrespectful names?' she asked.

I said, 'Across Asia, children call their parents pimps and whores. That is the way of the new generation, which behaves with insolence towards its parents, and the way of this continent, that knows no manners or politesse.'

'My heart – the heart of a mother – senses evil,' she said.

I said, 'The boy speaks from the unbridled madness of his heart. He who seeks to find meaning and hints and clues in these words strives after emptiness and wastes his time.'

She began to calm herself, slowly, until she recalled another matter and jumped to her feet. 'A man with a thick black beard – do you know who that might be?' she asked.

'No.'

'Before Salah began cursing and reviling me,' she said, 'he prophesied to me about the visions he has been having, and first among them was a man in elegant clothing with a thick black beard, and this man was a sort of prophet who leads the Jews to our land in order to wrest it from us. He is slick-tongued, this prophet, and he speaks to kings and aristocrats about creating a realm for the Jews.'

'You are speaking of an egg before it has hatched,' I said.

'Salah pictures him on a veranda, leaning over a railing, his profile dark, his beard thick,' she said. 'He even told me his name but it is hard for a speaker of Arabic to pronounce.'

In order to amuse myself, I said, 'And what else did the Prophet Salah reveal?'

Worried, she said, 'He saw a strange man standing on his head. And a woman with thick glasses and thick arms and a thick voice like a man's. And a man with a black patch over one eye. All these were enemies to our people.'

I said, 'Do you really and truly believe this nonsense, this gibberish? Can you not see, Afifa, the senseless alarm that is shaking your bones, the silliness that issues from your throat? Quiet now, my beauty, I am here beside you.'

She regarded me with tearful eyes.

I said, 'I know that many transformations are taking place on the estate. Your husband died in the prime of his life. Your son has been left fatherless. But, on the other hand, good days have befallen this house, an industriousness has taken hold of everything. The orchards are greening, fruit and flowers are blooming wherever the eyes behold. All these undoubtedly agitate your soul but, trust me, Afifa, everything is for the best.'

'And the boy?' she said.

'Do not worry about him,' I told her. 'I swear to you that I will correct his ways. Just as the trees of the estate are growing tall and proud, so too shall Salah bloom.'

'Amen,' she said. 'May these words pass directly from your mouth, which sprouts pearls, to Allah's ears.'

I took her fingers in hand and kissed them one by one.

Since I could see that she was still not completely comforted I filled my lungs with air, exhaled with a hiss and said those three short and simple words that every woman wishes to hear.

She fell into my arms at once. 'And I love you as well,' she said. She kissed me and whispered, 'Forgive me for all my thoughts, dear Jacques, love of my life.'

And I said, 'I forgive you.'

18 January 1896, Café Armon

Each time I come to the Café Armon the beggar-poet known as the Wildebeest appears from nowhere to keep me company, and I provide him with some liqueur or other spirit along with some morsel – *kreplach* or potato *varenikes* – to fill his grumbling belly. Today as well, like all the other days, he came to sit beside me and I plied him with wine while recounting my sorrows with regard to the strange boy at the Rajani estate, which I hoped one day to turn into a first-rate colony.

The Wildebeest bent his head over a scrap of paper and scribbled a few words, which he then handed to me.

I asked, 'And what might this be?'

He said, 'It is a poem of consolation to perk up your spirits, written here, on the spot, in your honour.'

I read the scrap of paper:

> Good cheer, my friend,
> Let's raise a toast
> And fill our glasses with wine.
> No longer shall we sit alone
> Miserable and crying . . .

The nature of the poem was, in my opinion, juvenile and idiotic, but as a sign of gratitude for the massive poetic effort involved in rhyming 'wine' with 'crying' I ordered a bowl of steaming stew for the Wildebeest, which he downed lustfully.

A child of one of the tenant farmers summoned me this evening, quite agitated, and since he had come to my window at a late hour – an act absolutely forbidden, as the tenant farmers are limited to the area of their huts – and since he asked that I follow behind him in close pursuit, I understood that something terrible had transpired on our estate; indeed, one event after another has occurred in the past few weeks, ever since the pernicious angel folded his wings and alighted on the naked roof of our home and began to dishevel all order and disrupt all love.

Despite the late hour and the darkness, all the tenant farmers and their wives and children were awake, milling about and talking in fearful, anxious voices, and when I approached they fell silent and the women gathered round me, rolling their eyes and pointing in various odd directions, and I paid no heed to the demands of anxiety, as it undermined my confidence, nor to the butchering knife wreaking havoc in my stomach, but instead I asked to speak in private with the men, in order to comprehend in language simple and straightforward what had happened, and they brought me to one aged gentleman, the eldest among them, who had been living on our estate from the day of his birth, and I looked into his eyes, watery with fear, and sat before him and, lo, his hands were trembling, and he said, You are still but a child, and if your mother hears of our encounter she will be overwhelmed with anger, but you must know that these things disturbing our peace have never before transpired on this estate.

He insisted that the wailing women be removed and the sobbing children be calmed, and when I asked, What is it that has transpired?, my small soul, that of a child, grew even smaller in the face of these giant hurdles placed before my every step, and the old man, in a voice about to shatter, said, One of our young boys came upon a walking spirit several days ago in the depths of an orchard, in the dark trees, and the pale, lifeless ghost prophesied to him in a thundering voice that our fate has been sealed and that all the tenant farmers will be banished from the estate to the north of this land, never to return, and the ghost described a long and placid procession, for this land will vomit us out without our having done any wrong, and our huts built of fiddlesticks and air, of straw and mud, which have served us loyally for ages and ages, will go up in flames to the last one.

The old man added that the child had been taken ill and was burning with fever, but since then other children, as well as a man and a woman, had encountered the spirit, and all were terror-stricken and bedridden, and the entire community was frightened and confused, for a dead spirit was walking among the trees and branches even though it is not the custom of the dead to rise up from their graves, and residents of the world to come do not visit residents of this vain and futile world in which we live. We are, he said, helpless and fearful of the worst, since the spirit is angry about a murder of which we know nothing.

At that point the women burst into the room, wailing, and they said in their sobbing voices, The land has cursed us and wishes to vomit us out, soon we shall no longer dwell in this place, we shall no longer be the children of this land, we shall no longer till the soil and the clods of earth and the furrows, and I, distracted, said, Return me to my home, why did you bring me out here tonight? To which the old man replied: The child burning with fever, the first to hear the ghost's prophecy, requests your presence, calls you by name again and again, through clouded breaths – Salah! Salah! – so will you agree to see him? And I told him I would, after which I was racked with regret, but the gaggle of women bustled me off after the old man, and I walked along, terrified, to one of the huts, where the sick boy lay, and he was no more than five years of age, burning with fever in his bed, and when he saw me his eyes filled with blood and he ordered his mother and father to leave the room, and when we were alone, just the two of us, he described for me, with ragged breathing and reddened cheeks and burning brow, exactly what the ghost had told him.

19 January 1896, the Rajani Estate
The mood at the estate is not the best. The Arab woman has not yet finished with being a *tuches face*. The boy is shut up in his room and does not eat or drink. And the maidservant has sequestered herself in her quarters, where she grumbles and rummages about. I, on the other hand, derive much pleasure from the diesel engine that powers the bucket pulley and the water that flows swiftly and easily through the wide irrigation channel. Even the eucalyptus trees are coming along nicely, and two almond trees that stand at the entrance to the estate have begun their stunning bloom.

Most importantly, I forgot to mention some excellent news: today three colonists who hail from Russia and speak the Hebrew language have joined me at the estate for the purpose of assisting with all the labour to be carried out. The first is named Menahem-Mendel, the second Asher-Yehoshua and the third Shimon-Yedel. All three have been combing the Land of Israel for the past month or two and do not wish to live the lives of farmers in any of the colonies, for they prefer that of the cities. Now that their money has run out and their stomachs have shrunk they were about to set sail for home but were kind enough to answer my pleas and those of their good friend the Wildebeest, and agreed to lend a hand. It is pleasant to toil as a team with workers better educated than the tenant farmers, who are as lumpish as beasts.

※

21 *January 1896, the Rajani Estate*
Today, at long last, the boy left his room and came down to eat with us. His mother was very excited and flushed. Salah was in fine spirits and ate with gusto, even helping himself to an extra portion of the fresh vegetable salad and the rice with lentils that Amina, the maidservant, had prepared. Amina has many shortcomings but she excels at chopping the tomatoes and cucumbers and onions very fine and seasoning everything with the Arabs' superb olive oil. Her Ladyship could learn many lessons about cooking from these Arab women.

When the meal had ended the boy stood and said, 'I have an important announcement for you.'

'And what would that be?' asked his mother.

'I have decided to read to you a story written from my own imagination, a story on which I have been labouring for long months and which no one has yet read.'

The Arab woman stared at him in complete surprise, then laughed in relief and said, 'This is truly joyful news, my sweet son, and we shall be pleased to take part.'

I asked, 'And what is this story about?'

'It takes place far away and a long, long time ago,' he said, 'in the Bedouin deserts during the days of the Jahilya, and the story tells of Rashid, a boy who lives there. Tomorrow in the early evening I shall read a small portion that I have translated into French especially for Jacques.'

I thanked him profusely, and with great satisfaction.

The Arab woman came to life and ordered the maidservant to prepare a special evening meal on the morrow and to decorate the house with branches from an almond tree and to serve excellent beverages, and she rewarded me with many kisses. Were it not for the late hour, and the fact that Her Ladyship was waiting at home for me to arrive and engage in sexual intercourse, I would have known the Arab woman fully. Still, this will certainly happen tomorrow after I have heard the boy's story.

In a voice filled with agitation, one among the guardsmen summoned Rashid this evening and led him to a darkened hill of sand, cool from the desert winds, and at the sound of his low whistle there emerged from within one of the tents pitched there two fellow guardsmen, their heads bowed and their gazes eager to detect any sign of a traitor or delator.

The first guardsman urged them on. 'Tell him,' he said, and they swallowed their spittle and were dismayed, so that Rashid asked them, 'What is it?' for he knew not what guardsmen such as these could have to tell a child like him, the wisps of whose moustache had scarcely begun to graze his lips, and they said, 'Like you, we, too, mourn the death of your dear father, murdered by the Hazraj, and we are distraught that he was buried in a sandstorm and died in the desert, but know you this: late last night, during the third watch, at a time when even the light of the stars turns dull and opaque and the desert winds whistle through the barren sands, there appeared before us a figure in the distance, armed with sword and dagger, and when we called out to it, "Who goes there?" and brandished our spears, the figure turned towards us and, lo, it was your dear departed father in the days of his glory, the sword at his thigh the very same splendid sword whose possession was claimed by the Hazraj, and your father's forelock was dipped in blood, his face that of a pale skull and his eyes were missing.'

The boy shivered and trembled uncontrollably and the guardsmen were dismayed at causing agitation to the boy's grieving and inferior soul, and Rashid asked them, with hope and fear, whether this was not a nightmarish hallucination, and they said, 'No, we two saw it as one,' and Rashid asked, 'And what did the spirit want?' to which they replied, 'It did not tell us. Only its gaze was sorrowful, sunk in bitter disappointment as if it did not expect to meet us but rather someone else.' And Rashid whispered, 'Me, 'twas I whom the spirit wished to encounter.' And the guardsmen said, 'That is what we, too, believe.'

The guardsmen poured Rashid hot water with herbs to keep him awake and he remained with them, bundled snugly in warm clothing, for the entire watch, in order to glimpse the ghost, should it reappear, for although the boy's hair stood on end in fright, he was determined to meet the apparition that night and speak with it, to learn its reason for returning from the land of the dead and hovering about with no rest or repose, as happens in stories and fables.

The hours passed, and in another moment the boy would fall asleep on his watch, for the monotonous cast of the wind and the lashing sound of desert junipers caused him to slumber, when suddenly the guardsmen tugged at his clothing and called his name and awakened him and said, 'There, there, look that way,' and a thousand pins pricked his heart for, just as they had described it only a few hours earlier, there appeared the figure of a ghost, troubled and grieving, whose broad thighs and great height and heavy sword bedecked with a jewel for each throat it had slit were precisely those of his dead father, and the guardsmen each put a hand on the boy to stop him approaching this bewitched spirit, and they warned him that deep, dark pits of salty and bitter water stood on either side of the hill and that by pursuing the ghost he would risk his life, but Rashid wished nothing more than to follow his father, to glimpse him one last time and perhaps to hear from him himself, or at least from the spirit that had claimed his form, why he was still roaming between this world and the world of the dead.

The spirit signalled to Rashid to follow him to a small, hidden valley, the very same level valley with treacherous earth and many traps and snares the length and breadth of it, and as they walked away from the encampment, with only the light from ancient stars hanging above them, the ghost turned its face towards Rashid and said, 'My son,' and Rashid asked, 'Are you my father?' to which the ghost replied, 'Yes,' and his voice trembled, and the boy could see that from the spirit's hollow eye sockets there was a flow of tears, and with them the strange knowledge that Father was crying, Father was crying.

The boy remained silent and the ghost said, with a bitter sigh that came from the depths of his uprooted heart, 'Rashid, my son, how rueful is my demise, for I have been condemned to the place called Al-Khoutma, the crushing disaster that is hell, the fire kindled by Allah,' and Father lowed and sobbed and said, 'All my fortunes and all my possessions were of no good to me, I shall soon burn in flaming fires, and the witches approach bearing wood for fuel, upon their necks a noose of strongly twisted rope, for roasting my flesh.'

All the while Rashid could not stop staring at the dead skull, whose lipless mouth and loathsome tongue continued to speak as if they were still in the land of the living, and he was filled with compassion for his father, who had never once spoken to him in weakness, had never talked from the depths of his heart of his troubles or his fears, and only now – after his death, on his way from one hell to another – was he speaking to him as a father to a son, and Rashid wished to caress the dead man's bony fingers and give him a word of consolation or encouragement, but the spirit silenced him: 'Our time is short: in a little while I will be forced to return to my prison-house, chained to the heavy trunk of a Jericho balsam tree, a tree that grows in the bottom of hell; its produce the heads of the serpents, its branches wormy and black. Now, my son, listen well and hear my words.

'Know that the whole purpose of my presence in the land of the living is to reveal this secret to you: that which has been uttered and pronounced of my death in a hero's battle, on the back of a swift-footed camel as I butchered our many enemies, all this is lies and falsehood a thousand times over, and the bitter truth is otherwise, that your mother, who pretends to be the loving wife, found another to whom to give her love, and he is none other than the Emir Omar, tall and ginger-curled; it was he who stole her heart with sickly sweet words and traitorous gifts so that together they conspired to bring about my death, and would that the curse of hell fall upon the head of this Omar and his flesh be torn to shreds and rot for ever in the shade of that cursed Jericho balsam tree; and he came to our home like a snake in the thorns and twigs and seduced your guileless mother into treachery and murder, and upon his insistence she concocted for him a toxic blend, a bowl of venom designed to shrivel the skin and stop the heart of he who drinks it, and when we went out to battle he arranged for us to stand guard together, lying in wait to ambush our mortal enemies, but when I paused to rest a bit and gather my strength for the big battle on the morrow, along came this man of malice, this son of a whore dancing on spider legs and, in the porches of my ears did pour the leprous distilment while I lay sleeping peacefully, and afterwards he did dispose of my body and told lies of a desert battle and, lo, I am dead and my body has rotted and my flesh is covered with worms and excrement.'

Once again the ghost shed tears and Rashid settled uneasily onto his knobby knees, and his father signalled to him that it was time to take his leave, and from the eastern horizon a pale sliver of dawn rose and the three worried guardsmen appeared on one of the hills, sighing with copious relief at the sight of the boy still alive and not trapped or drowned in one of the poisonous ponds, and the ghost grasped Rashid's shoulders, looked straight from his own hollow eyes and said, in a voice that would disturb

any heart and scatter any soul, 'Have you considered if he gives the lie to
the truth and turns his back? Does he not know that Allah sees? Nay! If
he desist not, we would certainly smite his forehead, a lying, sinful
forehead, and summon the braves of the army of hell.'

22 January 1896, Neve Shalom

The hour is late but I must none the less sit down to my diary
and write the events of this day.

My soul is fuming.

Suppressed rage, leaping flames and hot, bubbling water roil
and boil inside me when I recall the putrid, enraging, humiliating
and despicable act carried out against us by the boy.

Not a boy, is he, but a monster.

Not a monster, but a two-headed snake, a hideous worm,
vermin that must be conspired against and annihilated.

The evening set aside for the reading of the story we had been
promised began in a most pleasant fashion. The Arab woman
and I were seated, at Salah's invitation, in the reception room on
the ground floor of the house, where we chatted and laughed like
a pair of lovers.

In retrospect, there was only one worrisome sign, and that was
the boy, who, under false and evil pretences, required us to sit not
in his room but on the first floor of the house, quite nearby the
place where his father's lifeless body had been discovered.

Without knowing that the boy had rigged a trap of the
sweetest honey for us, the Arab woman and I tasted the excellent
delicacies prepared by the rummaging, grumbling maidservant,
and I even accepted a glass of wine bought from the Christian
Arabs of Jaffa, and in high spirits I said, 'Please, Maestro, read us

this story of wondrous romance, upon which you have been toiling these many months.'

The boy smiled a smile that seemed to me then warm and loving but which soon showed itself to be ignoble and derisive. Then, in a guileful manner I did not expect his juvenile brain to be capable of, he began reading the French translation of the story he had written from his own imagination.

I will not bother my diary with details of the ridiculous plot, with its tales of battling Arabs in desert lands, for it is well known that Arabs from the dawn of history love acts of murder and plunder and attach little importance to a man's life and honour. In the days prior to the coming of their Prophet Muhammad, in the period known by them as Al-Jahilya, the Arab tribes slaughtered one another without mercy, and it was in one of those battles that the dignitary El-Said Abu Rashid, father of the boy Rashid in Salah's story, met his death.

Rashid.

Anyone hearing the first lines of the story already knows that Rashid is none other than Salah and Salah is none other than Rashid, for Rashid, like Salah, is attracted to writing and poetry and, like Salah, Rashid loves and is close to his mother, and like Salah, Rashid is delicate and feeble and weak and, anyway, it is a known fact that in matters of literature, all the characters described are created in the image of their narrators, and any writer who denies this is merely lying to others and himself.

At this point in the story we were still listening with rapt attention. His mother was smug with satisfaction at his literary abilities and his capacity for translating his work flawlessly into the French language. Her cheeks puffed and her skin glistened with pride at this fruit of her womb so fluent in writing and reading, and she praised his talent, though as far as I was concerned his characters were far too simplistically drawn, even for the level expected from a boy his age; they contained no depth or emotion, functioning merely as paper dolls created from air, no life breathed into their nostrils. Another major fault in his writing is his refusal to staunch the flow of words, his dislike for punctuation of any kind, fashioning sentences that go on and on until one's breath runs out, scarcely a dot or a dash separating them for many long pages.

But then, only a few minutes into the story, my soul grew tense and distraught, for anyone listening to the next lines would understand that this was no traditional tale of days and people of yore, but a parable, and not just any parable but a twisted and nefarious parable of me and his mother and Salah himself, whose own father has recently died.

As for the plot, it is simple-minded and unrealistic in the most fundamental manner. After the father's death his ghost appears to the son, Rashid, in a dream in which the father explains that he did not meet his death in battle as everyone believed but – heaven preserve us! – he was murdered by his wife and her accomplice, her lover.

I was unable to comprehend how it is that a boy who spends all his time on an isolated estate managed to create such a strange story as this, and from what dark recesses in his troubled soul he concocted such a *mélange*. It seems to me that there can be no explanation other than the malevolent maidservant, who during the days and hours of peeling vegetables and frying aubergines and sifting rice took respite by pouring her lies and deceptions into the boy's ears.

But the worst of all was still to come, and my soul grew even more tense and more distraught at what words lay ahead. His voice quiet and soft, the boy proceeded to read his description of the lover who apparently had persuaded the woman to murder her husband – a fair-haired man who resembles me quite precisely. At once my breast was aflame, for this man was nothing if not evil incarnate. And the boy read of how this man spoke with eloquent flattery to the husband just before his death, and now the fire in my breast rose into my throat and my whole body was in tumult over this boy's spiteful rancour, his ingratitude, for how could he dare sling this muck at me, these terrible, perverse lies? Me! His good friend, his advocate, the one who toiled day after day with limitless patience to educate and encourage him, and bring him to the realm of happiness and joy, all of which I did even though he is not my son, not the fruit of my loins, does not even stir within me pure or natural feelings of love, while his father all the while sailed the seas and roamed the ports and spent time with whores and harlots. And I had but one desire: to plant a ringing blow on the pale cheeks of this wanton child. Instead I stood up and left the room and the entire estate so as not to hear even a single syllable more of the ill-conceived plot from his sick and feverish brain, a plot whose entire existence can be described in a single word: insolence.

23 January 1896, Neve Shalom
It is the middle of the night now. I am unable to sleep at all, so I rose to write in my diary, for the story written by the boy is greatly disturbing my peace of mind. Not because of the contrived plot or the fantastical elements or the fertile Levantine imagination that came together to create an enraging admixture, but because of the personal affront that scorches my throat.

For days and weeks I have toiled to cause the estate to flourish and be beautiful, to console the Arab woman on the loss of her husband, and even to bring goodness and benevolence to the citizens of the world. And what is my recompense? A sort of parable of wickedness designed to vitiate and humiliate me. Were I the boy's father he would already have felt a stinging blow from my arm.

Her Ladyship is twisting and turning in her sleep. All night she has been retching and threatening to vomit. But she does not vomit nor will she, for she has not fallen pregnant.

Witness yet another example of fantasy.

There is a wan and waning moon this evening, but its dull light is enough to strike my eyes blind, for I shall not be able to sleep, and my fingers creep towards the ink and the notepad of their own accord for the purpose of pouring onto the pages that which I cannot discuss with a single human being, for my soul is in terrible distress this evening, not from the good angel's angry departure from the reception room where he was listening to my story of a man like him and of a bowl of venom and of a murder by poison administered to the ear; nor is my distress derived from Mother's alarm and dismay, when she asked what it is that I have done, and her cheeks grew pale as a ghost from hell; rather, I am distressed by the searing knowledge, painful as a knife at my throat, that the good angel's fate was sealed this evening and the verdict is that he must die for the acts of covetousness and lust and adultery and murder that he perpetrated.

For days and weeks I had the angel for a good friend and escort, and he brought some of the sun's light to my life, for as a result of his pleasantries and his games and his mild temperament, my nightmares began to dissipate and I loved life more and I emerged from the loneliness of my room. But what is the value of friendship that contains no friendship at all, and what is the reward for camaraderie that is no camaraderie at all, for the man before whom I opened the hidden chambers of my heart, the man to whom I revealed my secrets and my afflictions, this man is nothing but a sinister snake, a liar among liars who spreads his poison among friends and relations alike, among his comrades and among those he loves.

Were I grown up and possessed of a manly body I would take up arms this very evening and strike him down, I would slit his throat and drag him by his forelock and raise his severed head and kick it into the *biara* so it would rest there and rot to the end of generations. Were I older, larger, with branching muscles and a deep voice and feathery sideburns, I would bash his head with a rock and bring about his demise. But what am I other than an orphan boy, small and weak and strange, with no strength in his loins, whose frailty is mocked even by the cats, a shell, a husk afloat on stormy seas soon to submerge and drown him?

24 *January 1896, the Rajani Estate*

My rage at the boy is not abating and the affront is not dissipating. For that reason I went to the Arab woman as she scrubbed her hands over the basin. At once I instructed her to have Salah apologise to me profusely for the slanderous and defamatory remarks he made about me. Further, I told her that if I do not receive such an apology I will leave my job as overseer and she will be alone to manage the affairs of the estate as she wishes.

The Arab woman, submerged in her melancholy, the light in her eyes extinguished and her face sour and dour, left off from her incessant scrubbing in order to defend her child, the act of a woman's love for her son gone astray, and she began to praise him, saying that what he read to us was only a story and nothing more, and there was no other intention or hint at anything beyond, for the boy is devoted to his artistry, which is carried out for the sole purpose of entertaining and uplifting the soul.

I told her, 'Even in a work of fiction one finds truth in the emotions, and in this case the boy hates me, loathes me, in spite of all the good I have done for him.'

With a small irritating smile of malaise she said, 'The boy loves you deeply. It is just that his illness and the death of his father have impaired his judgement.'

'So that is the reason,' I said, 'he portrayed me as a depraved murderer?'

'That is the way of authors and poets,' she told me. 'In the heat of creativity they write without thinking and in the end offend their loved ones.'

I began pacing to and fro about the room.

She pleaded with me in a hushed and saddened voice. 'Please, do not be so exacerbated. He is only a boy.' She thrust her hands into the basin once again, lathering and rinsing her fingers with great intensity until the skin began to peel away in patches.

I said, 'He must come to me no later than the tenth hour today for the purpose of apologising sincerely. Otherwise, I will leave you alone here with the tenant farmers.'

'I will summon him,' she said.

So, I will await this conversation and see what it brings. After these things come to pass I shall return to this diary to record the events that transpire. Although I am not a writer or an artist or a poet, my nose smells the scent of an impending disaster. Again and again I have read the scribblings in my diary for the purpose of finding the hints and sources of that ruin to come, but in vain. There is no way of knowing what Salah might be planning and what his heart – which rejects those who love him and hold him dear – intends for him to do. Time teaches us that there is no underestimating an enemy, even a boy, for if he wishes he can move mountains and sow great destruction.

Early in the morning I went to the tenant farmers and at once they gathered round me of their own accord, their hands pressed together in mourning and lamentation, and from their vexing words, which caused them increasing agitation, I was brought the bad tidings that last night, at the very hour when I was reading to the malfeasant angel about a character like himself, and caused him a tempest of emotions that led him to storm out of the room, the feverish boy gave in to death's rapacious lust, and in his final twilit moments he called out my name and made the stars and the breaking dawn and the swift-footed deer promise that they would not let this murderer escape, and with these last words, his mother weeping nearby, his soul departed, and the farmers were just burying him in a place quite close to the cemetery by the sea, on a sandstone ridge, where my own father is interred.

At once I recounted to them all that the child had told me on his deathbed, that the spirit they have observed perambulating in the orchards is none other than the ghost of my father seeking to avenge his despicable death by a faint-hearted man who did not even dare summon him to a duel but merely snipped the wick of his life as he lay sleeping in his own home, and the tenant farmers asked me, their eyes peeled wide, who this killer was, and I told them, The very same man who gives you your daily bread, the very same man who pretends to be looking after your welfare and that of the estate, and the dim-witted peasants acted as if they did not comprehend, so that I had no choice but to give them the name of the pernicious angel, known as Jacques, and they asked if this were indeed what the boy had said as he lay dying, if he had given Jacques' name, and I told them it was his and no other's, and the farmers asked why the man would take another man's life, and I explained that that is as clear as the light of day, for the man wishes to take the estate for himself and for his people, the Jews, and to replace my father in Mother's bed, and so, I told them, it is upon us to relieve him of his life. 'It is incumbent upon you people to rise up,' I said, 'and commit this act in my name, the name of an orphan, for I myself have never witnessed an act of killing and I have no idea how to rip a soul from its body, how to remove life through bloodshed, and to bring living, pleasure-seeking, moving flesh to the depths of depravity of eternal death.'

But the peasants said these matters did not seem plausible. They said, Even if there is some kernel of truth in all this, we are small and downtrodden, more lowly than the dung-heaps and the garbage, so who are we to judge between the *effendi* – your father – and Jacques? And what contact do we have with these great machinations, for we ask nothing more than the daily portion of beans and bread that satiates our souls? Now stop burdening our minds with talk of terrible mishaps and suffering and let us return to our work and our huts and our women. And I said, If you do not do as I ask you, he will rise up and banish you from your land, and everything you have built here will be set aflame. And the tenant farmers said, Even if this strange prophecy comes to pass, Allah sits on high and looks after us, keeping us safe from evil and from bandits. And if He does not come to our aid we shall spread prayer rugs and we shall pray and fast a great deal. And now, they urged, Cease from imparting your evil ruminations. Then, with shoulders pulled back and heads held high, they returned one after the other to their wretched homes, deaf to my impassioned cries and the stamping of my feet on the earth of the estate.

24 January 1896, the Rajani Estate, a few hours later
This is the entirety of a conversation I had with the boy today, which I wish to record so that I will not forget.

I swallowed my pride and ascended to the second floor, to the boy's room, because it was beneath his honour to depart from the ivory tower in which he can be found at all hours of the day and night.

The boy was sitting at his desk, bent over his papers and notebooks, clearly toiling hard at something that looked like an important letter, written in Arabic. I peered at it, but the letters of that cackling language, which look like bird droppings, were incomprehensible and I could learn nothing from them. Salah folded up the letter and thrust it into an envelope, which he placed at the edge of the desk.

'Hello,' I said.

He turned his face towards mine and responded in kind.

His behaviour had changed. That same confidence with which he had read the story to us was once again evident in his face. Rebellious fire sparked in his eyes. He had most certainly changed.

'Has your mother spoken to you?' I asked.

'Yes,' he said.

'Then I await your speech.'

'Speech comes with difficulty to me just now,' he said.

'I have time,' said I. 'I will wait.'

He said, 'I have heard a rumour that the story I told boiled your blood and for that I ask your forgiveness. All that I wrote was nothing but my imagination and nefariousness of heart. It is a work of fiction invented by the author. Any resemblance to people living or dead is purely coincidental.'

'This request for forgiveness,' I said, 'does it come from the bottom of your heart?'

He lowered his gaze. 'No,' he said.

'And why not?' I asked.

'Because you, too, have boiled my blood.'

I said, 'I will not comprehend this even if given all the time that ever was or will be for contemplation. What reason do you have to be angry with me? Is it not true that from the very first meeting between us I have done you nothing but good, good and more good?'

'It is true,' he answered.

'You yourself have admitted that time and again.'

'Yes, I have,' he said. 'But my blood boiled not for things you have done but for things you are yet to do.'

I said, 'Once again you are preoccupied with those prophecies of yours that vex your good sense.'

'These are not prophecies but knowledge, strong and true, of the future to come.'

'And what,' I asked, 'is the nature of this knowledge?'

He said, 'Do you recall the cemetery where my father is buried?'

'What about it?'

'In that very spot you and your people will build a large hotel, where people will come and go and where they will defecate and urinate without ever knowing that my father's grave cries out from the ground beneath them.' He continued. 'And do you recall the village from which you brought the diesel engine?'

'I do.'

He said, 'In that very spot you and your people will construct a large complex of buildings used for university studies and you will raze that village and pave over it with bricks and mud.'

'Enough,' I said. 'I have heard enough of this nonsense. Now you listen to me. It is the time to decide: are you for us, or for our adversaries? If for us, then remove from around your neck this scarf of anger and malevolence and don a garment of fraternity and honour. If for our adversaries, then we shall go and declare war one against the other. Which shall it be?'

He fell silent and covered his face with his hands.

I took advantage of this opportunity and silently stole the letter from the desk, slipped it into my breast pocket and departed from the room.

The good angel just now paid a visit to my room and a major confrontation befell us, for his blood boils against me and mine against him, and after he departed, as I sat at my desk, I drew two characters – one a large man, the other a small boy, the former golden-haired, the latter with dark curls – and each falls upon the other's neck, and the boy in my notebook asks the angel's forgiveness for all the evil he has done him, for the letters he has written to the Turkish governor and members of the Turkish police force, for the lies and deceit of which he has accused him from the depths of his imagination, for all the wrongdoing he has carried out against him with full intention and clarity of purpose, and the good angel asked, his eyes brimming with the tears of a victim, But why, Salah? Why have you perpetrated these evil acts? And the boy bowed his head and confessed: I myself do not understand. And the good angel said, Salah, do you know that in spite of your wickedness I love you still and for ever, for the time we have spent together is precious to me? And the smile on your lips is stored in my heart, and Salah promises him that he will burn the notebooks, every one, for the words – dead, mute, frozen on every page – are useless to one and all; only his love for the angel, the love of one friend for another, the love of an adult for a child, of a father for a son, is the root of all life, and for this he yearns, this he desires, and the good angel said, I know a poet from among my people who writes very pleasant rhymes that capture the beauty of the moment and awaken one to the din of life. Why don't you, too, Salah, try your hand at such poems, filling up your notebooks with psalms of glory and praise for the world and its magnificence instead of stories of days of yore? and Salah stroked his fair hair and breathed in his good and familiar scent and whispered to the good angel and to himself as well, I surrender to you, completely and fully.

25 January 1896, Neve Shalom
Early this morning I went to give the letter to my old friends Saleem and Salaam. It is their custom to sleep until the tenth hour of the morning, because their nights are filled with merry-making and debauchery in which men dress in the clothing of women and there are all manner of alcoholic beverages forbidden to people of the Muslim faith, and even acts of lovemaking that will ring in the ears and make the hair stand on end of all those who walk the straight and narrow path. Thus, I will not note them in detail here on the page so as to save them from discomfort and suffering.

Saleem opened the door for me, his eyes blurry due to the early hour, and he invited me into the room, which smelled strongly of overripe figs. After preparing coffee for the three of us, the two began to chatter about this and that of little consequence, a sort of prattle beloved among the Arabs as preliminary to the matters at hand.

Finally I told them to stop, and I related to them all that had transpired with the boy and the fantastical fiction that described me as an evil-doing man of the lowest moral standards who had conspired to murder and committed adultery.

Saleem said, 'There is a grain of truth in his words.'

'May Allah strike you down for that,' I said.

'Do you know,' asked Salaam, 'what the punishment is for adultery among the Arabs?'

'No,' said I.

Salaam said, 'If, heaven forfend, the boy writes of these matters to his uncles in a letter or telegram, they will at once appear here with a considerable number of armed men who will hang you from a lemon tree by your testicles.'

My body began to convulse. I waved the letter in my hand before them and said, 'In any event, the boy has been working hard on this missive, and I wish you to translate it into the French language for me.'

'Twenty francs,' they said.

Fury inflamed my throat and I shouted at them. 'Until when will you shake me down for every last coin I own? From the day I met you you have relieved me of two thousand francs, even more!'

They regarded me as if assessing me, then they pulled back the blanket on their bed to reveal their erect appendages. They said, 'Come lie with us and we shall forgo the payment.'

I gave them the money and departed.

This evening a door opened wide and behind it many more, all suffused with sunlight, and behind these were long corridors with yet more doorways, and I found myself walking this labyrinth, and I came upon what seemed to be an enormous sail held to earth by ropes at the four corners, and it opened of its own accord and from this I came to understand that all that had been revealed to me verse by verse, shard by shard, in dreams and nightmares and hallucinations, had now come together into a single map, whole and detailed, of the story that had taken shape, and that I was writing it down like a prophet warning his people of the destruction and annihilation yet to come.

The start of the devastation would be the loss of our land to our oppressors, the Jews scattered among the nations of the world, from among whom leaders and philosophers would soon rise to lead their people in conquering our homeland, not, as would be expected, by might and the trumpets of warfare (indeed, that nation is not known for its battle skills or its strength) but rather through acts of chicanery, subterfuge and deception, like the cobwebs spun by a battalion of green-eyed spiders; at first they will come in dribs and drabs, like the angel who came to us on his own, alone, and then they will begin to band together, erecting homes and whole neighbourhoods so that slowly, sneakily, cleverly, they will force the legs of my people to march, and they will shout derogatory names at them, will depict them horned and hideous, and the people will not heed the cries of the prophets and instead will shut their eyes and grit their teeth, and until the first among them awakens to the situation, the Jews will already have conquered much of the land, and they will have sunk in their talons and seated themselves on their hind haunches smeared with excrement, and the land will become contaminated with their filthy skin and their ugly souls, that Jewish soul despised among one and all that has been expelled and banished from place to place.

On a beautiful sunny day I escaped the confines of my room and rode my bicycle into Jaffa, pumping the pedals while my heart was plunged into the deepest despair at the thought of the war that will break out between two bitter rivals, and the stinging, humiliating Arab defeat and, lo, in my vision of things to come, the port of Jaffa teems with boats crammed full with children and babies trying to escape from the worms of fire rained down upon them by the Jews, and I entered the city's gate and walked among the souks and the cafés and the rising curls of *narghile*-pipe smoke and my heart filled with tears, for almost nothing shall remain of all of these, and without thinking I overturned a crate of fruits and vegetables and stood upon it, where I began to shout in my small voice, trying in vain to make myself heard above the din of shoppers and merchants, and I said to them, 'O people! O believers, people of faith! Open your eyes, rise and awaken: when the heavens are cleft asunder and the stars become dispersed and the seas are made to flow forth, then the land will heave its masses and hurtle them to distant lands, to dense and malodorous encampments built haphazardly, to be citizens of the diaspora for ever and ever, and nothing at all shall remain of this souk, and the flower market, and the street of the money-changers, and the street of the silversmiths, only abandoned buildings carved from the hill and dried-up gardens and springs,' and my throat burned with excitement, my veins throbbed, and little by little an inquisitive crowd gathered round me, and I pointed to the edge of the city, to the north, the site of our comely villages, our orchards, our excellent sea sand, and I said to them, 'There! That is where they will build their city from which they will banish us until not a single member of the Arab people remains,' and the passers-by and onlookers mistakenly took me for a jester and they laughed at the powerful words spewing from my soul, and some tittered derisively and said, 'Repeat those strange words you have spoken; the Jews will drive us from our homes? They are nothing but loiterers who knock at our doors asking for hand-outs,' and I recounted all my visions, like the one about the flock of birds sent to the skies by the Jews for the purpose of dropping explosive devices on Arab cities, and the crowd burst into laughter. 'Will that despised and worthless people then tame the birds of the skies?' they asked. And I said, 'Yes, yes, yes, no day will pass that they will not decimate our children and poison our wells, and he who kills Arabs will be seen as a hero in their eyes,' and the merchants raised a cry against me, for these words that came thrashing and gushing from me caused concern and anger among the shoppers, and one called out to me, 'If indeed this great wave of Jews will come to vanquish us, from where will they arrive? After all, there are but a few in Jaffa, and every day more of them run off for distant shores while they can,' and I answered them: 'They will come by the thousands, the myriads, from the lands in which they are scattered today, and many more will reach these shores when the nations of Europe rise up and slaughter them and banish them, so in turn they will come here to slaughter and banish us.'

And the gathered crowd called out, 'Enough! We have heard enough from you. Return to your home, boy, we are repulsed by your words,' but instead of heeding them I remained there and spoke up, in a voice meant to wake the sleeping from their slumber: 'A Jew came to our house and killed my father and bedded my mother. Now he has brought three of his friends to reside in our home. Just as he has done to us, so too will other Jews do to all of you. Your homes will cease to be your own, your lands will not wait for you, for the land will vomit out its waste and send you to great distances,' and at that point a woman quick to anger picked up a tomato from one of the stands and hurled it at my face, and then others in the crowd took up whatever they could find and did the same, pummelling me with all the good produce of Jaffa, and I continued speaking as though utterly mad. 'Your lands will not be your own! Rise and awaken! Take preventive measures! Push back the wolves and the jackals and the hyenas before they eat you and your carcasses! Rise up and destroy your evil enemies!' But the fury of the crowd only increased towards me so that in another moment they would begin pelting me with stones and fists and clubs and breaking my teeth and twisting my arm, for they do not love those who give good advice, and suddenly a Gypsy boy pointed me towards a small tunnel into which I crawled after him, and from there I reached my bicycle at the gate to the city, and I rode, wounded and dripping blood, all the way home, where I walked from door to door searching for a way in, banging at the echoing locks, which no one came forward to open.

26 January 1896, the Rajani Estate, a few hours later
My heart is riddled with paranoia because of the things written in the letter I found on the boy's desk, which Saleem and Salaam did indeed translate into French for me and leave on the doorstep of my house. I will record an exact duplicate in my diary, below.

Despite having been translated from language to language, the letter none the less preserves the unparalleled emotion of blind hatred and lust for vengeance in every version. Herewith, the letter:

Dear Illustrious and Honourable Uncles and Cousins of Beirut,

Myriad blessings upon you and your families. Many days and weeks have passed since I last heard from you or met you face to face, and I miss you greatly and hope that you are lacking for nothing and are well endowed with all the abundance and splendour heaped upon all the Muslims of the world by Allah and His Prophet, Muhammad, may He rest in peace.

I write this letter to you with a heavy heart, for grief and evil have befallen our estate.

The painful and distressing news of my father's death has reached you and you were most kind to send your condolences and a wave of tears.

At this time I must reveal an even greater calamity to you.

My father did not die a natural death; rather, he was murdered by a golden-haired man, a regular visitor at our estate. His name is Jacques, and if you come here at once, as I hope you shall, you will be able to identify him with ease, for he is a stranger among us, not an Arab. There is no way of knowing what other cunning plots the man is scheming but it is clear that he took the life of my dear and beloved father, and now all that is left is for him to sink his teeth into the holy earth of our estate. It has been made known to me that others of his people are fast in his footsteps to annihilate us, and if we do not rise up to kill them they will bring a calamity upon us.

Therefore, I implore you to come at once, without hesitation or mercy, leading legions of armed warriors who will avenge the desecrated honour of a dead man and escort a traitor to his death, for many are the sins of this man who fouls and contaminates our land.

I am but a child; my shoulders are not broad enough to carry out this onerous mission on my own and I have no knowledge of how one takes the life of a human being or even how to hold a knife and plunge it into the body of a miscreant, unlike you, who are all well versed in such matters of disposing of nefarious enemies.

Daily I shall gaze from my window awaiting your arrival. Please do not tarry, for this man is sorely dangerous, spending each day at our estate and walking me in circles while only Allah who sits in heaven knows what sort of thoughts of slaughter and carnage roam his mind.

Come quickly ere it is too late.

Expectantly, and with a cry of help, I am,

 Your cousin, friend and beloved,

  Salah Rajani

An Arab vendetta against my life is serious trouble, and for injustices I did not commit and which are the product of the twisted imagination of one who cannot distinguish between left and right, one who hears genies in every chirp of a bird, one who sees terrorising angels in every black shadow.

After consulting with Saleem and Salaam I altered the letter to read as follows:

Dear Illustrious and Honourable Uncles and Cousins of Beirut,

Myriad blessings upon you and your families. Many days and weeks have passed since I last heard from you or met you face to face, and I miss you greatly and hope that you are lacking for nothing and are well endowed with all the abundance and splendour heaped upon all the Muslims of the world by Allah and His Prophet, Muhammad, may He rest in peace.

I write this letter for the purpose of stilling your hearts from worry, for our actions have succeeded in bringing abundance and splendour to our estate. In the days and weeks to come I may, perhaps, come to visit you, and send greetings from Mother.

With love and longing I am,
Salah Rajani

26 January 1896, the Rajani Estate
After further consultation with Saleem and Salaam I went to the estate and returned the envelope to the place from which I took it on Salah's desk. Furthermore, I commanded that the boy, after sending his letter, was not to leave the gates of the estate or speak with anyone but his mother. I posted the Jewish colonists Mendel, Yehoshua and Yedel as guards to watch over his every move and had them confine the malevolent and plotting maidservant, who has led the boy in his malfeasance, to her tiny room, from which even the tip of her nose was not to emerge.

Salah's mother is preoccupied, endlessly scrubbing her hands with water and Nablus soap over the basin. I have commanded her to stop at least a dozen times, to no avail. This is certainly testimony to the unsound state of her mind, and for this reason I chose not to show her the contents of the letter.

My chest is filled with heavy sighs. Worry gnaws at me with gusto.

What shall I do?

My only hope is that the letter I wrote to my dear relations in Beirut, which I placed in an envelope and gave to Amina to mail by the speedy post of the Austrian consulate, will perform the task it was meant to and bring my uncles with great haste to the estate on a herd of ivory-tusked elephants from which they will alight brandishing sharpened swords and primed for battle, and they will approach me and say, Point out the man, the Jew who killed your father and defiled his bed, and I will nod in the direction of the good angel, at that moment lording it over the wretched tenant farmers, and I will say, That is he: know that by taking his life you are preventing a terrible calamity from befalling our people, for Jews around the world who witness the recalcitrant, justified battle of the Arabs will not hasten to journey here and dispossess us of our lands, and my uncles will smile nobly and with reserve and will draw their long and impressive swords and, lo, the good angel will regard them and smile innocently, as someone unaware of the hugeness of his distress, and only the pupils of his eyes will widen in mute astonishment when the sword is drawn at his throat, and a moment later his decapitated head will roll on the fresh and refreshing grasses of the Rajani estate, and no one save me will know that a single act of revenge will have saved thousands and tens of thousands of our fellow Arabs, for one event shall fail to lead to another and the calamity of the Arab peoples will never occur, and instead we shall remain tranquil and serene in the shade of the prickly-pear bushes and olive trees, tilling our land unobstructed, gathering honey and imbibing nectar and filling the granaries with grain for ever and ever and until the end of days.

26 January 1896, Café Armon, a few hours later

I set out for Café Armon in search of the Wildebeest; perhaps he would bring some solace and entertainment to my languishing heart. I found him there, haranguing a French Christian woman making pilgrimage to her saviour's burial place, and he was offering her three rhyming poems from his satchel that had been translated into the French language, while she gazed at him with puppy eyes and sensuous lips slightly parted, the scent of her perfume hanging in the air.

I swear I am still confounded by this attraction that women feel for the Wildebeest. After all, he possesses neither good looks nor princeliness, neither wealth nor glory, only his long body and an unkempt beard and foolish poems he pens as an afterthought. Perhaps they are drawn in by his artistic looks, for it is well known that he who plays with writing poems or stories or drawing pictures or dancing will also enjoy great success in playing with the women. Their passion rides such twisted rails that anyone seeking logic will be sorely disappointed.

The moment the Wildebeest took notice of me he ditched the Frenchwoman and hastened to me. And I ordered what he needed: vodka and *kreplach* and *tzimmes*, and we sat in the café overlooking the sea and I drank along with him to forget my troubles with the boy (to which I made no reference). The Wildebeest all the while fondled the behinds of the women passing by our table, and to the plumpest and choicest he added a lusty pinch.

I said, 'I find you in high spirits.'

'Not just high,' he said, 'but soaring.'

'Why so?' I asked.

'Look at the fishermen casting their rods, and the pleasant sea, and this excellent vodka. And look, too, at this,' he said as he produced five francs.

'What is it?' I enquired.

'A down-payment from the colony at Rehovot for a new poem written specially for them.'

'And what is the poem about?' I asked him.

'It is one of my best,' he explained, 'a song of love and desire for the Land of Israel that awakens the emotions of every colonist, who then opens his pockets and gives generously. Would you like to hear one verse of it?'

'With pleasure,' said I.

He stood to his feet and read with great emotion:

> 'Hear O Brethren, far and wide,
> Our vision is our land;
> And once we've gathered every Jew
> Our hope will be at hand!'

The patrons of the café had gathered around the Wildebeest as he read and applauded when he finished. He beamed. Who knows? Perhaps some anthem of hope will come out of this poet of the dung-heaps with his simplistic, juvenile rhymes. I ordered two more bottles – one for him and one for me – and I drank.

27 January 1896, the Rajani Estate

Mendel, Yehoshua and Yedel, the three eager spies I sent to watch over the boy, came back to me today with most distressing and heart-poisoning news. They had spent the day observing Salah as he went to speak with the tenant farmers, gathering them around him and inciting them. His timid and modest demeanour fell away as he stood on a small stool, flailing his arms and shouting, invoking the name of their god Allah again and again.

I asked the three what the boy had said to the peasants.

'We cannot discern this Arab cackling,' they said, 'but it is clear that he struck fear into the hearts of his listeners. The farmers began to kneel and pray in fear and awe in the manner of Muslims and they cried out from the depths of their throats in a way that we sons of Russia cannot hope to imitate.'

Afterwards, the boy returned to his house, with Mendel, Yehoshua and Yedel in hot pursuit, but instead of ascending to his bedroom he took a short-cut to a low mound of earth indiscernible to the untrained eye. He knelt down there and removed a small hoe from his pocket and began to dig until he unearthed a Gypsy-made dagger with a short blade. Then like a cat covering its excrement, the boy covered over the mound as if it had never been disturbed.

From there he walked towards the sea to the cemetery where his father is buried, my spies following after him. They claim that he had no knowledge of their presence and did not once take notice of them. The boy is quite a fast walker and my spies lost him on several occasions, but they caught up with him again. At the cemetery he sat facing the sea, then lit two candles, which he placed on his father's grave, and muttered a prayer. How great was the astonishment of Mendel, Yehoshua and Yedel when they saw the boy remove the dagger from his pocket and scratch his forearms with it again and again until the blood flowed.

Mendel wished to jump from their hiding-place and save the boy from this life-threatening act, while Yehoshua argued in the boy's favour, claiming that this was a pagan ritual practised by Muslims about to engage in battle. Yedel was undecided, so the three remained hidden, though not without arguing and wrangling *sotto voce*, so the boy would not hear them. In the end, Yehoshua was right: the boy staunched his blood with his blouse, dabbed a drop on his forehead, bowed down before the grave and raised his voice in Arab psalms, which sounded to them like ecstatic praying.

It seems the boy's mind is completely crazed, and if we do not save him from these hallucinations he will hang himself or jump from a window, taking his own life.

I must speak with his mother about this as soon as possible.

The idiot peasants are holding fast with their rebellion and have refused to raise a hand against the pernicious angel even though there are, among them, those who possess swords and daggers and have rich experience with slaughter and murder, and so I preached to them the speech I made from atop the overturned crate in the fruit and vegetable market of Jaffa and incited them to vengeance, and the farmers listened attentively, their pupils round with alarm, and they admitted that their fear of the evil angel is great but that they will never rise up against him to take their fate in their own hands, for the future is already written and determined like the pages of a book, and I beseeched them to give me a dagger or a sword or a even a jackknife and teach me how to grasp them, but the peasants answered as one that this was something they would not do, for they will not disobey Allah, nor will they disrupt His plans, and their only strength is that of prayer, and so to a man they laid down their prayer rugs and prostrated themselves before Allah, imploring Him to destroy evil-doers and avenge the deaths of the murdered and bring peace and tranquillity to their lands, and when I took my leave of them a flock of children pulled at my sleeve and told me of a hiding-place for deadly weapons perfect for the task that I desire to carry out, and they explained how to find it among the trees of the estate, and I thanked them and ruffled their hair in affection, for slowly the frightful decision to avenge my father's death myself is ripening in me.

From there I made my long way to Father's grave, to the cemetery on the sandstone ridge that overlooks the sea, and the gravestones stand silent – only the cats of woe moan mournfully in the salty bushes – and a lashing, tempestuous memory of the interment rises in my mind: here is where the adulterous wife stood feigning sorrow; here is where she tussled with the grave-diggers wildly and with renewed vigour; here is where the cypress and acacia trees swayed at the shrieking sound of the wind; and I knelt down to the grave, covered with a slab of cold marble, and said, Father, although I am alone in the cemetery I feel and know that eyes are watching me and my body, and I know that it is your eyes that watch my every step, and I swear to you that I will carry out your command and I will slay the good angel who comes to our estate so that your soul will find its eternal resting-place instead of roaming between the false world and the true one, between the living and the dead, and I offer only this prayer before you, that you will pass on to me the courage of spirit so that I may rise up against my enemies and kill them with my sword, just as you did on fleet-footed camels among the palm trees, and would that I were swift and determined like you in brandishing a spear and in matters of murder, and Father's hands protruded from the grave, cold and bony, and took hold of my fingers and placed in them a dagger that began to slash my flesh right and left, and he said to me, in the voice of death and hell, This is what you must do, Salah, there is nothing simpler. This is how one cuts flesh and this is how you shall take the lives of your enemies, and this is how our particular story will at long last be resolved.

※

28 January 1896, the Rajani Estate

Today I went to the huts of the tenant farmers and summoned them to the copious labour awaiting them in the orchards.

The smell of burning campfires greeted me, and wherever women and children noticed my presence they ran away as if a leper were approaching.

I made my way through laundry hanging to dry – the Asian sun was particularly bright today – until I found, hidden in one of the smoke-scented huts, all the menfolk, cramped and fearful. An uproar ensued among them when they saw me, their hair standing on end and their limbs trembling. I ordered them to rise to their feet, but none did. I shouted the few words I know in the Arabic language – *baraa* (which means 'outside!') and *imshu* (which means 'on your feet!') but they feigned ignorance or, more correctly, they did nothing to conceal the usual expressions of ignorance on their faces.

Suddenly a boy of Salah's age, the son of a tenant farmer, began to cackle at me in Arabic, and from all this cackling I understood that he wished to tell me something important. I had an interpreter summoned from Jaffa, since Saleem and Salaam were unavailable; it turned out that they were at the well-known Turkish baths, where they could take part in the acts of coitus they love so well. The interpreter, whose French was broken and battered, listened to the boy's speech and to what the men, who added bits and pieces, had to say, and in the end told me that the genie who walks the orchards has told them that he will take their lives if they touch even one of his trees.

I asked them whether it was Salah who had whispered this foolishness in their ears.

They muttered many things that the interpreter did not translate.

I said, 'Rise to your feet and return to work. Otherwise there will be consequences.'

Only then did the women appear, and with voices like crashing cymbals they wailed their Arab laments, so disturbing to the European ear, and sobbed about their foremothers, who had tended this land for years under the Rajani family and who had instructed them never, under any circumstances, to anger the genie of the orchards, or else their homes would be destroyed, for the genie loves above all other souls those of the young and pure and will not hesitate to take the life of one of the babies or toddlers if they do not obey his command, and he had already smitten one boy with a blazing fever.

'Cease,' I told them. 'Cease and desist from this blathering and nonsense. Rise to your feet at once and return to work or I will have you evicted to another land.'

They began to moan and wail and stamp their feet and clap their hands skywards but they did not rise from their feet to return to work.

I found Mendel, Yehoshua and Yedel and instructed them to find colonists like them who would come to the estate to work the land and to guard it against the Arab peasants.

The depravity of the pernicious angel is unbridled and insatiable, for today I heard him with my own ears, through the half-open door of the bedroom, shouting and hurling insults at Mother and repeating his threats that if she will not give him the *kushan* he will cut off her hands and pull her through the orchards by her ears until they tear away from her body, and he raised his voice and proclaimed that the estate is his, his for ever and ever, he is the one who has rescued it and he is the one who has brought it to glory and greatness and he who has turned a dung-heap into Paradise, and he claims that all the monies now flowing into Mother's coffers from the citrus harvest are there only through his wisdom and efforts, and Mother stammered and spluttered that in another moment she would surely fall into a faint, and all at once the pernicious angel softened and sat beside her and stroked her hair and said, From the moment I set foot on the land of this estate you tried to take advantage of me, to strip me bare: Jacques, save me, for my son has lost his mind; Jacques, save me, for the tenant farmers pay me no heed; Jacques, save me, for my husband has beaten me until I bled, and I have risen each time at the sound of your alarm and done what you have requested, and now, when this once I come to you to ask for something in return – a worthless piece of paper hidden somewhere among your treasures – at once you estrange yourself from me and wash your hands of me, and if this is what you see fit to do then I shall depart at once; remain here with Salah and Amina and the band of idiots known as tenant farmers on this estate, and Mother said, Jacques, no, please desist, wait, and he said, Oh, yes, of course, it is as I thought: you have no love for me, nothing of what I feel for you, you never loved me and never will, and she knelt before him and said, I love you, love, love, love, and I regarded this woman who was my mother and I no longer recognised her at all, sparks of insanity flashed from her eyes, the insanity of a widowed woman alone caught in the terror of this stranger, and I wished to burst into the room and shout, Mother! but my feet remained frozen to the spot, for in a hushed whisper she told him that she was ready to acquiesce completely and utterly, and in another day or two she would provide him with the *kushan*, which is to be found in the office of a man of importance in Jaffa, and she would pass the deed of the estate to him, for it is in his possession that the estate was meant to be, and now is the right time, and it is God's will, and the good angel took her hands in his and kissed each finger, then said, You are a good woman, good-hearted and incomparably beloved, and he embraced her with the voice of passion.

28 January 1896, the Rajani Estate, a few hours later
Time is of the essence now, for the earth beneath the capacious house is quaking and the estate is teeming with traitors and slanderers and sowers of evil.

I had already made the decision to evict the tenant farmers from the estate even before consulting with the Hovevei Zion leaders, who informed me that according to the law – that of the Turkish sultanate – these farmer peasants have no right to remain on the land by virtue of the fact that it is the Rajani family, and not they, who are the owners, even if they have settled here for a hundred years, or two hundred or three. After all, the owners may banish them at will and they must accept their fate and act accordingly at once.

This child playing his infantile games with me will come to see who Isaac Jacques Luminsky really is. In the future he will think twice and thrice before tangling with a man as superior and distinguished as I. I am familiar with all the ploys and wiles and ruses he has used in trying to incite the peasants, and the slanderous letters he tried to send to his relations in Beirut. Even his diary is now under my scrutiny and I am learning its secrets.

Still, I have decided to exhibit at least a modicum of European graciousness and goodwill by giving him one last chance to improve his behaviour before I take action. In the end we are neither strangers nor bitter enemies to one another but, rather, two people who wish for the same outcome: to cause the two objects of our love and affection – the estate and its exalted mistress – to thrive and flourish.

My eyes are trained constantly on the northern horizon, but the caravan of elephants ridden by the avengers tarries still and the days pass swiftly and a heavy shadow bloats the clouds and rains down fear on the house and grounds, for the evil angel has brought to our lands many of his confrères, all white-skinned Jews with malevolent gazes like his own, and they built themselves a wall and tower in which they reside, and they have banned the peasants from the *biara*, and they whistle loudly and act as lords and masters of our lands, and who will rise up and fight this gang of ruffians and their beastly leader?

My only wish and desire is to hear the sound of the trumpeting elephants, to feel the earth tremble beneath their weight, to witness the death of he whom I loathe, the pernicious angel, the saboteur, and to hear his tortured cries as he is trampled by the elephants, his body crushed and shredded, a mash of blood and flesh, while his soul hangs by a thread and his screams cause the sea and the rivers to quiver, but until now the skies are bright and cloudless and on the horizon there are no elephants and no camels, not even a lone blind mule for heaven's sake, and I vacillate between hope and desperation wondering why my relations are not doing as I requested in my secret urgent missive; perhaps they are dismissive of a letter written by a mere boy. Or perhaps they scorn my tortured soul, or never received my appeal because they are away from home, and this thought consoles me and breathes life into me, just as a last lick of fire raises orange sparks from the ashes, and to this splinter, this mere sliver of hope, I pin my life, and I shade my face against the sun that has sloughed off its grey winter doldrums and I am watchful for their clamorous, warmongering arrival, which will herald the end of the filth and stench that have spread throughout the estate.

29 *January 1896, Neve Shalom*
After a long day of travails and feeling exhausted and battered, I returned home to find Her Ladyship awaiting me with the news that her sister, Rivka, had sent a telegram announcing her departure for the Holy Land in another week.

'*Bon voyage*,' I said.

'Now come here,' she said.

'What is it that you want?' I asked.

'For you to carry out your husbandly duties,' she replied.

'I have no strength for that,' I said.

'Now,' she said, 'and no later.'

I mounted her but with no vim or vigour. I blamed the vodka and the Arab spices that were wreaking havoc on my intestines and churning my blood.

Her Ladyship grumbled, turned her back to me, covered herself with a blanket and fell asleep.

As for myself, I am awake, writing in bed by the light of a lantern.

This morning I murdered my beloved. I approached him in my most beautiful gown and my white scarf and tiny shoes, while behind my back a short, sharp-edged blade was hidden, and I extended my hands to encircle him with an embrace and I responded to his pleasant kisses, and my beloved, my precious, raises me up in his tanned and sturdy arms, his skin exuding the scent of his sweat, and I postpone my revenge and I tell him about his exploits in the pearl market of Baghdad, how he became publicly betrothed to another woman, a beautiful black-haired bride, how he showed preference for her over me, how he kissed her openly as the merchants cheered him on; but, no, in fact I feigned devotion, responded to his kisses, and my lover, my heart's desire, lays me down upon a soft bed of leaves padded with red flowers, and I am aflutter when he removes my gown and exposes my smooth thighs and the tiny soles of my feet, and he moves down to lick my toes, one after the next, and I place the blade under my hip, and we pleasure ourselves with the flavour of almonds and dates, raisins and apples, and endless sheets of dried and pressed apricots, and my beloved laughs thunderously and says, Leila, these are days of delight, and he drums his compact stomach, and the soft leaves under my bare back are convivial, and my beloved, my precious, says, You are my heart's desire, I swear fealty to you, pledge myself to you in eternity, and I ask him to tell me of his dalliances with others, of his nuptials, of the grand ceremony, of the red flowers in the bridal bouquet, of the bejewelled camels marching in procession through the pearl market; but, no, I allow his naked body to rest upon my own, the hair of his chest curling in my lips, my hand cradling the handle of the blade for the purpose of plunging it into his heart so that the blood will spray me copiously, a pleasant bath, and I will dip my finger in the redness and lick the hot flow of life and I will shout loudly enough to be heard throughout the Arab lands, Death! Death to this man who has been caught by surprise at the taking of his life, and his tongue dances quick acrobatic lies, but we are sisters of magic and bewitchment and we are faster than he, and we secretly lift the stinging blade and thrust it deep into his body, and we sing songs of praise and *lamentation, victory chants and dirges, for today we killed the good angel, murdered his soul.*

🌱

30 January 1896, the Rajani Estate

Today marks my first time to celebrate Jewish Arbour Day in the Land of Israel, and what a beautiful sight it is. The Rajani estate, with its trees and plantings and flowers, is clad in majesty. Four almond trees stand at the entrance, near the gate, and their pure white blossoms would capture any heart with their perfect splendour. May this diary forgive my meandering description of nature and vistas, but it is no exaggeration to say that bees are buzzing among all the trees while handsome birds coo on every branch. In spite of all its shortcomings, Asia contains much beauty.

The obstinate peasants are steadfast in their rebellion and refuse to budge, so I have assigned Mendel, Yehoshua and Yedel, along with five of their comrades come to assist with the labour on the estate, the task of planting many eucalyptus trees as is done by colonists in Zichron Yaacov and other places for the purpose of cherishing the seedlings and enjoying their goodness and taking pleasure in their beauty, and we sing a song in Hebrew. I am only sorry that the Wildebeest is not with us to teach us the new song he has been writing little by little and which will inject vitality into the hearts of its Jewish listeners.

The new colonists, whose names are not yet fluent on my tongue, had indeed booked passage to Odessa, but they have postponed their voyage for the time being since the estate pleases them, and when I told them about the lives of the farmers and vine-growers that await them here, their eyes crinkled into lines of joy and happiness and pleasant expectation.

I am faced with two tasks, one more urgent than the next. First, to bring in working hands to the estate to replace striking hands, and a youthful spirit of excitement to replace tired and broken labourers. And, second, to bring succour to this boy, whose soul is so terribly damaged.

After thinking on the matter extensively, I believe the right thing to do is to summon a doctor specialising in mental disorders and psychoses, for the purpose of hearing what the experts can advise in treating such a case, since the true love of an older friend has failed, in spite of his honest efforts.

From the day I spoke to my father in his grave, from the day I pricked myself with the blade, from the day I sensed his eyes upon me, observing all my good deeds and bad, I have been hearing dead Father's voice echoing in my head, and he commands me to do things that would cause any heedful ear to ring upon hearing, as in calling me to murder the good angel and then drown Mother and then draw a rope around my own neck and hang myself from it in my room, and I beseech him to leave me in peace, and he commands me again, and in fact I already comprehend that this is not Father but that swindling genie or some other malevolent spirit or thought that contains no truth or life, but this voice is stubborn and evil and doubts sprout on the bedrock of my soul, for perhaps Amina and all my detractors were right and I am in the grip of madness, and I gaze from a gaping hole in the wall to the heavens and lo, the trees have ganged together in groups of two and three and the sky has switched places with the earth and the birds caw viciously, and one raps at my window and says, Go out, Salah! Revenge! Do not tarry a moment longer or we shall peck at your flesh and eat your liver! And another bird hovers and flutters, then draws close to my face and says, All the birds are being deceitful and hiding the truth, and a third bird laughs and shrieks: Salah! Do what you think is best! And the birds are drunk, they fly left, then right, and whoever goes aright, for his own soul does he go aright, and whoever astray, to his own detriment does he go astray, and I fall to my bed and pound my fists, but their cackling gibberish disturbs my peace of mind, and I shut the window and wrap a thick blanket around my head and press it to my nose and into my nostrils, and the sweet absence of warm air suffocates my breath until my soul flutters, but the birds, the birds chatter still in their cacophonous chuckle, saying, Salah has lost his mind, Salah is taking his own life, Salah is hanging from a rope and his throat is suffocating and his soul is making its final gasps before disappearing into the dark thickness of death.

A few hours later
Although the Arab woman's face retains its sour pucker, her comportment in bed has slowly begun to loosen and she is returning to her earlier ways in earlier days, when she fearlessly took in what Her Ladyship was willing to receive only with the greatest of efforts and in terrible pain.

I showered copious kisses and expressions of love upon her, for which she was only too thirsty, and in honour of the holiday I brought her raisins and dried figs and apricots and other such delicacies of the Land of Israel, which I purchased in the Arab market, and I placed them between her toes, then fished them out with my tongue, and she laughed deeply, the first time she has laughed since becoming a widow, and when she asked what I was doing I told her it was a Jewish custom for celebrating Arbour Day.

When she lay tranquil and serene on our bed, I brought to her lips a pipe containing what is known here as hashish so that she would smoke it and become even more relaxed, and the Arab woman was happy and joyful and thanked me profusely and, like Esther with King Ahasuerus, I laid down all my requests before her and showed her that only good would come of them: on the one hand, we would for ever rid ourselves of these rebellious peasants who have set themselves against the estate's orchards and commerce and very existence; and on the other, we would do our best to help the boy overcome his delusions.

'What can we do for the boy?' she asked, pipe smoke in her lungs.

'I've had an idea,' I told her, 'to summon a doctor, since medical science has made such wonderful progress of late and it is possible to get a diagnosis today and treatment for what was once considered a curse from heaven.'

She grew sad. 'Salah,' she said.

I said, 'Do not trouble your heart. I will find the most expert of experts and he, with Allah's help, will bring a salve to the wounded soul.'

She kissed my fingers and gave her blessings.

'Where are you going?' I asked.

'To wash my hands,' she said.

I let her.

31 January 1896, the Rajani Estate
Today the expert arrived, none other than our old friend Dr Al-Bittar.

There was no other doctor to be found in all of Jaffa, and Dr Al-Bittar swore to me that he is an expert in the convoluted maladies of the soul, from epilepsy to melancholy and all other crazed sicknesses, and he even agreed to trouble himself with coming to the home of the patient, several miles outside the city.

The Arab woman was experiencing an attack of grief when the doctor arrived and thus was not on hand to greet him, so on my own I prepared him Arab coffee, well boiled and served with cardamom, as the Arabs drink it, and I sat with him on the ground floor and recounted the patient's maladies from start to finish. The doctor listened attentively, all the while rolling his string of blue *masbakha* beads and occasionally asking questions I found to be surprisingly intelligent, like what is the nature of the evil visions that the boy experiences during waking hours, and he expressed particular interest in the boy's delusions about the worm of fire he had seen, and I told him the entire story, how the boy was plagued with ungrounded suspicions that brought about the total disappearance of his loved ones, how a metropolis of Jews built on Jaffa and the Rajani estate would replace them and how a war would come and banish them all. Dr Al-Bittar was highly amused and laughed so hard that his *masbakha* slipped from his fingers and fell to the floor, and he said, 'Such wild imaginings I have heard only from the most disturbed of patients.'

Afterwards, the doctor asked to speak a bit with the boy, but this was a problem because Salah had locked himself in his room and refused to open the door. I spent an hour pleading with him, and even his mother came to beg him to come out, and all the while the doctor stood to the side writing notes to himself. In the end we gave up, and I returned to the ground floor with the doctor, to receive his initial diagnosis.

The doctor screwed up his face and bit his lips as if deep in thought. I understood from his behaviour that he wished to receive something, and I gave him some *baksheesh*, beyond the sum agreed upon. He thanked me for the coffee and promised to send his response within two or three days.

I thanked him and we parted company.

Not long after his departure I heard a door open upstairs and the patter of small footsteps descending the staircase. It was Salah, who came to the reception room where I was sitting.

Looking upon him I was saddened, for I recalled our first meeting. How great was the distance we have come from then until today! I thought of how he had said to me, in a voice as thin and quiet as a schoolgirl's, 'You are a Jew,' and how his cheeks reddened like a virgin's, and in my mind's eye I leafed through the pages of our shared history like a man reading a book in the evening, and with each page I turned his character changes, from page to page and chapter to chapter, and a deep sadness filled my chest for this deterioration of relations between us, for the love this boy had for me that was replaced by a taste for vengeance, and for the sweet secrets that became schemes and intrigues.

As if he were reading my mind and as if he were feeling as I, Salah walked silently, just like that other, first, time, to the cushions on which I was reclining and without saying a word made a space for himself beside me, bringing his head to my chest and his slender body to mine, and he sighed sweetly, the sigh of a boy seeking his father's consolation.

And in the silence of the night, in the light glowing from several candles, I stroked his soft cheeks, which no blade has ever touched, with the back of my hand, and also his closed eyes, which have witnessed the destruction of the world, and I whispered in his ear, 'I promise you, Salah, that we shall return to our former days of glory and everything will be rectified,' and he mumbled, half asleep, and I repeated, 'We shall return to our former days of glory and everything will be rectified, I promise you, Salah,' and Salah nodded in his sleep and dozed off at once, and how beautiful was his slumber and how beloved was he, and as I write this now in my diary I am filled with an abyss of sadness for all the loveliness and goodness that have disappeared, and all the ugliness and evil that lie ahead.

Once again the good angel appears to me in his good colours, for today he summoned to our home the important doctor with the dignified look from the Money-changers' Lane in Jaffa, and with a worried tone to his voice explained all about my maladies to the doctor while I spied and listened from nooks and crannies, and I am filled with compassion for the angel and his kind temperament, for his good works, for his guileless and innocent soul, and he did not even once think to mention the sins that have tainted my soul, how I desired to squelch that soul to extinction, how I wished it the worst of all fates, how I set obstacles and stumbling blocks before it and brought it grief and anger, all for naught, and all my villainous scheming springs out at me from my notebook, vulgar words tinged with madness written in ink, and I wonder who it was who wrote these lines if not a hideous boy, an ingrate who estranges himself from those who love him, and I decided to go to him, to the good angel, and curl up to him, but the doctor was still there, asking many questions and writing in his notepad, and the two said many wonderful things about me – that I am a good boy, intelligent – and I found myself in the throes of disgrace, ashamed at all the evil that has visited my soul, how I allowed the chattering of birds to make me question my own virtues, and I raced to my bedroom and closed the door, locking myself in – for how can I look at my loved ones, how can I gaze into their eyes? – and, lo, the angel and the doctor knocked at my door, and the great and virtuous doctor, who took the trouble to ascend to the second floor of our home, asked in his thick, warm voice, Salah, are you awake? And the good angel added a playful plea, but I did not respond, did not utter even a single word, for how in my blushing shame could I open the door to them?

The moment the doctor departed I left my room, buds of shame and disgrace still reddening my cheeks, and descended the stairs with the fear and awe of one who wishes to ask forgiveness but knows not how he will be received, and the good angel was looking at me, his expression one of sadness and disappointment for all the terrible things I have done to him, and pictures formed in my mind – how he fluttered his wings at me and came to me in my room, how he sat with me on the sandstone cliffs by the sea while our happy future spread out before us from one end of the horizon to the other, how I made a bitter error in accusing him of deceit and terrible acts – and a feeling both puzzling and terrifying at once rose up inside me that the two of us, the good angel and I, I and the good angel, are nothing but fictional characters trapped inside a dreadful book written over many pages, and we change from page to page, from chapter to chapter, as the eyes of others – readers – watch us at all times, and hands turn the pages of our story then lay us down by the bed and talk about us, and what do they think of us? Do they bear us a grudge? Are they angry with us? Do they judge our characters, and are they as unforgiving as we of ourselves? And when these new thoughts threatened to wash over me completely, I put a stop to their din and drew near the good angel and placed my small hand in his large one, and the good angel smiled wanly at me, already forgiving me my disloyalty and bad deeds as those of a boy who knows nothing of the way the world works, and I laid my head on his chest, and the good angel sighed contentedly, a deep, rolling purr that is the satisfied sigh of pleasure a father takes in his son.

2 February 1896, Neve Shalom

Early this evening I brought Saleem and Salaam to the tenant farmers at the Rajani estate and asked that the menfolk assemble round one of the smouldering campfires, sparks blowing in every direction. We gathered around the last of the glowing embers and I read the edict issued by the mistress of the estate, Afifa Rajani, whereby the men were ordered to cease their labour on the lands of the estate. All fell silent. It seemed at first as though the farmers had failed to understand, perhaps due to Saleem and Salaam's rapid translation, or perhaps due to some other reason, and the stupid expressions on their faces and their complete inaction (they did not budge from the campfire) attested to their appalling lack of comprehension. Therefore I asked Saleem and Salaam to explain quite clearly that they have been instructed to bundle up their belongings and leave the estate first thing in the morning in one week's time.

The women and children had begun to gather by this time, curious to know what the meeting was all about, and in fact it was the wives and other women who were first to comprehend the meaning of these tidings, and they began tearfully to embrace one another, casting their eyes about in sorrow and longing at this land they had occupied for so very many years, from the days when they had arrived from Egypt.

I am already well acquainted and familiar with the Arab and his manner of expressing joy by loud hand-clapping and banging on the *darbooka* drums, and his manner of expressing grief through uninhibited wailing of a nature unacceptable in my native land. To my great surprise, however, their custom this time rested on the foundations of nobility and culture. The tearful women did not burst into mournful cries of lamentation, stifling their moans instead with silent tears, like a man who accepts his calamitous fate reluctantly while at the same time making his peace with determinism.

To accompany their gentle, collective crying they asked my permission and, as I watched in astonishment, they brought from their huts several eastern stringed instruments and raised their voices in heartbreaking song. I recorded the translation of the words in my notebook, for they made me sad as well, these songs of mourning about their bad luck, which has led to their dismissal from the land of their birth and that they must leave behind all that is dear to them, all of their dreams, and find themselves in a new land.

They added more wood to the fire and made a kind of Arab candle, which they hung about. In their mourning and grief they continued their lamentations.

It was then that I understood for the first time, with all my heart, just how bound the Arab is to his land.

The child of one of the tenant farmers rapped at the blinds on my window and I opened them, late at night, and the child said to me, Ruin and destruction have befallen us! And I said, Has the ghost stricken you again? Know this: it is no ghost but the product of your own imaginations and superstitions, at which the boy burst into tears and said, Ruin! Ruin and destruction, for an edict has been issued evicting us from our land, and I went out to him from my room and we descended the tree together and hurried to the peasants' encampment, and all the while I attempted to extract bits and pieces of information from him. Was this the handiwork of ghosts and spirits? I asked, and the boy said, No, a man of flesh and blood, the selfsame murderer we feared to stand up against, and when we arrived at the huts the entire community was sitting around a smouldering campfire and wailing, and when they caught sight of me the women rose to their feet and clapped their hands to the sky, and the men rose, too, and said, There he is, there he is! Salah, the prophet, to whose words our ears refused to listen! and the grey-haired old man stood up from his crouching position on the moist earth of the estate and bowed down before me so low that the tip of his nose kissed the tip of my shoe, and he said, You are our prophet; words of truth flow from your mouth and we are an obstinate people, soulless and complacent, who failed to follow your lead, and all the while I heard these words and at the same time did not, for these tidings were not at all clear to me, nor did they make sense, and only after I implored them did the peasants reveal to me that it was the good angel who demanded their eviction, and that their pleas were unheeded although they have nowhere else to go, for the earth of this estate has been the place where their feet have trod for many years; rather, with a hardened heart and clenched fist and pursed lips, he told them to leave in the space of seven days, and their huts would be razed, and I abhor the angel's cruel ways, for the farmers have children and babies, and there are the infirm and disabled and other wretched souls among them – where will they go and what will they do? for they will die of starvation and the hard-ships that lie on the road ahead – and an ancient flame of fury ignited in my chest, for my stories and dreams did not lie, in fact all were true, and now the true face of the angel was revealed, this man masquerading as honest and good is nothing but an evil oppressor with a heart of stone who wishes to strip us and our sons of all we have, and my father's spirit, which I had tamed, now grew strong in the chambers of my heart and called out to me, Salah, kill the snake before it breeds and multiplies, cut out its heart, sever its limbs, and the birds flew about chattering merrily in the pale night sky, and they said, Salah, rise up and behave like a man, for this is the hour for courage in which the brandishing of a single sword will thwart the schemes of an enemy, and I was overwhelmed with emotion and I stood upon a jagged boulder and called out to them, O peasants, O people, awaken and rise up, for it is not too late! Even if the edict has been issued all hope is not lost, for we can take the path of rebellion and resistance, the path I prophesied to you. Rise up and arm yourselves against your destroyers before all is lost, and the birds and the eagles and the vultures will accompany us and they will hurl stones and fire and brimstone and they will kill all whom they are asked to kill, and my tongue prophesied in such high language that the simple-minded peasants could not comprehend the meaning of my words, and I called to the children to gather in a single group and bring their torches and swords and knives and daggers, but they remained hidden behind their mothers' skirts, and the men remained seated on the earth, and the old man relaxed his shoulders and bowed his chin and he whispered, Salah, we believe your every word but we are unable to respond, for this is the edict that has been issued against us, and Allah's will can be changed or challenged by no man, and so all the people returned to their circles around the campfires and sang an old song of a farmer separated from his land and a wanderer who sails over the seas, never to return to his home.

9 February 1896, the Rajani Estate

The task has been successfully completed. Today the tenant farmers were evicted from the Rajani estate.

First thing this morning they stood as ordered by their huts, all their bundles beside them. The children were silent, the men's heads were bowed. Only the women continued searching between the rays of sunlight for any last thing left behind – a cracked clay mug, a blackened scarf, a tattered shoe.

As if to raise the volume of the tune that had been resounding in my head all night, the women stood round the last, fading flames of the campfire and sang mournfully, in hushed tones, the words that the Wildebeest had translated for me:

> 'Farewell for ever, vineyards,
> And days of lilied grace,
> No longer shall we gaze upon
> Your fronds of leafy lace . . .'

They set out on their journey in a long human trail of perfect silence, unlike the days of their noisy rebellion, to a place decided upon by their elders, the fertile valleys in the north of the country, where an *effendi* awaits them with hard work weeding and watering the good earth, and as the train of people moved along the path that wound past the *biara* towards the gate and from there northwards by the banks of the Wadi Musrara, and as the women calmed their babies, and children showered their parents with innocent questions, I suddenly caught sight of the boy, Salah, silent and tense, moving among the verdant trees of the orchard, then standing at the edge of the now-abandoned village, holding his dark head in his hands and crying bitterly.

I crouched behind the poisonous leaves of the oleander bush the entire day, rubbing my eyes in disbelief at this satanic sight, for here was the pernicious angel accompanied by many of his Jewish accomplices, and they shouted loudly, vulgarly, commanding the men to come out of their shacks and stand in the gathering-place, and the women and children were assembled elsewhere, and then the accomplices made a thorough search of the ragged clothing worn by the men, for the purpose of removing rings or coins, and they fetched from the ground anything that fell there or was forgotten, such as wretched jewellery or worry beads, and they piled everything in sacks that they took for themselves, and I watched this scene and failed to guess or fathom its source – was this pure villainy, or the momentary blinding of power? And where was Mother? Why would she allow her lover to rob and plunder thus? And where was Father's ghost? Why was he not rattling his bones and cleaving the tree-trunks to topple the good angel and bury him beneath? And his disciples were mocking the peasants as they stood gathered there, and as they looked on, the accomplices raised torches lit from the dying campfire and touched them to the huts, and tongues of fire lapped at the straw and stubble, at first with hesitation and then with growing eagerness, and the flames incited one another until the huts of the tenant farmers surrendered utterly, and the sparks passed from one roof to the next until only a few minutes later the entire village had been razed, eaten and consumed by countless sparks, and the peasants stood motionless, watching, but the angel's accomplices were already prodding them along, and they were banished for ever, and a cloud of smoke rose and billowed upwards from the scorched shacks and dying embers, the last memory of long days that once were and are no longer, and nothing remains of them now but the ashes of a few ramshackle buildings and blackened rings of charred straw and burned leaves.

Late winter to early summer, 1896

10 February 1896, Neve Shalom

Bad luck gives way to more bad luck, and grief follows grief.

Today, towards evening, I returned home early after paying a visit to the offices of Hovevei Zion in Bustrus Street to ask advice. Upon reaching my house I found the door slightly ajar, and at once I was aflame with suspicion as to the reason, daring not even to venture a guess. I approached on tiptoe and from where I stood unobserved, I could hear Her Ladyship's voice. She was not speaking French, as she was wont to do with her Arab clientele, but rather was engaging in linguistic gymnastics in Russian. A man's cloying, fawning voice responded, and it belonged to none other than my dear friend and companion the Wildebeest.

I continued to stand there, and from the other side of the door I could hear the sound of lips sucking and smacking.

Wrath and fury passed from my heart to this man with a black soul, who pretends friendship but who, like a snake slithering through thorns and briars, will not hesitate to use his poison against even those who support him and wish him well. As if he had forgotten the many times I had provided him with a hand-out of food to stoke his wildebeest belly, and as if all trace of brotherly love I had bestowed upon him had disappeared, this man had moved in darkness and taken advantage of my absence from home to pleasure the body of Her Ladyship, the fairest of all women.

I burst into the house and found the two of them bent over a sheet of paper, holding hands and jabbering, laughing.

I said, 'What is transpiring here, deep inside my house?'

The Wildebeest waved me over with his broad hand and said, 'Your dear wife is helping me with the missing first line of this poem, which I am trying to finish.'

The poem was written as follows:

> La la la la la la la
> The hope is an old one, upon us enstamped:
> To return to the land of our forefathers
> To the city where David encamped . . .

Her Ladyship was blushing and did not open her mouth.

Post-haste I told him, my face drained of colour by rage, 'Take your quills and ink and leave this house. Do not return here.'

The Wildebeest's eyes opened wide above his thick dark beard, and he said, 'Friend, we were labouring over nothing more than a rhyme, and a line missing from this poem.'

I said, 'Take up your rhyme and your line and your kisses and depart at once!'

Once more he swore he had engaged in no licentiousness with Her Ladyship. He was persuasive enough to arouse the envy of the best actors from the Vienna Opera.

Again I ordered him to leave the house at once and to keep his hands away from my beloved wife, and I tossed in a curse wishing him failure in finding the first or last lines for his wretched poems and then, for good measure, added some blasphemy in Russian.

The Wildebeest bowed his head and left the house in silence. Her Ladyship locked herself inside her clinic, consumed by guilt.

Strange noises interrupted my sleep this morning, a low moaning and grunting, so I took the dagger I keep beneath my pillow for the purpose of murdering the pernicious angel, and I descended to the ground floor only to find this noise issuing from Mother, and she was saying, Leave me, you bitch, Away you daughter of a whore! And the maidservant Amina was struggling to hold her down with her coarse hands while I stood to the side in gaping wonder at the filthy world and all its nasty, ugly surprises, for these were two women who were fighting, and Amina was slapping Mother's cheeks and telling her to calm herself while Mother called her a cow, a bitch, a worm, and she spat in her face and in the end she overpowered the maidservant and dashed from the house, Amina shouting after her, Please, mistress, I beg you, and I pursued her, fearful and trembling, for Mother disrobed as she ran and was now completely bare, her pale white skin shining in the early-morning sun and her breasts waggling as she ran, crazily from side to side, and the upper, hirsute line of that black triangle called out for all to come, and Amina caught sight of me and said, Hurry, hurry, Salah, follow her, and we reached Mother with a last burst of vigour and caught her by her hair just before she could pass through the gate of our estate, and Amina covered her with her dress, which Mother had hurled onto the road, in order to hide Mother's shame, and Mother shouted, To the river! To the river! to bathe there and be rid of impurity, for ants and scorpions were crawling across her skin and making their terrible scampering noises, and we managed, with great difficulty, to return her to her bed, and Amina took the initiative and shredded a sheet into strips and said, Tie her up, Salah, quickly, and like Amina I wrapped the strips around Mother's hands and fastened them to the bed, as the room filled with Mother's terrible screams: To the river! To the river! And Mother cursed me – oh, would that I had not heard her, and if I had to hear her then would that I not recall – until Amina thrust a ball of cloth into Mother's mouth and tightened the knots and piled a blanket and pillows on top of her and whispered, There, there, mistress, enough now, and Mother, sweaty, a wave of fury in her glassy eyes, moaned low and darkly from her strangled throat, and Amina went to the pantry and returned with a small jar of smelling salts, which she put under Mother's nose, and the noise and shouting slowly receded, and Mother acquiesced to her saviours, and Amina instructed me to loosen the knots a bit while she removed from a hidden drawer a small plate of tobacco mixed with hashish, which she rolled in a thin piece of paper and lit and passed it to Mother, so that she could imbibe its sweet smoke, and Mother fell into a quick, deep sleep, her eyes rolling like marbles, and Amina said, Salah, my good boy, do not leave your mother's bedside, for her soul is ill, and I said, I will do as you wish, and I stood at Mother's bedside until she opened her eyes and I held her hand and kissed her fingers, which I had not done in a very long time since I had been preoccupied for so long with my own torments and with Father's death and with the sins and crimes of the pernicious angel until my own mother, who gave me life, was forgotten to me, and only now I noticed her wounded lips and the darkened skin of her face and her wan and gnawed fingernails, and I said, Mother, together we can over-come all those who wish us harm, and she awakened from her sleep and smiled sadly and asked that I release her from the shredded sheets and pleaded with me to bring her water from the basin, and when I moved the cup to her lips she looked to the bottom, to the water swirling there, and whispered, in a growing snarl, To the river, Salah, I wish to bathe in the river.

I write these lines by the light of a withering candle in the small hours of the morning. Once again my sleep has been disrupted.

For hours I tossed and turned in my bed and bored my nose into the pillow until I could stand it no longer and decided to take action, arising from the bed and leaving behind Her Ladyship in a sound sleep. I seated myself at the chest of drawers in the foyer, opened my diary and began to stuff it full with all the babble and balderdash flooding my soul.

My thoughts circle one another like a mad dog frothing and foaming as he chases his own tail. Perhaps by getting these words down on a blank page I will begin to make some sense of them and reduce their sting.

One particularly meddlesome and troubling thought is that the boy's uncles are hot in pursuit, poised to cut short my life. I must remind myself that this is nothing but foolishness: for one, Salah's original letter was never sent to them. And furthermore, even if it was sent by him or by someone else (and who would that anonymous person be who would lend a hand to such a matter?), his relatives would certainly not lift a finger to help, for they are citizens of Beirut and Salah lives in Jaffa; they are preoccupied with their businesses and he with his stories. Last, in the highly unlikely event that they were to come all the way here, they would find that I am absolutely innocent and pure. Not a man in this world could remain unconvinced of this truth.

While I am still busy calming myself with these respectable justifications, another more lamentable thought visits me and ruins my peace and joy, and I am ashamed even to record it in writing but will do so none the less. My soul quivers as I recall that work of fiction, that amalgamation of words read by the boy that evening, since which I seem to see but do not see, seem to hear but do not hear, seem to feel but do not feel, the sight or voice or body of a man who has been interred and now walks the land of the dead and who, in the eyes of my soul, in the throes of neurosis, follows in my footsteps to avenge himself.

Mother was becalmed by the curling smoke of the hashish, but in the hours hence her face turned gloomy and she sobbed and cried, so that we were forced to tie her again to the bed and to keep our eyes upon her at all times, and this morning, when Amina had to leave the estate for a short while, I stood by Mother's head and smoothed down her hair, and Mother whispered to me in a seductive, misleading voice, Salah, Salah, my son, bring me a knife so that I may peel an apple, remove these strips of cloth from my hands so that I may rub my eyes, and then she bawled and said, Salah, my sins weigh heavily upon me, I pray that your father is sitting in the Garden of Eden with forty virgins combing his hair, and I wish that he will forgive me my crimes, and then, burning with fever, she began to hallucinate and talk nonsense and she said to me, Quickly! Before the maidservant returns, bring me some poison that I may drink it to the last drop, and I said, What are your sins, Mother? And her cracked lips parted as she enjoyed a brief and bitter laugh, and she said, The *kushan*, the deed to the estate, I handed it over to the pernicious angel; witless, I went to the home of the Turkish governor and removed the signed deed and gave it to him so that now our estate, everything we own, has been placed in his hands, and we are weak, thin-necked birds trapped in his fists and subject to his goodwill and benevolence, and from the very day I was wedded to your father – may he rest in peace – when I was taken from my dolls to be his bride and he brought me to his home, his estate, he showed me the footpaths and rolling grasses, the orchards and the groves and he made me swear an oath that in the event that his departure from this ephemeral world preceded mine, I would not abandon even a single clod of the earth of this estate for the rest of my days, for the Sufi mystics who sanctified it made this prophecy: when its lands are lost, the estate itself shall vanish. And he who breaches this oath will endure the torments of hell and a curse will visit his life and death, and any man, innocent or evil, who takes this estate for his own shall know no peace. His sleep shall be disturbed and his nights filled with madness like a ship forever careening this way and that on the stormy waves, and a scream erupted from Mother's throat as if she were a woman giving birth to a thousand genies, and with a strength I did not know she possessed, Mother tore away in an instant all the cloths binding her to the bed and shrieked, Here he is, the angel of destruction come to take us from our land, to expel us! Salah, take his life, here he comes, he is on the threshold of our home! Salah, save your mother, and I hastened to revive her with her smelling-salts, and the sweet curling smoke from the hashish pipe that had stood by her bedside all the while filled her with its goodness and her tension receded and she fell into a deep, deep sleep.

And when Amina returned to Mother's bedroom and I told her all that had happened in her absence, a plan took shape, for we would stand against our enemies as one, and Father's ghost had commanded that we behead the pernicious angel, and Amina revealed to me that in the small garden near her room there are fragrant evergreen oleander bushes, whose flowers capture all hearts with their beauty but whose leaves are tinged with poison, And now, my young son, you must go out and concoct a potion with these poisoned leaves; soak them in hot water and remove from them a distilled essence, for we are but two women and a small boy in this large house and the strength in our bodies and bones is weak, but by using our clever minds we shall overcome our enemies by placing this concocted essence in a pot of tea or a cup of juiced lemons, and when the pernicious angel comes here tomorrow or the day after you will invite him to your room and give him to drink from it until he finishes the last drop, and only then will all the evil that has befallen the estate disappear, and your maladies and those of your mother and all the nightmares that may befall our people shall not take place, and our Arab brethren shall live in peace. And she kissed my forehead and said, Do not fear, Salah, dear Salah, and she made me swear to do thus, and I kissed her fingers and swore the oath.

12 February 1896, the Rajani Estate
Today Dr Al-Bittar's diagnosis arrived.

He wrote a disturbing missive to Salah's mother about a malady nesting in the boy's soul that will one day take hold of him, a mental disease, a psychosis that, left untended, could erupt aggressively, with disastrous results. He continued by mentioning the address of a very pleasant rest home that caters to all those who suffer from frayed nerves, the hot springs nearby the town of Tiberias, on the shores of the Sea of Galilee. If the boy were to stay there for two or three weeks he would be cured of all his maladies.

The Arab woman spent the day weighing the possibilities over and over again as to whether to send the boy to that place, for the separation from her precious son would be very very difficult for her, and her heart – a mother's heart – would long for him incessantly. At first she wanted nothing to do with the missive, then she glanced at it, and finally she seated herself and learned the words of his diagnosis, every one of them. And still she vacillated.

On the one hand, his absence would break her heart. Even visiting the curative springs would be out of the question since she could not manage the tortuous journey and its dangers. On the other, she could not help but witness the hugeness of his suffering at the estate and the enormous pitfalls to his health. He had no other children of his age to play with; the only other person occupying a place in his world was that evil-eyed maid-servant who had stuffed him full of fears and anxieties of the worst kind; from every corner and angle he was reminded of his father's death. And if this were not enough, his dead father's belongings, his empty clothing, his strong scent still lingering in the rooms evoked delusions and fantasies that depressed his soul.

The Arab woman showed me the doctor's letter but did not ask my opinion and I offered none. But I will admit this to my diary: should the boy depart for one week or several I would not be grief-stricken. His presence has grown loathsome to me. I have had enough of his terror-filled prophecies, his slander about me, his enraging stories and the sanctimonious expression on his face. Let him go to this place of rest and bathe himself in the sulphurous pools so that we may have some peace, for heaven's sake.

But I spoke none of this to her. In matters of this nature a mother must come to her own conclusions.

13 February 1896, the Rajani Estate
The Arab woman gathered more information about the sanatorium. It is a place of great warmth, which banishes all sickness and degeneration.

One woman from Jaffa had sent her son there to be treated for moon-sickness and sleepwalking. He was cured, and is now the owner of a sweets stall in the souk. Another woman dispatched her mother-in-law to the sanatorium and the old woman was cured of her imperiousness and meddling. Everyone assured Afifa of the merits of the mysterious curative waters, invisibly enriched, that restore balance to mind and body.

Furthermore, the springs contain gases and vapours from the belly of the earth that smell like a boiled egg, and their properties are excellent in calming the nerves.

Afifa also heard that European aristocrats, including Emperor Franz-Josef himself, made it a habit to visit the baths at Baden-Baden for the very same purpose as those at Tiberias.

⸙

16 February 1896, the Rajani Estate
Today at last we spoke of the matter. The Arab woman smiled glumly and said, 'Jacques, I have come to a decision.'

'And what would that decision be?' I asked.

She said, 'I must send Salah to the curative springs. My heart tells me that all the grief that has befallen my son stems from his proximity to his mother and his lack of proximity to his father and other people. Something has gone awry in him from his very foundations, which needs the treatment the doctors will prescribe.'

My heart filled with compassion and love for this woman's courage and determination.

'However,' she said, 'I must secure the boy's agreement. I will speak to his heart, tearfully, with kisses and embraces, but with the firm knowledge that this is good and true advice.'

To which I said, 'I agree.'

At long last the pernicious angel visited us today, and his arrival at our home provoked an immediate bustle and commotion. Amina hastened to squeeze the lemons and add to them molasses and sugar water, which she poured into drinking glasses and gave to me, and together we opened the jar from which wafted the bitter scent of oleander, and she poured a little into one of the glasses, and the poisonous drops were diluted by the lemon wedges, and I sat down to my books and my diary and I wrote in them as is my wont, and there was a knock at my door and I opened it with a pounding heart, but it was not the angel, only Amina come to inform me in whispers that a plot was being hatched, that the angel was wheedling Mother into sending me to a sanatorium for a week or two to soothe my despondent soul, my frayed nerves, my aches and pains, and after discussing the matter quickly we resolved that I would agree to all requests for the purpose of appeasing him, and thus we would succeed in convincing him to sip our poisoned concoction, and Amina kissed my cheeks and pressed my body to hers and said, You are a young man of courage, daring and bravery; would that all the sons of our Arab nation were strong and determined as you, and she wished me luck and said she would be in her room praying to Allah for the success of our enterprise, and I could feel my knees shaking and a cold sweat dripping from my brow, and I hastened to seat myself at my writing table to ponder my friends, written in black ink, for they are my consolation and my succour.

The minutes ticked away and lengthened, as I listened for the sound of the angel's footsteps, the footfalls of a man condemned to death, on the stairway approaching my room, and I laughed in my heart, deep inside myself, at the foolishness of this scheming man about to fall into the hands of a small child, and a deathly breeze shook the folds of the curtain, giving its blessings to this act, and the branches of the carob tree visible through the window formed for a brief moment the shape of Father's face – his thick eyebrows, his green eyes, his black-bristled jowls – and just as I stretched my cheek towards him to receive his kiss, there was a knock at the door.

It was the angel, as excited as a child, a flash of fear flickering in his eyes, and I asked him to be seated next to me but did not yet offer him refreshment from the lemon drink sitting on a wooden shelf in my room, and the angel was the first to speak, saying, Salah, you are like a son to me, and you know how very much I have worried about you, and I coolly cut into his words and said, I know already about your plan to send me away to the restorative baths, and the angel said, What is your response? and I said, I agree in full to this idea, for it is a good one; my soul is indeed tortured from the time of my father's death, so much so that I can no longer discern what is truth and what is fiction, and voices resound in my soul and my brain like genies perched in trees or spirits in the river, and if I spend a day or two or three in the sulphurous pools the waters will surely bring back my peace of mind, and the good angel looked upon me with a smile of surprise, patted my back, and said, You are a friend, a true friend, and the glass of lemonade winked at me from its place on the shelf, its potent mixture murmuring, biding its time impatiently until it could make its way down the angel's throat, past his Adam's apple and into his stomach, where it would dry up his blood, and I said to him in a trembling voice, Please, friend, help yourself, for friendship and fraternity are ours to share; drink up and we shall recall our days of glory, and the good angel smiled at me and took the poisoned glass in hand and waved it in joyous salute, and in another moment he would bring the lip of the glass to his own and he would be granted a kiss of death, but he had a sudden change of heart and returned the glass to its place, and said, Let us embrace, and so we did briefly, and he whispered into my black curls, And so this shall be the end to our enmity, to which I replied affirmatively, We are friends, beloved to one another, and he said, I can see that you wish to tell me something, and I wanted to tell him, Yes, good angel: drink! Drink from the glass you only just put down, drink to the bottom until there is nothing left, go to sleep in my bed for ever and ever, but instead of these words, others issued from my mouth: All I wished to say I have said already, and how good is it we have returned to our former state; tomorrow morning I shall depart, at your command, for the restorative springs, and there I shall be cured of all my ailments.

Several hours later
The Arab woman returned from the boy's room after a very short time, with these words in her mouth: 'He seems agreeable, but wishes to see you.'

I said, 'Then I shall go to him at once.'

I knocked at his door, my heart pounding furiously, for it is impossible to know the secrets of his heart or when he will erupt like a volcano.

To my great surprise, he was seated as usual at his desk, quite peaceful, his room the fortress for his thoughts. He did not so much as turn his head towards me. I could see only the nape of his small neck and the curly black hair covering his skull. I cleared my throat as if standing before a dignitary, and said, 'Salah.'

'Please be seated,' he said.

I sat down next to him. He placed his hand in my own, and I held it.

'So is this the end of our story?' he asked.

'What do you mean by that?' I said.

'Have all our chapters been written?'

I said, 'No, since many more shall be written,' which he, the great author, was still writing and polishing.

'And yet,' he said, 'our story has come to an end.'

'What do you mean by saying such things?' I asked.

'I am leaving here with no intention of returning,' he said.

'But of course you shall return,' I told him. 'In two weeks' time.'

He said, 'Just as you banished the tenant farmers and your people will expel the Arabs, so too are you banishing me from this place.'

'You must know, Salah,' I said, 'that this malignant voice issuing from your body is none other than a nervous disease, the neurosis for which you must be sent to be cured.'

He fell silent, as if considering these matters in depth. Then he asked, 'What is the nature of this place to which I am going?'

'It is a place of healing,' I told him, 'the excellent waters of which will bring you tranquillity and rest. See for yourself: we have only spoken of these hot springs and the pleasant sunshine and already you are more at peace and a brightness has lit your face.'

He sighed heavily.

I asked, 'Are you still disturbed by visions of the future?'

'I no longer know what disturbs me and what does not,' he said, and sighed again.

'Why these heavy sighs?' I asked.

'I have good tidings for you,' he said.

'But good tidings need no sighs,' I said. 'And what is the news, anyway?'

He said, 'Your wife is carrying your seed in her womb. Nine

months from now a girl shall be born to you, a baby with blue eyes and a soft tongue and plump cheeks and a sweet scent. Her beauty will captivate all who gaze upon her, and all will covet her. It will not be long before she clucks her tongue and calls out to you, "Father, Father," and you will take the baby girl onto your chest and you will kiss her copiously.'

I was overcome with joy, and in another moment I would have kissed the boy on his brow and on his cheeks, for I was filled with astonishment at how he could know such a thing. He had never seen Her Ladyship, nor could he have imagined her existence, so how could he have guessed with such wisdom and cleverness these machinations we had been carrying out in secrecy that would bring us a child?

While I was still rejoicing with myself, the boy told me he had another tiding for me, less good than the first.

'What is it?' I asked.

He pinned his dark gaze upon me and from under his thick black curls said, 'She shall live but two years.'

19 February 1896, the Rajani Estate
Praised be the Lord who sits on high and answers our prayers: the boy has gone.

Saleem and Salaam were kind enough to serve as his escorts this morning on a northbound wagon. I provided them with Dr Al-Bittar's letter, so that they may present it at the sanatorium. The trip to Tiberias will take them three days, after which it is their intention to remain an additional day in one of the Arab villages near the springs, a gathering place for Bedouins who enjoy thrusting their sexual appendages into the orifices of goats and who know something about doing the same to men like

Saleem and Salaam. In short, they will return in a week's time to inform me that everything went according to plan and the boy is where he is meant to be.

The Arab woman comported herself with restraint and parted from the boy without these unnecessary Arab customs, but there was no way to prevent the old maidservant from performing the entire repertoire – the beating of her ageing, ample breasts with her fists, the tearing of hair from her head, the waving of veils until the figure in the wagon could no longer be seen and was nothing but a speck on the horizon, black and thin.

After Salah's departure the Arab woman had but one wish: to sequester herself moodily in her room, to remain there until she was done mourning their parting, and of course there is no need to mention that she would not agree to wear any festive garments, would eat no delicacies, and would not allow a man to enter the gates of her womanhood. I told her that I would respect her wishes.

She shut the door and covered all the windows.

Waiting for me at the entrance to the estate early the next morning was a wagon harnessed to two brown-browed horses, and Mother was leaning upon the good angel's shoulder and repeating words he had whispered in her ear, that it would be good for me to get away for a short while, these two weeks, to the curative springs, and that this was her will, and that it would be a blessing for me and for everyone else at the estate, and that she wished me good luck and success in my departure and upon my return, and I looked deeply into her eyes and it seemed she was slightly cured of her madness, and she was sleeping the nights through and no longer stripping off her clothing and running amok to the river, and a resigned acquiescence had settled on her every limb, for I am still young and unversed in the twisting ways of the world, and perhaps this counsel from the adults is sound, that among those vapours from the hot, curative spring water, the shadows tormenting me and my life will be drowned and obliterated, and the good angel stood in the gateway of the estate, his eyes bright, his hair like spun gold in the morning light, and I gazed upon him, at his splendour, at the halo around his head, and I thought, One day long hence, as I draw my pen across the page as a writer or poet and I recall these early, gloomy days of my childhood and everything that has happened to me at this estate – Father's death, Mother's madness – the good angel shall be the hero of the story, the first among heroes and lovers in this plot, and he will walk the holy earth proudly and vanquish his enemies, beheading them, and how lucky I am to have taken refuge under his wings and been swept up in the embrace of his arms, and how lucky I am that he came to this estate to beautify it and return it to its comeliness and brightness, and at the very moment I was thinking these thoughts a flock of crows took flight above the orchards and flew noisily in every direction, their black feathers floating to earth.

In the wagon, those two wastrels known to all the residents of Jaffa by their dandified manners were awaiting me, but Saleem and Salaam lay sleeping there, confused and drowsy due to the early-morning hour to which they were unaccustomed, and they did not observe me as I rose to the wagon with my small bundle, nor greet me in any manner, only coming to life when the good angel pressed many coins into their pockets and whispered something into their ears and presented them with a letter to be delivered, and then we departed to the place I hoped would be a balm to my soul.

We jostled along winding roads as the coachman hired by the

good angel led the pair of horses while Saleem and Salaam slept enmeshed, their snoring growing louder, and I conjured to mind all my prophecies of this land, about the rivers that will fill with putrefaction and muck, about the orchards that will be uprooted and covered with stone and mortar, about the villages that will be razed and will vanish, and this all seemed quite unreasonable, unfathomable, for I could see farmers working their fields and the sun in the heavens shining powerfully and the trees with many deep roots, and all was in place and at peace for eternity, and I was gripped by a strong belief that my malady was indeed a mental illness, and just as Mother's nerves are feeble, so too are mine, and I thanked God that the good angel did not drink from that poisoned glass, and I made up my mind that if the ghost calling himself my father appeared before me once again I would not allow it to lead me astray but, rather, I would strip it of its traitorous clothing and put it to shame and torment it until it disappeared on its own and left my heart and my mind and allowed me to live a simple and suitable life, the life of a small boy living on an estate with his beloved mother.

And with the low, slow murmur of these calming thoughts against the backdrop of the monotonous jangling of the wagon as it made its way to Tiberias, I too fell into a light slumber and from there to a long and pleasant sleep, which, to my great pleasure, was bereft of dreams and visions, the only brief interruptions being the occasional call of the coachman or the snorting of the horses.

23 February 1896, the Rajani Estate
A delegation of dignitaries from the Hovevei Zion group came to the estate today for the first time.

They dismounted their horses and tied their reins to the repaired and freshly painted fence. I opened the gate for them and said, 'This is the titled land I have been describing to you,' and I indicated that they should follow me on the twisting path recently widened by the colonists in my employ. I led them to a low hill carpeted with Oriental flowers, and I pointed out the many acres of land and told them, 'Here, alongside the capacious home of the Arabs, will be constructed the first colony in the Land of Israel built on good and healthy earth,' and I scooped up a handful of soil to pass among them, for them to enjoy its aroma and richness, and they all applauded and laughed heartily.

The Hovevei Zion members, led by the head of the organisation, David Kumar, joined me on the mound and patted me excitedly on the back and praised me. Yehoshua Eisenstadt, with his gaze both dreamy and piercing, shared memories of bygone days when all eyes were upon the estate but the reigning *effendi* with the red tarboosh had sabotaged all attempts at making a deal. Even David Kumar was adulatory, and he allowed himself to pick from the ravishing flowers of the estate, entwining them into a beautiful wreath even though there was no fair maiden to whom he could present it.

The assembled Hovevei Zion members began discussing the poet with the thick beard who wrote wonderful rhymes that would cause the heart of any Jew to tremble. They asked if I was acquainted with this man, who dressed as a pauper and was remiss in his grooming.

'This man is an evil-hearted womaniser,' I told them, 'who fornicates with married women. It is best to steer clear of him.'

The silence that followed made it clear that my words had hit their mark.

Along with the members of Hovevei Zion there were

surveyors and Arab labourers who would erect the colony's buildings on the side of the small hill next to the house. Here, a pleasant breeze from the sea would enable the Jewish colonists to enjoy their time of repose after long days of toil. Their homes would comprise three or four large and pleasant rooms with a pen and coop at the back and a vegetable garden at the front for the colonists' daily sustenance so they would have no need to visit the Arab souk.

Building would commence as soon as the bureaucracy was taken care of and the building permits obtained. The people from Hovevei Zion gave their assurances that one of the organisation's benefactors, Baron de Hirsch or Baron Rothschild, will provide generous funding for the construction of this commendable colony, to which I refer (only to myself) as the Luminsky Colony.

I was pleasantly surprised by the sudden appearance of Her Ladyship, accompanied by her sister, Rivka Blumstein, whose ship arrived several days ago. Her newness in this land is evident in her every foolish misstep.

Rivka said, 'My sister wrote to me a great deal about this garden in which you spend all your time.'

'I am indeed well spent here,' I told her.

'And is there a woman on this estate?' she asked.

'Only an old maidservant and an Arab madwoman. Now, take the lovely wreath from that gentleman's hand,' I said as I placed my hand under her elbow and led her to Mr Kumar.

Her Ladyship looked about her with a scowl on her lips, her expression beginning to show signs of *tuches face*.

'Why the sour look?' I asked her.

'I am not sour,' she said.

'And yet your face is not putting on its best expression.'

She said, 'This estate is not to my liking.'

'The people from Hovevei Zion seem to like it well enough,' I said.

'An evil spirit emanates between the trees,' she said, 'and wreaks havoc. The paths are narrow. An awful stench of old goats and rot and urine rises from the house.'

'Do not worry,' I told her. 'This building will be razed to the ground, and in its place a thick grove of eucalyptus trees will be planted. In the basin of the pool we will make a lovely lagoon with a bridge and a boat. Nearby will stand the secretariat building, hewn from bricks and sporting high windows, and that is where you and I will live.'

She said, 'Isaac,' and suddenly turned pale.

'What is it?' I asked.

'I'm feeling terribly weak,' she told me.

I led her to a bench, where she twitched and convulsed. David Kumar, trained as a doctor, caught sight of her distress and came to her side at once. He whispered into my ear, 'Is she with child?' I told him I knew not. She was given water and this made her feel better at once.

As we sat there, the Arab woman came out to the veranda of her home wearing a black robe with a veil to cover her face. She looked upon the assembled crowd as someone looks upon gathering clouds, and said nothing. Earlier I had come to an agreement with her that a very handsome home would be built for her on the slope of the hill in the style beloved by the Arabs, with a flat roof and arched windows and an opening in the roof for the smoke of the wood-burning stove. I do not know whether her eyes met my own, whether she caught sight of Her Ladyship – the other wife – seated on the bench gripped with nausea, or her sister and the doctor leaning over her, for Afifa quickly returned to her room and did not come out again.

For two whole days we made our way as warmth and softness and comfort enveloped the three of us in the wagon. Mother had never told me of the beauty of this land – the fertile plains that give way to moderate hills, the small lakes that dot the wooded areas, the whiteness of the streams with their excellent water and the good-hearted farmers – for I had never before travelled such huge distances, and Saleem and Salaam told stories of the great Sea of Galilee awaiting us at the end of our journey, of its sweet water and the tall hills surrounding it, and they told me, too, of the miraculous, magical baths there, which can turn hardened hearts soft and ill eyes well and scattered thoughts to sharp, and Saleem embraced me in his tanned and muscled arms and pointed to an envelope he kept in the lapels of his garment stuffed with money to keep me in good style when we reached our destination.

And even though I knew all the while that Saleem and Salaam were fabricating stories and telling tall tales and half-truths and all manner of exaggerations drawn from their imaginations, the stories were as pleasant and consoling as the kisses Saleem bestowed upon Salaam and Salaam bestowed upon Saleem, and on the first night of our journey, when we pitched our tent in the woods, the two went out silently in the dark and, with a warm wind whistling around them, fell into one another's arms.

Alas, our travels were not to go smoothly or pleasantly, for on the second night, when we had completed half our journey and after the horses had been roped to a thick tree and the coachman had gone off to sleep in the tent and I was bundled inside the wagon and night fell and the only sounds to be heard were the croaking of the frogs and the chirping of the crickets, I was suddenly awakened by a sharp cry, and at once I was gripped with the fear that this was the voice of the dead shrieking in my ears, come to find out why I had not yet raised my dagger to kill the good angel, and I shook my head to rid myself of this cursed ghost and dispatch it to the dark and boiling pits of hell, but at once I heard the coachman and Saleem and Salaam shouting in terror, Bandits! Bandits! and through the trees I could see the figures of men surrounding us – four, perhaps five or even six – several of them slicing the reins of the wagon, others driving the horses away, and the coachman cried out to Saleem and Salaam, Surrender! Raise your hands! Otherwise they will kill us all! but Saleem and Salaam ignored his pleas and called out to the bandits, Your lives are in peril! and they charged them with daggers drawn, and a scuffle broke out and men were fighting one another, their wrath spilling, and I sprang from the wagon in terror and hid among the scented leaves of some prickly bush, and as my eyes grew accustomed to the darkness I could see the silhouettes of men duelling, swords and clubs brandished, until finally there was silence, and I remained hidden all night, shivering with cold and fear, and every rustle sounded like snakes to me, and every cackle like poisonous toads, and it was only my two friends, Leila and Rashid, who were able to console me at that time, Leila in her pure white gown, which she waved about playfully, and Rashid, as he lowered his head to my chest, his deep, regular breathing calming my soul just a bit.

24 *February 1896, Neve Shalom*
The signs of Her Ladyship's pregnancy are multiplying.

Not only has her woman's cycle ceased functioning but her exhaustion and nausea have increased as well. I pray with all my heart and soul that this be a son, a son who will take shape in her womb and, of course, grow to enjoy longevity and bring to life children and grandchildren and live on this land.

But while good tidings surround me from every side – the colony that is forming and the pregnancy that pleases Her Ladyship – my heart feels no joy, for each time I wish to ponder my good fortune I picture Salah and his evil words and demonic prophecies, and the things he told me are seared onto my soul and in my gut and on my breast.

I have never before encountered such unbridled malevolence, evil that has no benefit to the evil-doer other than the strong desire to bring evil to others. Would that all his curses and prophecies were to fall on him himself and on his family and his nation the Arabs henceforth.

It is at times like these that I miss the Wildebeest. If we were to drink vodka together by the sea I am certain my cares and worries would be forgotten, at least for an hour or so.

When the first light of day pierced the thick woods a scene of sheer horror was revealed to me: Saleem and Salaam lay on the bare ground, the coachman nearby, his throat slit. Their trousers had been peeled away, their chests naked and exposed, their innards spilling to the ground to serve as food for the flies and the ants.

I could do nothing but cover the dead bodies with a little dirt and leaves and say a short prayer for their tortured souls.

I stood there a while longer lost in thought, then I took Salaam's coat to put on my body and over my head to shade myself from the blazing sun and returned to the woods.

Saleem and Salaam have not yet returned from their journey to the hot springs. I wait desperately for clear knowledge of the boy's placement at the sanatorium, but have had no word as yet. They no doubt went to misbehave with the Arabs and Bedouin in their strange indiscretions, as it is known that where sex is concerned man's heart is tugged and pulled from the straight and narrow more than in any other matter. I shall wait a little longer for them to come and deliver their news.

I lost my way in the dark, thick forest, and out of fear and anxiety I did not dare go back in the same direction to risk seeing those three murdered bodies once again, and only Salaam's heavy coat, redolent of his sweaty scent, remained with me from the wagon and the journey and all the glorious plans to cure me peaceably, with hot, flowing water at the distant springs of Tiberias, and as I walked along, hunger began to gnaw at my stomach, for I was alone, lone and alone among the moderate hills, and in this uncultivated land I found only yellow and red wild flowers and grasses and leaves, but nothing I could use for food, so I hastened my footsteps towards the sun, southwards, towards Jaffa, to the site of our own Rajani estate and its orchards, and I imagined how I would return home and throw myself upon the bountiful fruit, and Amina would serve me a soup of legumes and rice, and then I would ascend to my room, to my stories and poems, and all would return to its proper place, peacefully, and as I walked along, the weeds grew taller and it seemed I was walking further afield of the paths and byways made by human beings, and I turned back and shaded my head from the burning sun and my tongue flopped from my mouth in search of water, but there was none, and I did not know whether I should dig in the damp earth to salvage a few drops from there or to continue walking until I reached a settlement, and the thoughts tumbled about dizzyingly in my head, one biting the tail of the next, and from all this confusion and heat I sat on the ground to steady my breathing and to calm this vortex of thoughts, and suddenly I remembered the envelope hidden in the jacket stuffed with money for my stay at the spa, and if I could find a shepherd or farmer or woman who had gone astray I could bribe them with it so that they would rescue me and return me to my home and my mother and my fine room, may I never leave it again, and when I squeezed the inside pocket, I found an envelope in the pocket and inside the envelope a letter, which said the following:

To the El-Mussad Mental Hospital, Nablus

I hereby deposit in your able hands my son, Salah bin Mustafa Rajani of the Rajani estate near Jaffa.

The boy is stricken and is incapable of discerning between right and wrong, truth and fiction, past and future, reality and imagination. It is my unenviable obligation to inform you as clearly as possible that in spite of the innocent appearance of my only son, he is in fact very dangerous to himself and to those around him. Once, he created terrible unrest in the fruit and vegetable market of Jaffa with his odd prophecies of wrath, and another time he set out to drown himself in a pool of water at our estate, and yet another time he set fire to the huts of our tenant farmers and caused them to flee for ever from our land, sowing destruction and chaos.

On the orders of his physician, Dr Al-Bittar of the Money-changers' Lane, who has already informed you by post about my son, I will ask that you keep him in your hospital in a locked and guarded cell so that he may not harm himself or others and may not bring about strife and contention.

With the tears of a loving mother fearful for her son, I append to this letter one thousand francs for the purpose of covering his expenses for a period of seven years. Would that his complete recovery will come long before that.

Respectfully,

Afifa Umm-Salah Rajani

A great peal of laughter issued from my body at this man with no sense of honour whatsoever, for he is more contemptible and despicable in my eyes than the worms that wallow in sewers of excrement, and sullies with his words and actions the pure air and the holy land, and from this laughter and scorn and contempt I understood that I would devote the very last of my dying powers, those of a small child who gazes in wonder at the filth and depravity of the world, to erasing the memory of this dastardly enemy from our land, now and always, and I tore the letter to pieces and I spat upon those lies and sent them flying in every direction.

27 February 1896, Neve Shalom

The colonists toiling at the estate refused to work today and came to me in a state of agitation. I asked them what had happened and they said, 'Al-Roch! Al-Roch!' and they were now speaking the Arabic language, and I struck my forehead as a man in the throes of desperation and said, 'Now *you* are declaiming that senseless verse?'

Menahem-Mendel, Asher-Yehoshua and Shimon-Yedel and the other five colonists turned pale, and they began to describe a ghost that would strike them on the back and cause them to err when pruning the trees and weeding.

I asked them, in the most level voice I was able to summon to my throat, 'Are you as stupid as the Arabs that you believe in the existence of ghosts? For shame!'

The colonists bowed their heads but did not take back their words.

I told them to show me where to find this *Al-Roch*. In silence we walked among the trees, and I moved aside the branches hanging low with grapefruit and lemons and citrons, my heart all the while chilling with scorn and spite at these superstitions in which humankind believes and how they deceive not only the ignorant peasants but also the very best of our own, the educated classes of Europe.

At last we came to the eucalyptus saplings, very near the western edge of the estate where we had cut back the prickly-pear bushes and planted a small and pleasant grove. 'Well, what is it?' I asked.

They said, 'Stand still and listen.'

Against my better judgement I stood among them, fury igniting in my heart at their great stupidity and my bad luck, and the wind passed between the trees and growled in their branches, and I tapped my foot to show my impatience and turned my back to leave. At that very moment the colonists began chanting in Arabic, '*Al-Roch, Al-Roch*,' and pointing to the leaves that had formed at a distance the shape of a man walking, then dropping dead.

'I have had enough of your nonsense,' I told them. 'Return to work at once – or you shall all be dismissed.'

Today is the Purim holiday but joy has eluded me. The month of Adar, famous for mirth, has brought no happiness or gaiety to me.

This evening we attended a Purim ball held at the home of an acquaintance in Neve Tzedek, the honourable David Balivsky, a teacher at the Hebrew school of Jaffa. This Balivsky, who has a jingling walk and the soft speech of a pampered woman, spent a month or two staging a sort of *Purimspiel* extravaganza. For that purpose he enlisted all his male pupils and dressed them in women's clothing as part of a farce about the people and customs of this land. For example, he made fun of the Arabs' eye diseases and their ululations at weddings and, contrarily, their shouting at funerals and referred to them all as Haman and Vayzata and all the other oppressors of Israel. The appearance of the young actors did not make a favourable impression upon me at all, for there is no benefit or advantage to mockery and satire whose arrows are pointed at others. Let Mr Balivsky put aside that which preoccupies him at the moment and take a critical eye to the indolent ways and pointless education he has been instilling in his students.

As always in such situations, Her Ladyship was radiant and allowed all the men to dance attendance on her. I had the pleasure of meeting Yehoshua and Olga Henkin, who, three or four years ago, bought the lands of Hadera and took ownership of that colony's title. They have become quite boastful about it and strut around with bloated chests. I would like to see them deflate.

Dr David Kumar was engaged in an energetic conversation with his colleague Dr Haim Hissin. The lands of the Orient have many maladies, and the doctors here will always be kept busy. The doctors told me that my friend the pauper poet is very angry with me. I told them that he ceased to be my friend a long time ago, and I turned my back on them in outrage.

But there is no bad without some good. For the purpose of fulfilling the commandment on this holiday to drink to the point of inebriation, the host brought a short and swarthy man by the name of Nuriel. He is of our Yemenite Jewish brethren who came to this land some fifteen years ago and assimilated into the people here with ease. In his pockets he carried mint candies designed to set European tongues aflame. And he knows how to prepare and serve a sort of Yemenite wine laced with all manner of herbs and spices that is extremely potent.

'Hello and good evening, Nuriel,' I said.

He answered, in his guttural Yemenite accent, 'Drink up, my friend,' for with his discerning and practised eye he could see that I am fond of the drink.

'What juicy stories can you tell me?' I asked him.

'For one,' he said, 'there is our host, Mr Balivsky, may God bring a curse on his head. At this very moment, Haman the wicked is taking his revenge on him with a long, hard rod. If you go up to the bedroom on the second floor you will see Vayzata, too, pricking him with his pitchfork.'

I have found a new friend.

Lucid and alone, I spent the night on stones and plucked leaves, and with clarity of thought I made plans for how I would kill this enemy and all the many enemies to follow, for my hesitations had vanished, and only one purpose remained: to rescue our people and our land from the plunderers and pillagers, the wolf wrapped in sheep's wool, in the manner that my forefathers would rise up early and confront their oppressors, for the Muslim has no better way than to stand face to face with his foe, brandishing a drawn dagger, razor sharp, and to call out in the name of Allah and shred the miscreant's body, and these thoughts I pondered and contemplated all night long, how I would mete out his sentence: if by poison then I would have to consult with an apothecary in Jaffa, and if by sword or dagger then I would have to purchase it from Gypsies, and if by strangulation then I would have to put my ten scrawny fingers to work and strengthen them, and slowly I was able to make a plan, for I recalled the days of the Jahilya and the early days of the Koran and the noble manliness and the customs and manners and rules it brought on its wings, and it was already clear to me how I would cut down this enemy.

And once I had made this discovery, Father's ghost revealed itself to me in a dream, and he was neither angry nor wrathful but determined and clear-headed in the manner of a person who has accepted his fate, and Father whispered to me, Salah, these visions you have been having this long night are pleasing to me, and I raised my eyes to gaze upon him and I said, in a dry whisper, Father, it is Allah's wish that I reach the estate and take this man's life, and the ghost bowed its head with a slight smile, and before it disappeared it motioned silently to show me the way so that on the morrow I rose up and went in the direction it showed me, and before me I found a small path that led to a tumbledown lane, and from there I spied women carrying baskets on their heads and heard the bleating of goats and the whistles of cheeky young men and I ran towards them and called out, Jaffa! Jaffa! Take me to Jaffa! But I tripped and fell on my belly and my face filled with dirt, and I picked myself up with waning strength, and a woman shouted, Give this child some water! And good people came to moisten my lips and give me spring water, and sad-eyed children surrounded me, and once again I called out, Jaffa! Jaffa! And these peasants seemed not to understand my words but they continued to ply me with water to revive my soul, and with renewed vigour and a clear voice I said, My name is Salah bin Mustafa Rajani; I was the victim of a foe and fell prey to the heinous actions he carried out for the purpose of stealing my family's land, and now, if you really and truly believe in the way of the Prophet, and the dream of Paradise and the fear of hell guide your thoughts, then please, bring me back to my home, for my mother has been left alone, and there are many who wish to take advantage of her, and passers-by stood looking at me in astonishment, for the Arabic I spoke was pure and literary and flawless, as if Allah's verses were falling from heaven and landing straight on my tongue, and all the listeners were gripped by a holy spirit and they escorted me to the main road at once where wagons and horses and donkeys were moving at a snail's pace, and they raised their voices and stopped the flow of humans and beasts with their bodies until they found a man willing to put me atop a camel's hump in his caravan, and I perched there among the freight and baggage and shouted to the leader of the caravan, Would you give me a dagger or short sword that I may use for the purpose of killing a Jew who murdered my father and raped my mother, so that I may restore my sullied and scorned honour? And the man turned his head towards me in wonder at these odd matters, but when he caught sight of the cool and pellucid expression on my face, he said, Boy, open the box tied up in a kerchief behind you and choose your weapon from the many you will find there, and I peered into the box at the new daggers, shiny and lustrous, and chose one with a handle ornamented with curling purple grapevines and green leaves, and I placed it inside the pocket of my coat and then I put my soul to sleep so that I would garner strength for what lay ahead for me to do at the Rajani estate.

1 *March 1896*
Saleem and Salaam have not yet returned.

The closer we got to the Rajani estate, the more I could feel new strength surging through me, and the dagger I grasped tightly in my hand was throbbing with excitement at the solution I had found to the unwieldy plot of my life, so that I now knew that upon my return to the estate I would no longer hesitate or vacillate; instead, I would bring to my father's spirit, and the spirits of my sons and their sons all yet unborn, both goodness and salvation, and the caravan of camels travelled slowly, steadily, until we passed over Wadi Musrara, and my heart clenched with feeling at returning home, for the trees of the estate appeared to be bowing their heads as if downcast, hoping for assistance from him who had not yet come to help, and I thanked profusely and wholeheartedly the kind man who delivered me after a distance of two days from the forest of the murdered bodies to my home, my grand home, and for the dagger presented to me with love.

I arrived in the evening and found two despondent figures there – Mother and Amina – and they were milling about, tearing out their hair, until they caught sight of me, and the look in Amina's eyes was wise while Mother's was glazed and hollow, and at once I noticed how her skirts were torn and her forearms scratched and bloodied, and Amina cried copiously, but I said, Both of you – quiet, hush: is that man hereabouts somewhere? And they said, Yes, and I said, In that case let us go to my room and we shall discuss matters quietly so that no foreign ear may hear us. And when we entered my room I carefully closed the blinds and shut the door and recounted everything to them – about the letter sent with the lovers Saleem and Salaam and the scheme and the coachman – and Mother began to sing strange songs of rejoicing, songs for weddings, and she clapped her hands, until suddenly she started to shiver and her skin turned to gooseflesh, and we sat her down on my bed and covered her with a blanket, and I said to Amina, We are Arabs, a people crowned with honour and glory, our forefathers marched through the desert and slaughtered all their enemies by their swords, and in days of yore they ruled in every land, from the east to the west, and we will not allow some defiled and despicable Jew and his race, whose ways are of scheming and intrigue, to plunder us and strip us of our estate, and Amina asked, But what is it that we can do, for we are nothing but two women and a boy while our enemies are bitter and cruel-hearted? and I told her that I had been giving thought to the very fact that there can be no happy ending to this story but a call to duel, and I told her I planned to invite my adversary to meet me at this hour the next day, and we would stand facing one another with daggers drawn and the best man would prevail, and Amina threw her hands into the air and said, Salah, my good child, you are walking towards your own death, for this man is tall of stature and quick of movement, and if you attack him with your sword he will not hesitate to behead you, and I said, God who sits in heaven has instructed me in these matters, and even my father's spirit – may he rest in peace – will give me strength and daring to fall upon my oppressor, for we are sons of a heroic nation suffused with glory and known throughout history, and as I spoke I was overcome with weakness and felt that I was about to faint into darkness, and Amina hastened to depart from the room, and she brought me bread with olive oil to soak it, and Mother came awake from her mad spell and said, Salah, I listened to all your plotting and I give you my full blessing that this act of murder go well, and that tomorrow at this hour the end of this story will be at hand, and the man you fittingly call our adversary and oppressor will no longer walk among the living, while all his faithful disciples will disperse and our days of goodness return.

꙳

8 *March 1896, Neve Shalom*
The story of my life seems to me to be the poor scribbling of an unsuccessful author and not in any manner truthful. I had believed, until recently, that my life and all my days were a sort of comedic romance, even a good stage play, and I could imagine the spectators, in *pince-nez* and evening dress, laughing in enjoyment at all my antics with Her Ladyship and other women, the seductresses, and my male competition, and fraternity and love, for all these contain much to laugh about.

But days such as this one cause me to think otherwise, that this is no comedy in which I have the starring role but a melodrama that may end at any moment in bad fashion, with war and death and disaster, and if not a melodrama then a tragedy, and if not a tragedy then the worst of all: a farce, which awakens the contempt of the spectator or reader and turns me into a villain and scoundrel, an adulterer and a man of evil. And what is the meaning of this? A man trapped inside a tragedy suffers and everyone cries with him; a man trapped inside a farce suffers and everyone mocks him.

All this comes for the sole purpose of providing an explanation to my diary of the truly strange event that occurred today at the estate, and that is, in short, that the boy, as if in a bad dream, or as if he were some twisted character in some story for fools and the gullible, returned home. Where did he come from?

What happened to him? Did he reach his destination? And, if so, what was said to him and what was not? And what became of the letter from Dr Al-Bittar? Where are Saleem and Salaam and the coachman? And the money given for expenses along the way? The answers to all these I do not have. In this corner of Asia – where there is no proper governance and no order and men do not behave justly and righteously and might makes right – there is no way of knowing what awaits around the bend, what wonders and obstacles will befall the innocent wayfarer.

He was tired and dirty, his eyes hollow from hunger and exhaustion, his face scratched and streaked with blood, his hair dusty, his clothing tattered and torn, but he was still living and breathing and walking on his own, his trusty escorts missing.

I was the first to take notice of him as he entered the gates of the estate on shaky legs. From a distance, at that twilit hour, I had the mistaken impression that this was some wounded soldier with a bloody bandage wrapped round his head, a malfunctioning rifle hanging from his shoulder, and for the briefest of moments I thought to steal into the house to find a dagger or knife or club to meet this evil head on, though it was doubtful I could have done anything. Just then his mother stepped out onto the veranda and I hid myself among the branches so as not to pique the boy's anger.

The Arab woman moaned through tears of joy and called out his name, her voice breaking when the boy turned his face away from her and refrained from returning her hearty embraces, and from his flushed complexion and his dreamy eyes the mad delusions and torment of one who is insane were clearly visible. He responded only to the old maidservant, who appeared, cackling, from her locked room only when she caught wind of the commotion taking place. She wiped the blood from his face and applied fresh bandages and she cleaned away the mud and the muck. The women pressed in on him and asked, What happened to you? In Allah's name, tell us! And Salah, leaning on the arms of the fleshy maidservant, was barely able to ascend the stairs into the house, and I walked behind the three of them as a shadow, taking care not to be seen by the boy for I feared he would turn hysterical, which might cause his fever to spike and he would lose what remaining strength he had.

Upon their entrance to the house the boy murmured, in his hoarse voice, which had gained some maturity in the short time that had passed, that he wished for bread and water and olive oil, which he ate and drank voraciously, and a foggy darkness descended on the estate like a thick blanket, pulling long shadows over the walls and into the folds of the carpets and curtains.

The boy tried to say something further, even mentioning my name, the many syllables wearing him down – Lu-min-sky – but the women hastened to silence him for his blood was weak and his face wore a shocking pallor, and they pulled off his tattered clothing and began to tend his wounds and scratches and spoke to him in their language with great emotion, and I could hear my name mentioned again and again, each time with a grimace or a scrunching of the nose so that it was clear they were not speaking favourably of me.

In full agreement with one another the women led the boy to the second floor, to his room, and as they supported him on the way upstairs Afifa suddenly sighed and began to sob and cried out, My son is dead! My son is dead! But Salah answered her: No, I am yet alive, I have not yet returned my soul to the Creator.

They extinguished the candles in his room and let him fall into a deep sleep and for an hour the two women spoke between themselves, often sobbing and wiping their noses, and they brought low stools and sat beside his bed for the purpose of reciting all manner of verses from the Koran which were clearly meant to be incanted at the bedside of someone in deep distress.

I left there with a heavy heart and a feeling of terrible confusion and sadness and anger all mixed into one like some vortex of freshwater and seawater, of clean water and sewage.

On my way home, to Neve Shalom, the heavens opened and the *malkosh*, the last rains of the season, stormed around me so violently that the legs of the mule I was riding collapsed time and again so that the beast and I were swept into the roiling waters of Wadi Musrara, but in the end we were spared drowning in the slippery mud and made our way slowly south back to Jaffa and the homes of the Jews living at its periphery.

I entered my home on tiptoe and blessed my good fortune at returning to sane and decent people, the sons and daughters of Europe, and to my own family. How agreeable it was to see that Her Ladyship had gone to bed and was deep in tranquil slumber, and the foetus in her womb was also sleeping soundly, floating in warm and pleasant water, and Her Ladyship's small belly, which did not yet show signs of her pregnancy, rose and fell with her slow and measured breathing.

I stripped off my clothing and climbed into bed naked, eager to cleanse myself of the filth of such a troubling day, to breathe in the sweet breath of my beloved wife Esther, who has never given me a moment's unpleasantness while I have mocked her, alienated her, cheated on her through no fault of her own, but there awaited me a terrible surprise, for another man was installed there, and he lay, fully clothed, alongside Esther, his head on her pillow and sleeping peacefully as if this had always been his place, his bed, and I felt a terrible shriek welling inside my breast, and if this were the Wildebeest I would strangle him forthwith, and it made no matter to me that I would be found guilty and placed in a Turkish jail, and I pulled back the blanket in one swift motion, a sharp-bladed knife in my hand poised to behead the adulterer, but the figure sleeping there was small, in fact not a man at all but a boy, a small boy with black curls scattered across the pillow, dirt and mud covering his cheek, and he was wearing not a soldier's uniform but a child's clothing, and a small notebook, a diary in which he wrote in a dense hand, had fallen from his grip and lay open on our sheets, and I laid myself down quietly so as not to make a commotion or awaken their deep slumber, and three words, three words that contain much tranquillity and fear, poured into my head just before I was taken into sleep's deadening arms: Salah has returned, Salah has returned.

The site of the definitive battle is the cemetery, Father's burial place, on the cliff facing the sea, and I can picture it as it unfolds: here I shall stand facing my adversary, here I shall attack on his right side and here from his left, and Rashid, son of the desert, appears before me and incites me to commit this act of murder and slaughter, this is how to flay his skin and this is how you shall eat his blood-soaked liver, and you shall serve him as food for every beast of the field and every bird of the air, and I clutch Rashid's tunic and tell him, Rashid, I do not desire this man's liver but rather the redemption of my family and my people, my fellow Arabs and Muslims, for if I do not stop this enemy with my body, with my right hand, if I do not kill him for us in this twilight battle, great destruction will befall us all, a turbid wave: flocks and flocks of his people will dispossess us of everything we own, for this is the hour of truth, and if we miss it then our fate is sealed for ever, and *en route* to the quiet cemetery, where Father's bones turn and turn one atop the other and weeds sprout through his cheeks, I caught sight of two people there digging with pickaxes and spades, and I greeted them warmly, for they sported the turbans worn by devout Muslims, and at once I understood that these were a pair of grave-diggers, their faces lined but their lips creased with laughter, and they greeted me in return, and I asked, What is it that you are doing here? And they said, We are preparing two graves for final burial, and I asked them who the two were destined for interment, and they said, This we know not; in the morning we are told how many graves to dig and off we go to dig them, and in the evening we bury the dead and then lave our hands and go to the Jaffa whorehouses to gladden our hearts, and I peered into a grave, to its depths, and it is narrow and dark and I can see roots and small bushes growing there and swift-bellied worms, and the grave-diggers laughed and said, See, boy? This is the end of glory, a place of rot and blight under the earth, and their laughter resounded again and they said, This is a sweet lesson for us: eat, drink and be merry in the company of women, for our days are short and the darkness is great and after it comes nothing, no hell, no heaven, not twenty virgins or one hundred, only this narrow chamber covered with clumps of earth, each bitter and grainy, and they asked me, Have you encountered a female's sweet orifice, the moist pit, the tangled darkness that is the origin of man's actions? And I fell mute for I knew not with certainty what they intended, only that their intentions were vulgar and the lobes of my ears turned bright red, and then one of the grave-diggers cried out in surprise, for his spade had hit some bone or skull from a neigh-bouring grave that had become exposed due to the strong rains, and he uncovered a face and then a moment later lifted the hollow-eyed skull from the ground and laughingly kissed its mouth and said, Do you know whose skull this is? and I regarded them with nausea and fear, for this game was imbecilic in my eyes, and the grave-digger said, This is the skull of a beautiful young woman who died before her time, whose black hair was long and shiny and whose eyes sparkled with passion, and many were the men who hoped to fall into her net, but she took her own life by drowning herself in the El-Ouja river, and a wave of heat rushed through my chest, for many long years ago, when I was just a small child of five or six, I had known that young woman, daughter of the nearby village of Sumeil, and her name was Naima bint Naim, and how often had she gathered me to her and fondled my curly locks and whispered sweet things in my ear, and now my eyes were regarding what was left of her, and the grave-digger said, What is wrong with you that you are silent? Have you swallowed your tongue, have you lost your senses? and I came near him and took the skull into my trembling hands, brushing away the flecks of soil and tangled roots, and where was her marvellous hair whose plaits were of fresh flowers, and what had become of the lips that whispered words of sweetness and comfort and consolation against a cruel world? and the grave-digger said, Take her to your bed, caress her brow and kiss her foreshortened nose, for while it is true that live women pleasure men with their flesh, they torture them even more so with their mouths and tongues so that it is perhaps better for man to cavort with the dead ones from whom they may derive at least a small measure of pleasure, but I returned the head of Naima bint Naim to him and the grave-digger looked into the depths of her eyes and said reproachfully, Do not roll into your neighbours' graves, young lady, for they are all dead and their flesh has withered and they will no longer stand erect, and their bones are crushed and dry, so now return to your grave and lie there.

The boy has not yet awakened. His mother and the maidservant did not leave his bedside the whole night long. I have little information, for the Arab woman is brief and succinct in her communications with me, though I cannot know if this is because she shares the hatred her son feels towards me or because of her feeble nerves. She merely informed me, her brow pale and her face ashen, that the boy is burning with fever and his body is terribly weak. There is no way of knowing if she speaks the truth or whether this is one of the fantasies that spew from her gullet.

Today is a day of great significance, for it was decided that this shall be the day for the laying of the foundations of the colony's first buildings, the homes of the farmers and vine-growers. For that reason, all hands were occupied with digging and laying planks of wood on the side of the hill, and many wheelbarrows came and went and tools were piled in heaps.

The first to arrive were the Egyptian labourers, tyrannised by their Muslim taskmasters, and in their work-worn faces I thought I could see the visages of the tenant farmers who once worked here but who have gone to a different land, and a red blush filled my soul. After them came the surveyors, followed by colonists and the members of Hovevei Zion with dignified appearance and bloated bellies. A great, rejoicing tumult engulfed the estate, and before my very eyes I watched as the colony I had dreamed about from my first day in the Land of Israel began slowly to take shape. One large pit signified the site of the clerks' office, another the synagogue. Here is where the farmers' homes will stand and here the vegetable gardens. The Arab taskmaster led the Egyptian labourers from pit to pit, deepening the foundations with their spades and hoes.

But my spirit did not rejoice at all.

10 March 1896, Neve Shalom

The boy awakened from his deep sleep and his urgent first request was to see my face at the earliest possible moment. The women toiled in vain to dissuade him from this request, for they felt the excitement would sap his strength entirely. In the end, it was decided that late this afternoon, just after sunset, I will ascend to his room for a tête-à-tête that his mother has limited to a mere half-hour so as not to bring the child to complete ruin.

This evening our foe and oppressor will come to the house and I have instructed Amina to send him straight up to my room, and I will invite him to a decisive duel, his impending death, an act of man against man, and the twisting vines on my dagger are aflame, and to pass the time until he comes I went to consult with my friends the genies who reside in the streams and rivers, for the purpose of receiving strength and magical powers and witchcraft from their watery hands, but the king of the genies no longer lives in the *biara* of our estate since he was forced to depart from there because of a noisy engine installed by our foe and oppressor, so I went to search him out in Wadi Musrara, but he was not there since the wadi is not deep enough and its vegetation is insufficient, so I went northwards alongside its moderate flow to the place where it meets the freshwater river, El-Ouja, the site many years ago where, the villagers say, broken-hearted Naima bint Naim drowned herself, and I peered into the water at the fish and the water-buffalo splashing about and I called to the king of the genies and tossed breadcrumbs on the surface to tempt him to come forth, and I asked the creatures of the river if they had seen his splendid palace, its pointed spires and many faithful servants, and I looked about to catch sight of the watery staircase leading downwards to its gates.

The genie was indeed nowhere to be found but he had left clues for the well-informed, such as the sudden flight of a flock of swallows and the mysterious whisper in the branches of a carob tree and the strange shape of feather clouds in the sky, and these signs led me to follow the river to a certain bend, to a place where the water is very deep, and once there I removed my tunic and stood on the bank and dipped my toes in the water and waited for him, like a fisherman dispatching his pole, until finally the water began to quiver and a ripple of foam appeared and the green eyes of the genie flickered there and I called to him, O good friend, is it you? to which he replied, 'Tis I, Salah, and I said, Where is your palace, and the watery staircase, and the water spirits who stand watch over you at every side? and he said, Hard times have befallen us, my friend, for since the time that we were stripped of our home in the *biara* on your estate my flock was dispersed in every direction, and only after much toil was I able to find this new home, which is being built slowly, and how difficult it will be to return to my days of glory, my time of splendour at the bottom of that pool by the orchards, where I ruled the fish and flora with an iron fist, and even the flight of birds, which I determined from my home in the depths.

And I said, My days on earth, too, are far from pleasant as they once were, and I told him about the Jew who was bringing disaster and destruction upon my family and my life, and about the duel for life or death that would take place the next day, and the genie praised my spirit of valour and told me the tree-dwelling genies would share their powers with me so that I will be courageous and swift-footed and determined, thus able to bring the enemy to his demise, and at once he commanded a pair of swallows to disseminate his promise among the spirits and the trees and the rivers, and I asked, What shall I do if God will not stand with me, if Fate is blind and clearly will not give me the upper hand? and the king of the genies smiled sadly at me with his green eyes and said, If that is so then you shall descend to me, to the depths, as I invited you to do in the past, for your place at my side, on a throne, is reserved for you, so that you may become a resident of this river, which is not as sweet and pleasant as the *biara* but which none the less contains water-lilies and lovely flowers, and its flow is good and steady, and if ever worse times even than these shall befall us, we may dive to the invisible depths, to the containers of dark and hidden underground water that pass in channels beneath the earth, and we may establish there our own colony for ever and ever.

Several hours later
The hours beat loudly and my soul grows tense and anxious. And what is the remedy for this but a drinking partner?

By the sand dunes near the sea our acquaintance the Yemenite, Nuriel, has set up a poor man's kiosk where he sells lemonade and orange juice to passers-by, and for the true imbibers he has a special and strong wine that might even contain hallucinogenic mushrooms and other poisonous drugs.

Short and swarthy Nuriel greeted me warmly upon seeing me.

I said, 'Do you have some time to spare me?'

In his large-hearted fashion and Yemenite accent he said, 'My days are spread before me like a bolt of cloth that has no beginning and no end. It is only you people, Ashkenazim, sons of Europe, who enclose time inside minutes, and minutes inside hours, and hours inside days, like prisoners in their cells.'

So I spoke to him at length about my journey to the Holy Land and my first days here, how I arrived with a rebellious bride, how I searched in vain for a good and healthy garden, how my path crossed serendipitously with that of the estate, how I came and went there, and caused the wife to become ensnared in my net, how I turned the boy into my friend, how the *effendi*, lord of the estate, met a sudden death, how matters continued to this very moment in which I was explaining all this to Nuriel on the Jaffa beach, with a bottle of Yemenite wine. Nuriel listened attentively, wiped his mouth on his filthy shirt, and said, 'Your mistake, Mr Luminsky, is that you know absolutely nothing about Arabs.'

'Please explain,' I said.

'I lived in Yemen alongside Arabs,' he told me, 'and I know their ways intimately. They are sons of the desert, long ago the most courageous people on earth, but in our modern times there is nothing left of their former vigour. Their charging horses and battle cries have been replaced by laziness and stupidity, and all their leaders are slack and ineffectual. Nothing is left but their lust for power and honour. In every interaction with them you have proven yourself to be weak and worthless, lacking both power and honour, and that is why they behave as they do and fail to be grateful to you for your actions. There is nothing more despicable to an Arab than a man who scorns honour.'

'Then give me some advice,' I said. 'Where should I lead the conversation I will have with the boy?'

'Show him your might,' he told me, 'and do not refrain from raising your hand to him. Hide your weaknesses and insecurities. Be aggressive and strong. That is the only way to free them from the shackles of their madness.'

Surprisingly, his sharp words awakened me, encouraged me

and were pleasant to my ears. I thanked him for the liquor and
the conversation and set out for the estate.

The good angel entered my room today on tiptoe, and I paid
careful attention to his tall stature, his golden hair, his white
teeth, his sparkling blue eyes, for the purpose of finding among
all these the signs of a bloodthirsty foe, a killer and tyrant, a
persecutor and despot, and I glanced at his fingers, which write
libellous letters, and at his tongue, which produces pearls of
poison, and how loathsome and repulsive this all was in my eyes,
and I held myself in contempt for having followed him blindly,
how I had seen in him a true friend and comrade, how I had been
his doormat, and, speaking sweetly and with flattery, the good
angel asked why it was that I had not gone to the restorative
baths and where it was that Saleem and Salaam had disappeared
to, and it was clear that his curiosity was mixed with fear, but I
gave no clue; instead I merely dropped hints into my words and
feigned exhaustion, though I told him that his most recent
scheme – to have me shut away in an asylum for seven years –
had been revealed to me, and the Jew regarded me with astonishment and said, Salah, have you returned to your imaginings? and
I mocked him in my heart for the dull game he was playing with
me, and I said, Enough of this nonsense: tomorrow evening I
challenge you to a duel, and the Jew said with even greater false
astonishment, What is the meaning of such a duel? and I said,
We shall stand with daggers drawn and we shall fight until the
better of us wins, and he laughed derisively and said, Do you take
me for an Arab, that I would slay a man without trial? and I said,
You are a man whose soul is blasphemous, a man of no honour
or pride, and I curse you and your countrymen that you may die

the death of curs each and every one of you, and the Jew said through pursed lips, I will not stand for such vulgarities on my estate, and I said, You are a cur, son of a cur and a bitch, and yours shall be the grave of a dog, and the angel's face reddened and I continued to harangue him, saying, Your mother in Russia is a whore visited by all the men there, and you are a bastard, a bastard child of a whore, and he pulled me from the bed and grabbed my arm and said, You shall desist from this insolence and this baiting and all this other childish behaviour of yours, idle your tongue or I shall beat you until you are blue, and I said, Cur, cur, son of a cur, your mother is a bitch and a whore and every Cossack in Russia parts her legs and visits that black triangle of hers, the whore's, and the good angel raised his arm and planted a stinging slap on my face, but I continued to curse him, and he slapped me again and again, and at the sound of this commotion Amina came racing up the stairs, shrieking, He is killing the boy! He is killing our boy! And the good angel shouted, Go away, you heinous creature, and he slammed the door in her face, and he said to me, with bloodshot eyes, Take back everything you said or this shall be your burial, and to my thunderous silence he punched me in the face, and there was a salty spray of blood on my tongue and shards of a crushed tooth, and he brandished his fist once again and said, Take back everything you said or you will for ever regret the curses you uttered, and he commanded me to go down on all fours and ask his forgiveness, and I, with my broken tooth and bleeding tongue, looked straight in his eyes and said, You evil, wicked man, if there is the heart of a man and not a woman beating in your breast, and the blood of heroes and not mother's milk flowing in your veins, if there is yet a drop of honour left in your malevolent soul, then come tomorrow to the cemetery, to the arena, the duel, to fight for your wretched life, and my foe cast me a brief glance, laughed derisively and said, So may it be, we shall meet tomorrow, and he departed, slamming the door behind him.

🦂

A few hours later, the Rajani Estate
This, then, is the conversation that took place today between the boy and me.

Under the influence of my talk with Nuriel, versed as he is in the ways and mentality of the Arab, I went to the boy's room on the upper floor of the house, where the odour and the walls and the window have become loathsome to me. The boy lay in his bed like a worm in horseradish, quite ill and exhausted, but from the moment I entered the room he glared at me haughtily.

'Who is so audacious,' he asked, 'as to build on my estate without my permission?'

I said, 'I shall not engage in conversation with you unless you show proper respect.'

He gazed at me with a look of astonishment.

I sat down and said, 'This estate belongs to me now, and to the labourers and the guards, and not to some runny-nosed wall-pissers.'

The boy groaned.

'Further,' I said, 'I do not know why you disobeyed me and did not reach the baths where I ordered you to go, and I have no intention of listening to your excuses in this matter. The moment you have recovered and can stand on your own two legs I will give you your punishments – one corporal, the other spiritual – which I will decide when the time comes.'

He said nothing.

The boy propped himself on the pillows and rose up a bit,

making himself taller. His body was worn out, but his eyes shone with rebellion and his face was full of wrath. In a thin and weak voice he began to abuse me with vile curses, adding that I was demonic and he would have to kill me. 'Tomorrow at this hour I challenge you to a duel, at the site of your grave. Now leave, you cur, depart from my room, and do not defile my home and land any further.'

He lay down again in the bed and closed his eyes.

In a state of great consternation I took my hat and left the room as he asked me to do.

I wished to sleep this evening in peace and tranquillity, powerless and flaccid, before the fateful day tomorrow, but Mother kept sleep far away from me, poor, wretched Mother, whose intentions were excellent and who wished to look after me and heal me, Mother, whose waning sanity is now gone, and the entire night she screamed and shouted and undid the knots we used to tie her down, and I, still half sleeping, rushed to her room, and there was Mother dancing naked upon her bed, and Amina and I tried in vain to clothe her, and even the smelling-salts and hashish pipe were to no effect, and when at last she calmed down and agreed to sit upon her bed and drink a little water, the candle in the lantern blew out and a strange wind rustled the curtains and low whistles shivered under the floor tiles, and Amina shrieked and said, A ghost! A ghost! It's a ghost walking about the room, and she tried conjuring and witchcraft to dispel the ghost but for naught, the ghost merely mocked her with strange scraping noises from the bed and a ringing of wind chimes, and just then Mother's hands grabbed hold of me and, lo, her fingers were cold and lifeless and her face turned yellow and wore an expression I had never before seen there, and the wispy hairs of a beard appeared on her chin and her cheeks hollowed and her hair grew dense and wiry, and she opened her mouth as a prophesying mule and her voice was that of a man's, of Father's, as thunderous and angry as in life, and her eyebrows stood on end and she wore a hideous expression on her face, and she shook my body back and forth and called out in his voice, Salah, Salah, my cursed son, how long will you sit idle? Why did you not engage in battle at this very hour? and I said in a strangled voice, Father, my beloved Father, please wait just one more day, only one more day, and that will be the end of this scoundrel, for tomorrow, early in the evening, we shall stage a duel, and Mother shook me in her arms, which were as strong and sturdy as a man's, and Father's voice burst forth from her throat once again, Salah, every moment that you tarry is like another thousand years of suffering for me, and my strength is waning, Salah, for I shall walk for ever between the living and the dead and my soul shall know no peace, for my son, issue of my loins, has disobeyed me and will not avenge my death, and as she spoke these words, Mother's fingers climbed up my neck and tightened into a stranglehold, and Amina screamed and said, In Allah's name, let go of the boy, and I shouted to the maidservant, Run and light a lantern and drive away the ghost and throw salt in its eyes, for this is not the ghost of Father but an evil genie who lives in the carob trees, one of the wormlike angel's disciples come to ruin us before the duel, and Amina hastened to the kitchen and did as I bade her, and she threw salt and lit as many lanterns as she could and whispered verses good for dispelling ghosts: There is no god but Allah, alive and well/He sleeps not, nor slumbers/His throne fills heaven and earth/And He is the greatest and the utmost, until Mother's grip loosened and Father's voice evaporated from her throat, and I said to him before he departed,

If you are indeed Father then I shall hereby swear before you once again that tomorrow evening I shall kill him, I shall wipe his memory from the earth, but the ghost was already gone, and the first rays of dawn appeared in the dark sky, and I embraced Amina, for she is the last friend left to me in this strange and filthy world through the gates to which I wish I had never passed.

11 March 1896, the Rajani Estate

Today I went to see Nuriel by the sand dunes at the edge of Neve Shalom, not far from the Muslim neighbourhood of Manshiyeh. I found him at his kiosk pouring libations from his stock of Yemenite liquor. The moment he saw me his eyes lit up and he called out my name. The Yemenites, and our other Oriental Jewish brethren, are fond of exhibiting their emotions publicly. I find myself genuinely liking them in spite of their similarity to the Ishmaelites. I have even heard that this Nuriel has fathered ten children, five of them girls, and that the eldest is a ravishing, black-skinned, black-eyed maiden and sexually quite enticing. Nuriel told me, *Tfadaal*, help yourself, and he placed a large bottle next to me.

I took a very full swig and said, 'This and that transpired in my conversation with the boy, according to your counsel. Now are you free to hear the rest of the story?'

'Yes,' he said.

'So here we go,' I said.

The day after you and I talked, the boy spent the day under lock and key in his room on my orders so that he would cause no damage or bring ill-will to himself or anyone else. So, too, with his mother and the maidservant, because I told myself that it was better for them all to sit in their rooms than to hurl their curses at me.

The work at the estate proceeded smoothly. The Arab labourers appeared with planks in their arms and began to pile sandstone rocks one atop another in order to form thick walls for the farmers' quarters and the secretariat, and I derived much satisfaction from watching them. Even the colonists left off from their work to praise the Arab workers for their meticulous building skills and speed, which are rare among the Jews.

Shortly before sunset I filled my lungs with air and thanked God for this tranquil and pleasant day of small pleasures.

I was already harnessing my horse for the journey home when one of the colonists came running up to me, his lips quivering with fear. He was pointing to the west, to the eucalyptus grove, and was unable to utter a single syllable beyond one lone word: *Al-Roch*.

An old flame of fury ignited inside me. I raced to the grove, where I found the other colonists huddled together and moaning blindly, '*Al-Roch! Al-Roch!*' and I shouted at them to stop this nonsense, and I picked up a small branch and entered the grove. 'Show yourself!' I shouted. 'Evil spirit, I'll send you back to the depths of hell!' And a small, malevolent *Al-Roch* slipped among the trees like a ghost and I called to the colonists, 'Quick, help me catch it!' but they were paralysed with fear and unable to move, so I chased the *Al-Roch* myself to slay it, remove it from this world, and while running, it began to laugh in the satanic and mocking manner of a boy, calling to me, 'Luminsky, your day has come. This is where you shall meet your dog's death.'

I picked up a larger branch and waved it in every direction, but the boy's laughter did not dissipate – in fact, it grew louder, once in my right ear and then suddenly in my left, always in that annoying tone of provocation and taunting, and I called out to him, 'Salah, come for your punishments, one corporal, the other spiritual,' but he continued to tease me and lead me on, and in the growing darkness he began to throw small, sharp stones at me from behind the trees, like David and Goliath. The first whistled past me and did no damage but the next were painful and dangerous, even life-threatening, for the boy had climbed into a tree known only to him and from there was better able to aim for my face, and a sharp pain ripped through my lip as it split in two, and the boy began to laugh his scornful laugh again, and said, 'Yours will be a dog's death, Luminsky,' and rained down more stones at my face, and soon I would be blinded right there in the middle of the groves and orchards, and the colonists could hear my cries of pain but were too frightened to react, certain they would find me being swallowed whole by a monster or a genie.

The clean handkerchief I keep tucked into my breast pocket soaked some of the blood from my face, and after I had mopped the sweat away I called into the air, 'Salah, you coward, show your face,' and suddenly I caught sight of his legs as he sprinted ahead of me, and I raced after him, but the boy – who had feigned exhaustion, lying half dead on his bed – was as fast as an arrow and kept well ahead of me, and by this time my fury was boiling, and I wanted to destroy him, to impose a bitter, evil punishment on him. In the meantime, my tongue felt a new spray of blood from my gums where a red, hot hole gaped in place of a tooth that had been shattered.

I turned this way and that to see where he had gone, my legs nearly giving way and causing me to fall into the deep pits dug there, and I could hear the lapping of the waves past the sandstone cliffs, for we had reached the cemetery, where the *effendi*, Salah's father, was buried, may God's curse fall on his head. Tall cypress trees and other Asian species of great beauty surrounded it, and at the top of one sat Salah, one leg crossed over the other, a store of small stones in his hand, which he hurled at me, one after the other.

I shouted at him, fuming, 'Come down at once and take your punishment!'

He glared at me in defiance.

I went to climb the tree but I was too tall and clumsy. And the boy hurled stones at me. So I sat down on one of the headstones engraved in Arabic and covered my head with my hands.

At the sound of rustling I opened my eyes. Salah was standing proudly before me, a sharpened dagger in his hand. 'Good evening, how nice to see you,' he said, mustering malice.

I said, 'I would have preferred to meet you under more pleasurable circumstances.'

'At least,' he said, 'your death will be an easy one, since the blade of this dagger I am holding has been dipped in the poison of the oleander bush. It will claim your soul just as soon as it reaches your blood.'

'Tell me, little boy,' I said, 'do you really wish to take the life of another man?'

'I do,' he said, 'since it is in place of thousands of lives yet to be taken, and to avenge my father's soul, may he rest in peace.'

'He died a natural death, Salah,' I said. 'A natural death. You have no right to blame others. In fact, you hated him, hated him your whole life, and this hatred you have turned into hatred of me.'

He said, 'You murdered Abu-Salah.'

I said, 'I did no such thing.'

'Lies, lies, a thousand times lies. You shall meet your death here,' he said.

He shouted the famous Arab cry *Allah akbar*, which means 'God is the greatest of all', and is popular among those who kill themselves as they kill others, and he brandished his unsheathed dagger in the air.

As the appointed hour approached, my body fell prey to a terrible fear and my knees buckled and the dagger in my hand seemed suddenly thin and feeble, as if the tip and the blade were not enough to kill a man, and I breathed deeply and heavily and kissed Amina as she sobbed in her room, and she kissed me back and kissed her Koran as well, and I went to the cemetery, where our duel was to take place, and evening had already fallen, and a dark moon began its path across the heavens and blackness reigned and the lapping waves and the chirping crickets could be heard from time to time, and I was not there long before the angel of death and destruction appeared from behind the eucalyptus trees he himself had planted, and he stood at his full height wearing an expression of anger and inscrutability, and he carried a sharp wooden rod, a kind of spear, and he told me, I did not come here to kill you but to mete out your punishment, for the estate is mine and I am like a father to you and you must obey my every command, and the insolent words you spoke to me demand one hundred lashes, to the point that your skin flows with blood and you wish to die, and I said, You are grotesque, infinitely grotesque, for without mercy or compassion or hesita-tion you would attack a child, an orphan, and this after you have had adulterous relations with his mentally disturbed mother, and he said, Not one but two hundred times I swear I shall strike you this evening until the residents of the cemetery grow fearful and rise up on their shaky bones to save you from my wrath, and I did not answer him but instead I picked up stones from the pile I had amassed earlier and, under cover of darkness, I tossed them at his face until the pernicious angel was livid and said, Come here, Salah, you mad dog, I swear I shall beat you until your soul departs your body, and his shouts and flailing arms and the sharpened rod he held gave him the look of an angry giant, and I climbed a trusty tree, aided by the genies residing there, who also made sure that every stone I hurled met its mark on the giant's face and brow and eyes, so as to blind him in the war, to kill him in this heroic battle and mostly to draw him towards the trap I had set for him where the deep graves had been dug, and I had spent much of the day covering these graves with leaves and dry branches to serve as a death trap, and the angry giant fell for my scheme, for he went looking for me in the trees to catch hold of my small feet and uproot them from my body, and I made sure he caught sight of the shiny hem of my tunic in the dark gloom of the cemetery, and his eyes nearly popped from his head when he stepped onto the trap and fell abruptly through the leaves and branches into the pit, still alive, and from the groaning I could hear from below I knew he had sprained and broken his leg and had no more strength left and was now subject to my mercy.

And I descended from my spot on high with the tree genie and drew near the angel with the dagger in my hand, and I said, I hope these clumps of earth of yours are pleasant to you, Mr Luminsky, master of the estate, and he completely changed his attitude and his language and said in a quiet voice, Do you wish to kill me? and I said, Yes, for there will be salvation and redemption and succour for the entire world, and he said, Not by the dagger or the sword, Salah, but with your fingers, those long, thin, delicate fingers that have written scores of poems and stories and have painted the beauty of this land with a brush: cast away your dagger and strangle my throat, for the sweetness of their touch will carry me to the tortures of hell, and I regarded him in the grip of magical powers and I knew his words were true, and I threw the dagger to the ground and drew near him, and he stretched his neck out before me, and it was thick and reddishly tanned and scented with sage, and I placed my hands around it in order to cut off the air he breathed.

(*Continuation*)

I took a brief pause to drink from the Yemenite wine. Nuriel gazed at me intently with his wide-open brown eyes, and there was saliva dribbled onto his beard and his skin as dark as an African's. 'Then what happened?' he asked.

'What do you think happened?' I said.

'That's clear and simple,' he said. 'If you did as I suggested you took hold of the Arab's arm and you gave him a double share of a beating on his buttocks.'

I said, 'What you have described I did not do.'

'You are as dumb as a rock,' he said. 'You Ashkenazim are beyond all hope. One hundred years shall pass, even two, before you grow accustomed to the mentality of this place in which we live. So what did you do?'

'As the boy waved the dagger about I sat on the ground in the manner of Muslims at prayer. I removed my shirt, bared my breast to his unsheathed dagger and told him, "Kill me."'

As I write these words on the pages of my diary the tears pool on my cheeks and mix with the laughter of relief, for life in this world has become despicable to me, from the day of my birth I have found nothing in it but ugliness and evil, and how heavy upon me is the burden of life, the need to suffer with forbearance and obsequiousness the mockery of other children, the stupidity of scoundrels, the scorn of braggarts, the poverty and vulgarity of the poor and downtrodden, and what purpose is there for all of these if no consolation is forthcoming – no kisses from an untrustworthy mother, no companionship and affection from a knavish friend, no love from an absent father, and what should a boy or a man or a person of great age do, how shall he pass his days in such a state of torment, how could he not wish for his own death?

And instead of my wretched life I am reminded of the entreaties made by the king of the genies who resides in the river, and they resound from the beak of every bird and from the song of every fowl, begging me to join him in the depths, and this is what we discussed and agreed upon and that I wish to carry out, and so, in the middle of the night, I arranged and folded my clothing and bade farewell to the room I loved so well, and I took one last look at my small bed, the bed of my childhood, and at the window that opens to the carob tree, and at the walls that lean towards one another like beggars seeking shelter from the rain, and it was here that my most wonderful and beloved days were spent, not with Mother's embraces or an innocent girl's kisses or the good angel's friendship, but with my friends who reside in the pages, Rashid and Leila, and their friends and friends of friends, and these are characters written on a page and they have no souls but none the less they live and breathe and love even better, in my opinion, than any other creature on this earth, and I sniffed at the leather bindings of the books and at the good and familiar scent of my diary, written over a period of many days, and at the wooden bookcases that fill every wall from top to bottom, and I shut the door.

From there I went down to the first floor, to Mother, who lay on her bed of excrement and urine breathing noisily, and I kissed her ringed fingers and fluttered my fingers in her hair, taking eternal leave of her, for we two are made from the same stuff and the journey of life burdens her greatly too, and I thanked her for all the nights during which she did not shut an eye on my behalf, and I asked her forgiveness with regard to my hideous illness, which caused her so much grief and worry that it had rendered her mad, and I was overcome with sadness to know what Mother never will, namely that she will spend long years in a wretched and filthy bed with no one at her side.

And it was in Mother's dark-drenched room, by the light of a lantern, that I went to her wedding chest, the one in which she stored her trousseau and other personal treasures she had brought from her parents' home, and there, among the linens and pillows and quilts, I found her pure white wedding gown with its fringed pockets, and the gown had been fitted for a child of no more than twelve, its hems embroidered with dolls in bright colours, and I disrobed carefully and donned the gown, and Mother gurgled and sat up in bed suddenly, both asleep and awake, as if she had taken notice of me and my odd actions, and I cried out to her in exultation, Look, Mother, a miracle has happened to me, for the sleeves of the splendid dress and its narrow tailoring fitted my small body perfectly, and I curled my hair and painted my lips and stood there in all my beauty, on my day of great joy, and from the garden of the great house I could hear the rising and falling sounds of a happy tune and the strings of a violin, and this was the song for a bride and groom on the day of their wedding, and I looked from the window and it was as if I could see the many invited guests before me, dignitaries from across the land and the Turkish rulers from Jaffa, and there were tables laden with the best of everything.

My mother was the one cavorting with the groom in the

mincing steps of a girl and he in the black leather shoes of a young man, and as they danced all their future troubles were forgotten, along with the bad, black days of quarrels and the endless travels from land to land and sea to sea, and the music faded and was replaced by the lamentations of mourners at Father's death and the funeral procession to his grave, and from there a scroll is unravelled and revealed to me the chronicles of life in its entirety, the future generations as they come and go, and interspersed with their dance, I see first my own death, wet and watery, on the broad steps that lead down and down to the depths of the good river, and then the rest of Mother's miserable life in a ramshackle hospital with no relative or kinsman to care for her, and from there, with increasing speed, the life and death of the angel and his daughters and their children, and all the events yet to take place, and the rivers yet to fill with blood and then their polluted silence, and the land is flooded with sewage and stones and fences and moral decay and spiritual decline until the huge and glorious end, which is a source of both worry and consolation.

And I put on Mother's shoes, the gold ones in which she danced in better days, other days, and I rose up and left the house and the estate, and the heels gutted hollow circles from the flesh of the earth, but I laughed at everything, for I am headed to a holy palace, to the throne, and the birds bless me on my journey and the clouds dance in the dark skies and slide from side to side, and I am possessed by a feeling of great relief, for the millstone of my life has been removed and my dreams and visions will quite soon disappear and vanish, and I laugh like the pealing of bells, free and unencumbered, from now on a friend to the fish and the birds in their schools and flocks, and to the water creatures and the river ghosts who live through all eternity underfoot of the humans who walk the earth.

This is sweet happiness, to be spared from the jaws of the world's filth, but it contains no small measure of sadness, too, namely the sadness for Rashid and Leila, those friends of mine trapped in the pages from which they will never be rescued, for not only was I the author of their lives but also their sole reader, their first and their only in this whole wide world, and with no eye to witness the bitterness of their fate they will die along with me, and no man will breathe life into their stories, and Leila and Rashid tug at the hem of my gown in the evening breeze and they plead with me to return to my room for this one last good deed, that is, to finish their stories and give them closure and purpose, for without these they, too, will walk between worlds, from shadow to shadow and from darkness to darkness, like ghosts condemned to endless wandering, never to find their eternal resting-place, and I considered and reconsidered in my tall-heeled golden shoes and my dress as it pranced about with the evening breeze, and I decided to return to my slumbering home in order to open for the last time the door to my room and to sit before my diary and my books, to repay my characters for their long and faithful friendship, and to bring about their dénouements before bringing about my own, for there is no task more honourable to an author than fashioning an ending, tying together the loose ends of a plot, closing all the circles, paying back the scoundrel what is due him and granting mercy to the righteous for his righteousness, bringing the deceased to the land of the dead and leaving the living in life, and not forsaking the edges and fringes of any character mentioned in some offhand way or in some superfluous sentence but, rather, bringing all of them under his wings and writing each one's story to completion, so that even if I myself, the author, live not, at least they, the authored, will, if even for a moment longer than I, for with the turning of the page and the ending of the chapter and the closing of the book, they too will meet their deaths, contained in leather binding and ink spots.

✤

Salah has disappeared and no one can find him.

His room was locked all night long after he fell asleep beneath his quilt and his mother had kissed his forehead, and only in the early morning, when he did not answer the maidservant Amina's summons to the breakfast meal, did they come in hysteria and helplessness to ask my advice. I stood to the side of the door and rapped loudly, calling his name. The boy did not respond.

'I shall smash the lock and break down the door,' I informed him.

The boy remained silent.

I ordered the colonists to bring a sort of iron rod which we used to crack open the lock and break down the door. It opened with a groan.

We entered into the room, Menahem-Mendel, Asher-Yehoshua, Shimon-Yedel and I. The boy's room stood silent and wan, the bedclothes rumpled, the window open, the curtain billowing.

I had them search under the bed and behind the commode and the cupboards, but the boy was not hiding there. It appeared that he had leaped from the sill to the branches of the nearby carob tree and from there descended to earth. Yet another of his juvenile pranks.

I instructed the colonists to search for him in every nook and cranny of the house, but they came up with nothing, even though they poked about in the ancient, labyrinthine secret passageways of the house, one of which, they informed me, led right to the Arab woman's bedroom, which would give a person the chance to spy on the occupant.

Menahem-Mendel showed me the Arab woman's wedding chest, which was open and had recently been plundered. We brought the mother, who had been distraught all morning long over her errant son, and she discovered that her wedding gown was missing.

I ordered the colonists to search the premises. Again, they found nothing. Only that his bicycle was not there and that it had left a path leading out of the estate.

Salah, it seemed, had run away. So be it.

I told the colonists to return to their work. Just as the boy had run away, so too would he return in an hour or two, or at the very latest, in a day.

A few hours later, Neve Shalom
As I walked through the Arab souks in hope of finding Salah hiding among the stalls there, I heard people talking among themselves in Arabic about some new matter whose nature I had not yet discerned. Without intending to I went to the Money-changers' Lane, where I had first met the boy, quite near the office of the pair of pimps, and I was flooded with thoughts and memories of that meeting – how he was standing in the doorway, staring at me with his piercing gaze, and how I mistakenly thought he was feeble-minded, though perhaps he really is, for in spite of his mind and his wisdom, his soul is disturbed from its very foundations, its roots. I was still in the grip of these thoughts when an Arab woman wearing a veil began to pull out her hair and moan and cry out in Arabic.

She continued her moaning and was joined by three other women, a wretched trio of beggars clinking their tin cups for coins from passers-by, who kicked up a wailing lament that brought our brethren, the Jewish money-changers busy exchanging foreign currencies for *bishliks* or francs, to the entrances of their shops. From the noise and the tumult it became apparent that this was a funeral procession, and in no time four drunk vagabonds sauntered by carrying two bodies, and I was overcome with horror and sadness when I realised that these were none other than Saleem and Salaam, and I ran to one of the money-changers, who was sucking pistachio nuts between his teeth, and I managed to obtain the following information from him: as Saleem and Salaam had made their way on the Nablus road, robbers had attacked them and taken their money and ripped out their intestines, and thus their rotting, stinking bodies lay in a forest until a passer-by noticed that even in death they were entwined, embracing, so that it was clear these bodies belonged to Saleem and Salaam, and the Turkish officials were summoned to return them to Jaffa for a proper burial. At hearing this news my legs trembled and nearly gave way, for if this was the demise envisaged by the great author for these two minor characters, that they might adorn the heroes of the story, then what was to become of Salah and Luminsky, and when would their hour arrive, and when it came, in what mantle of terror would it be cloaked?

A few hours later, the Rajani Estate
This has been an awful day.

The boy has not yet returned to his home and I am consumed by thoughts of woe. In despair, I walked the grounds looking for him, dead or alive. I recalled a prophecy he had once made that he would meet his end in the pool where the mule pulled the water-hoist.

Night had already descended and darkness reigned, and I walked there alone. I stopped the diesel engine and there was silence. I peered into the depths of the pool to see if the boy had drowned there, if the water had taken him for all eternity, but it was too dark to see so I stripped off my clothes as I had once done long ago with Salah, and jumped into the cold night water, my senses dazzled, and the branches of the water-trees seemed like venomous snakes, and I dived down and down and opened my eyes in the depths, and there was a blackening figure lying there, coiled like a foetus, and my heart jumped as I pushed myself lower and lower, and the figure seemed to be that of a lifeless boy, and as I approached to touch it it rolled over and I saw its face, and the eyes flickered in the seaweed and its laughter rippled the waves, for this was a genie, the genie of pools and lakes that the peasants would warn about, that it strangled babes in their beds, and this genie bared its teeth at me and drew near to suck my blood, and its watery arms snaked around my neck, and as quickly as possible I rose to the surface and sprang from the pool, snatching up my clothes and dashing from there while I still could, and the genie's laughter echoed behind me, and the trees closed in on me from every angle and direction, and my eyes popped from their sockets in deep astonishment as the orchards lined up in whole battalions, their roots serving as legs and feet, their branches now hands for beating and lifting, and they chased after me in earnest, to bring about my demise, and it was as if the entire estate was bewitched, producing genies and spirits at every juncture and vomiting me out.

Today was a day of grief and disaster. The boy is dead.

Arab shepherds from the village of Sheikh Munis found a strange figure wearing a white wedding gown floating down the El-Ouja river, into which the Wadi Musrara runs. At first this appeared to be the body of a heartbroken young maiden who had taken her life by drowning herself in the deep blue waters of the river. But upon closer inspection they discovered that this was a boy wearing a broad white dress spread like a fan over the wavelets, soon to be worn by the fish splashing about there, with all manner of shells and seaweed and green algae clinging to its folds. The shepherds jumped into the water and pulled the boy from the water. They removed his clothing but his eyes were glazed over and his skin was white and bloated, so that it was clear his soul had already departed.

A different group of shepherds that had passed by earlier told of a maiden they had spied from a distance, and she had entered the southern part of the river where reeds and marshes grew green and plentiful, and there she had removed her shiny shoes and held the branch of a sturdy oak that grew over the water, all the while humming sad tunes until she hurled herself into the water, flowers clutched to her breast.

The Arab shepherds related all this but I never saw the boy's body, for it was being held in the village and had not yet been returned to the estate. No one informed Afifa that her son was dead, but it was clear that her heart, the heart of a mother, had already told her the truth. In the past few days she has been walking from room to room of the house, her hair dishevelled, a yellow flower stuck in a buttonhole, muttering nonsensical words to herself. Even without Dr Al-Bittar it is clear to me that this miserable creature has lost her mind.

Were I a poet or an author I would imbue these pages with all my grief, or pour all the torments I feel now onto the page. But my hand is truncated and the pages are nothing but pages, so the only thing left for me to do is to read them again from beginning to end and to marvel at their conclusion.

The members of Hovevei Zion heard the news and came to ask what would become of the colony, which was destined to become the loveliest of all colonies in the Land of Israel, with its tremendous potential to be a paradigm for the entire colonisation process here.

I responded feebly, telling them my strength was gone, my blood drained, and sadness had completely poisoned my insides. Deep down I had already made the decision to leave this place, removing myself from the estate for ever.

How beautiful are the waters of the Tigris, its banks lined with palm trees, the fronds of which reflect in the greening waves, and I collect flowers on my way to him, the famed red flowers growing since time immemorial in Baghdad, as well as strangely shaped yellow flowers and orange flowers with squared stamens, and all of these I gather into a wreath, which I braid into my hair, and passers-by regard me with concern and worry and tell one another that this is the lovestruck young woman who walks by the Tigris singing songs to herself in a voice loud and clear, and as they watch in astonishment I dance and prance about, turning wildly, wringing my wrists and shaking my hips and belly, for this is a dance of seduction woven into a dance of mourning, mourning the unrequited love of my youth for a merchant of magic who passed from town to town, and with every movement of my foot and every note of my song my great love foams and froths, and where will these fountains and springs lead me but to the good river and the palm trees bent over its banks? and I grasp a trunk and hang from its fronds, its meaty leaves, and wedding songs jingle on my

tongue, and against the backdrop of this mêlée of senses the waters of the Tigris pass beneath my bare feet, and my white tunic flutters in the breeze and the petals of many flowers waft in the wind, and in my heart I wish that this moment will never end, for thus I shall be suspended between heaven and earth, above the river, singing to the memory of a love that is gone and shall not return, drowned for ever like the waters of the river as they plunge to the depths, and as I sing with great power the palm fronds break and I fall to the water's abyss, to the gurgling vortex, and its touch is cold and bracing, and the song still resounds in my throat, for even if this love drowns, the song shall live for ever, and the cloth of my dress is so heavy and the water surges forward with gusto, filling the pockets and folds and I am dragged downwards, downwards, beneath the surface, and the blue waves cradle me passionately, pushing a wet tongue into my mouth, and as this sweet water passes to my throat and lungs I rejoice and call out to the river to take my soul, for death is preferable to my life, and I press the flowers to my bosom, to my breasts, and I bleat with a mouth now filled with water and a throat now sweetly clogged and an emptiness of the darkest blackness, and black-haired I float upon the river Tigris, my eyes wide open but my soul departed, and my cut flowers are now beaded with water droplets, and they are still alive and they shine brightly even as they are swept along by the river, from wave to wave, from bank to bank, and they are stripped of their petals and their stems wither and only the song I sang before my death will continue to be heard from the mouths of shepherds and wanderers and passers-by.

A few hours later, the Rajani Estate

A caravan of Arabs brought the body to the estate and placed it on the ground floor, in the same place in which the body of the boy's father had lain just a few months earlier. According to Muslim tradition, the body of the deceased must not be kept waiting for burial, so Salah had to be buried that very evening.

His mother did not come to greet him; she wandered about the paths of the estate muttering and mumbling strangely. Even Amina the maidservant did not come to lament and wail. She was too weak.

The Arabs bearing the body gazed at me with mixed expressions of respect and deep hatred. I told them to leave me alone with the body.

They complied.

I closed the door behind me with a pounding heart.

On a wooden pallet, which looked like an altar, his body lay under a grey blanket. I peeled away the sides just a little.

Until today I had never been so close to a dead man, not to mention someone who had been as dear and beloved to me as a son. His lips were pale, his cheeks bloated with water, and to my horror his eyes, dead and glassy, were still wide open. It seemed that the Arab shepherds were not possessed of the most basic manners that would have obliged them to close the eyes. So I pulled down the lids but could not bring myself to gaze into the pupils for I feared that the piercing, heartbreaking look I would see there would not leave me until my dying day.

Now there is great tumult and commotion in the house as the hour of the burial approaches. This will be sparsely attended, neither by peasants nor dignitaries. Afifa and the maidservant will not be present. Only a handful of the shepherds who found him will carry the stretcher and bear him the whole long way to the cemetery, to his final resting-place, where he shall find the tranquillity he never found for the entirety of his brief life.

❧

Father's mare neighs at me when I draw near and mount it and gallop it to the sand dunes, for this is a day to set the world on fire, to punish the wicked as they deserve, and we sail through the desert breeze and breathe the good and curative dust, each intake of air bringing courage to carry out what needs to be done, and the horse nods and smiles with her full mouth of teeth, for this matter, this scheme, is proper and good, and in the afternoon, when the sun hangs full and burning in the desert skies and all the tribesmen are shut tightly inside their tents and curled up in heated sleep or sipping water or preparing coffee, I sit high upon my horse near a palm tree and proclaim, O tribesmen, may Omar be cursed! But no one seems troubled by this pronouncement, apart from two runny-nosed, black-eyed children who leave off from their game, so I call out more forcefully this time, O tribesmen, may Omar be cursed, for he murdered my father and committed adultery with my mother, and three old and toothless women step from their tents to curse me for disturbing their rest, but I call out, even louder this time, until Omar's son Nader appears with a dagger in hand and says, If you continue to shout such nonsense I will slit your throat, for you have insulted my father's honour and that of my family, and I say, Summon your father and I shall slay him here and give him the death he so deserves, and by this time the men and other members of the tribe have risen up and stepped outside their tents so that a circle has formed between the two of us, and the onlookers watch with curiosity to see how this challenge will be resolved, and I say, It was your father who murdered my own, as was revealed to me by his ghost, trapped as it is between heaven and earth, and Nader says, Bring us swords, and at this time Omar and my mother emerge and stand with the crowd and Omar says, What is transpiring here, and I say, Your son has challenged me to a duel, and when I am finished with him I shall come after you, you villain, you scoundrel, for you are a messenger of death, and Mother throws her hands into the air and says, In Allah's Name, the boy is addled in the wake of his father's death, forgive him his troubling behaviour, and now, Rashid, come home, for your mother's sake, and I say, You are not my mother, you are a bitch in heat for Omar's seed, and the men grow excited at the thickening quarrel and toss swords to me and to Nader, and a battle ensues, between us, between our clever swords, and at times Nader takes the lead and attacks while I draw back, and at other times it is I who attack and Nader who withdraws, and Father's spirit buzzes in my ears and imbues me with courage, and with a jump and a juggle I spear Nader's heart with my dagger and kill him, his blood spurting, and Mother faints, and I call out, Omar, now it is your turn, for you are an adulterer, obstinate and irredeemable, a murderer of fathers, and Omar drips sweat and his eyes shine with fear, and he takes up a different sword provided to him by his friends, and he charges with the intention of beheading me, but I hold him off, this man who is nothing more than an admixture of faint-heartedness, and his face and body are covered with scratches and in another moment I will ring out the final, victorious blow, which shall reverberate through all his organs and limbs and bring about his death, but just then Omar commits an indescribable act of villainy, for his sword has been secretly tipped with the poison of a desert bloom by his cohorts, and the blade shines with green venom so that a single tiny scratch on my shoulder renders me weak all at once and my blood runs dry and ceases to flow, and I call out, Oh, I have been poisoned by this scoundrel incapable even of fighting a just battle with his enemies, and Omar stands facing me, his legs parted, his sword plunging deeply into my neck, and the poison and venom froth inside me, killing me and bringing an end to my story, but with the remainder of my strength I turn the poison-tipped blade towards him and when my eyes shut I know the deed has been done properly and Omar the evil has fallen to the sand of the desert, fallen and died, and my father's soul is tranquil and appeased.

18 March 1896, Neve Shalom

The boy's burial is over and done with and now I am hidden

away at home in Neve Shalom. When Her Ladyship caught sight of my startled, frightened face she desisted from her usual tyranny. I have told her nothing of the boy's prophecy about the child in her womb, but this I know for certain: from the day of the baby's birth and until it has completed two years of life, I shall know no peace.

The colonists, before being sent home never to return to work at the estate, helped themselves to various objects from the house that would aid them in the future, such as bed linen and toiletries and trifling *objets d'art* and copper jugs and glasses, as well as pages from Salah's room they would use for burning to keep warm or for cooking. One of the colonists found an envelope with my name on it and hastened to bring it to me. Quickly I understood that this was a farewell letter written by the boy before he set out for the river. He wrote:

To my friend the good angel, the angel of destruction, the saboteur, the beloved,

In my passage to the world of truth I shall no doubt discover for myself the sins and crimes of those who walk the earth, and thus I shall know with utmost clarity whether you are my father's murderer, as the ghost whispered in my ear, or whether this was a false and libellous accusation, as you claimed.

Whether you committed this crime or you did not, know that you still sinned against the soul of a boy who loved you truly and innocently, a boy who opened the window of his soul to you and to whom you were as an older brother or a beloved father, a man to be revered and emulated and admired for his body and his mind and his speech, but you threw the fruit of this beautiful love to the winds and acted according to your inclinations and your greed for the purpose of taking over and ruining our home, you usurped a garden that you coveted for yourself and your people, so that you could establish a colony there, or a town or who knows what, and what is left of all your toil and of your plundering dreams, what is left but a woman with a sorely disturbed mind and a grand house in a state of ruin and neglect and a boy about to die on the water steps of a great river?

Once you told me, my friend, that even you, like me and like many others, keep a diary, and in it you write everything that transpires and you record your thoughts and emotions. I would give thousands upon thousands of gold coins to read that diary in order to shed light, even if only a weak light, on this soul that contains softness and love along with cruelty and evil, and appears on the outside to be an advocate of peace and a lover of all creatures but from within is rotten and vile, like those oranges at our estate still hanging from the branches but already shot through with rot and mould.

There were seven pages of this, densely written, all in the strange language of a tortured soul hanging in the balance between life and death. He laid out his prophecies again, too, some of which I had already heard, the simple-minded tales of war and worms of fire and all manner of other calamities and misfortunes, but now he included new ones that had been revealed to him.

And what was the nature of these new visions? To begin with, prophecies about my life, such things as the grief of losing our baby daughter but the consolation of bringing three more lovely daughters into the world, followed by their children and their children's children. As I read those lines they began to seem true to me, and my body trembled for it might well be that the boy was right about everything and knew the truth of all the ages and all the actions and all the secrets.

After that, on the next page, he described the war between the Jews and the Arabs, how it would grow huge and cause enormous suffering and bring about horrible death, and how it would end, and these lines held within their folds one message that was both wondrous and awful, and caused my soul to flutter as if ready to depart:

> I shall never be privy to the contents of your diary, but another diary, which exists and is revealed to me, is the one not yet written of the chronicles of future days, and it contains acts of glorious heroism as well as sin and injustice, and at the head of all these is the war that I have been predicting but which no resident of Jaffa has been willing to take to heart.
>
> In this missing, absent diary, available only to the eyes of a prophet, I can see all the actions of your people, the Jews, and they will continue to come to this land in small numbers, as I have said, and they will remove the Arabs and push them from their livelihoods, then from their lands, and we and our descendants shall proffer our hands in peace but our offers shall not quickly be answered, and in their place will come skirmishes and tussles and strife, to be replaced by murder and slaughter, and I cried to witness the enormous wave of blood that will bathe this land, and the sweet earth that will become polluted with slain and uprooted bodies.
>
> And there shall be twelve wars between you and us, the first of which is a war of fire in which you will gain

the upper hand and banish us by sea; next shall come the war of dry birds, and the war of bitter lakes, and the war of wickedness, and the war of the east, and the war of the hill-dwellers, and the war of those who hold the horns of the altar of sacrifice, and the war of the besieged city, and the war of the sheaves, and the war of the ivory-tusk elephants, and the war of the burrowers, until the last war, after which—

I laid down the letter and sobbed deeply and bitterly, for these were events that would take place in the future, some one hundred or two hundred years hence, but they appeared to the reader as implausible vicissitudes but somehow also as absolutely possible. He closed the letter with the line of a poem he penned for me, free of charge.

14 May 1896, Neve Shalom
For a full month or two I have written nothing in this diary for fear that by touching these pages I will once again bring a curse upon my head.

But today is a special day, the day on which we are leaving Jaffa and travelling northwards to the colony at Rosh Pina. The Jewish Colonisation Association offered me the position of head of the colonists and to be responsible for setting up new colonies, and I was tempted, and accepted.

Her Ladyship was particularly understanding and agreed to our departure from Jaffa. She was well aware of my grief and mourning and my broken spirit, and her noble soul saw fit to close up her thriving dental practice and travel far north with me. For this I am extremely grateful to her.

Were I the only party involved we would have left at least a month ago, but we were forced to wait for the nuptials of Her Ladyship's sister, Rivka, née Blumstein, to David Kumar, a fine couple. The wedding took place last night in the synagogue in Neve Tzedek and was attended by the élite of the Land of Israel, for David is the head of Hovevei Zion and the bride captures every heart with her beauty and grace. A rumour has already spread among the residents of Jaffa that we shall soon be gone, and our joy at this match and its celebration are tempered by the sadness of departure. Many of the men reminisced of time spent with Her Ladyship in the cafés, and their wives took liberties and placed their hands on Her Ladyship's belly and wished her well and offered advice on how to ease the pain of childbirth.

The bride took notice of my mood and said, 'Your face is sad and sallow. Is this your wedding gift to us?'

'No,' I said, 'but know this: your husband shall be a famous doctor among the Jews and hospitals shall be named for him. You will be happy together all your days.'

She embraced me; tears were in her eyes. I kissed her hands and left.

Today we loaded our belongings onto a wagon that will take us north and we padded it with many pillows to make Her Ladyship and the foetus comfortable. The Arab movers carried everything from the house to the wagon, back and forth, back and forth, and I was astonished at how, in so little time, we had managed to fill our sacks with so many good things – Her Ladyship's dental equipment; my books and diaries; Her Lady-ship's dresses, sewn by Arab women; and all sorts of wonderful things we purchased in the souks. And when we were safely on the way, my heart filled with the hope that for many long years I would not need to set foot in this city again or visit its alleyways, for the memories of these strange days, which are recorded in this diary, have seared my soul, causing it to become unmoored and agitated.

And yet when we passed the colony of Sarona, near Wadi Musrara and close to the gate of the Rajani estate, I could not help myself, in spite of Her Ladyship's orders, and I told the horseman to stop the wagon and I took a side path that led into the grounds of the estate.

The sign once posted there had fallen and was broken and the gate stood open, hanging loosely, indications of neglect everywhere. From the day of Salah's death no one had worked the land of the estate, since the colonists had been sent packing; some had returned to Mother Russia while others had emigrated to America, each to his own strange destiny.

I walked slowly, sinking into the mud, bad weeds springing up on all sides, and suddenly the house came into view, its windows shattered, goat and mule dung on the veranda, its rooms covered with soot from the many fires lit by passers-by taking a break in their journey and preparing coffee or a meal.

One day in the future perhaps some man – Jew or Arab – will discover the beauty of this fine estate and will adorn it in finery, but for now it is nothing but a home to insects and reptiles and the fruit flies so satiated with all the rotten fruit.

As we made our winding journey northwards, Her Ladyship slumbering, her head on my chest, I gazed at this strange land – in which Arabs live in tin shacks and huts and large cities, and here and there a smattering of Jewish colonies – and I wondered how it is that lovers can become enemies, and a pleasant twilight breeze can become a hot eastern wind, and I envisaged rivers and streams filling with pollution and filth, their waters poisonous and dangerous, and land parched and burning, and encampments overflowing with people, and at the time the boy's prophecy, which he wrote about in his farewell letter, echoed in my ears, and that wondrous and awful demise he described seemed to take shape before my eyes, and I repeated those few lines he had written about the future, and I could hear his serious voice, and a mixture of blessings and curses, and my thoughts led me to the baby in Esther's womb, and before the tears could reach my eyes I grasped Her Ladyship's fingers and reassured myself that this was a false prophecy made by a tortured soul who had taken his own life, and still I knew that every night, to the end of my days, at the hour I would sink into bed and fall into the bosom of sleep, his image would visit me.

Just then Her Ladyship awakened and she said, 'I need to pass water.' I had the coachman stop the wagon at the side of the road. Her Ladyship lifted her skirts and did what she had to, and her manner was cool and haughty, cold-hearted and determined, and I knew these were the same traits of character that would help her withstand the crises to come, and I was overcome with love for her.

Before we left Jaffa for this new chapter in our lives, which I hoped would be better and more successful than its predecessor, I wished to locate the man I had banished from my life and for whom I felt pangs of guilt for having behaved towards him badly and unfairly.

I asked after the Wildebeest in all the Jewish quarters, but no one had seen him or knew where to send me, for he had left no tracks or traces. There is no way of knowing what will transpire from day to day concerning a man with no wife. Without the bonds of marriage he is as a driven leaf, puts down no roots, flits from place to place, from nectar to nectar.

Then one day an urgent message came to the house by way of

one of Nuriel's sons. He told me that the Wildebeest had just bought a bottle of Yemenite wine from his father's kiosk and if I came quickly perhaps I would find him there before he began his wandering from place to place.

I hastened to the kiosk, but the Wildebeest had already headed for the port so I raced over the sand dunes of the Manshiyeh neighbourhood and passed through the teeming souks and made a path through the many Arabs carrying on business there, touching the wares and examining the livestock, and at last the Wildebeest appeared before me as I turned a corner. His back was stooped and his beard full, his clothes were dirty and he looked dejected and desperate.

I put a hand on his shoulder. 'Friend,' I said.

He gazed at me with empty eyes and frowned in disappointment.

'I have come to ask your forgiveness,' I said.

'You are an evil man,' he said, 'just like this land.'

'I slandered you without cause,' I said. 'Forgive me.'

He said, 'If I forgive you or I do not, it is all the same, for I am leaving here for ever.'

'To where?' I asked.

'America,' he told me. 'Perhaps my luck will improve there. All the strength and energy I have expended here on the colonists, male and female alike, has brought me nothing but failure.'

'Nevertheless,' I said, 'let me pass on this prophecy, which was given to me, and know that it is true: you will be a very famous poet, and your poems will be remembered for ever.'

He said, 'I have despaired of poems and stories. I have found no consolation in them for life's evils. Now leave me be for my ship sails in an hour.'

'And what about the poem that caused such strong feelings in all people?' I asked.

'Wasted effort,' he said. 'I never completed it.'

'Well,' I said, 'here is the missing line: "Our hope has not yet vanished."'

He savoured it for a while like a man tasting the sweet fruit of Paradise. His eyes flickered for a moment before extinguishing. He embraced me warmly, then ran for his ship.

I watched as he hopped into one of the Arab boats that passed from pier to pier. Downcast colonists and red-skinned Russians joined the boat and a sea breeze sprayed saltwater.

As they pulled away towards the ship anchored in deep water, the muezzins raised their voices from the mosques of Jaffa, their trilling call to prayer inspiring awe up and down the port.

Before the last of their calls had died out, the Wildebeest's boat had disappeared into the horizon of the rocky sea.

Epilogue

Isaac Luminsky left Jaffa for the north of the country, where he worked as a high official helping to settle the Galilee for the Jewish Colonisation Association. His eldest daughter was born at Mishmar Hayarden but died after only two years from the complications of an intestinal disease.

Luminsky devoted his life to two ambitious and contradictory goals: the first was the massive purchase of land in Palestine, especially in the Lower Galilee, from Arab *effendis*, a process that left the tenant farmers dispossessed of their livelihood and of land they had worked for years. These lands were later used for the Jewish villages and kibbutzim that carried the banner of socialist ideology.

His second goal was the advancement of rapprochement and appeasement between Jews and Arabs in the Land of Israel, which he carried out in a lively, energetic and often controversial manner.

Salah Rajani was buried alongside Saleem and Salaam in the Muslim cemetery that overlooks the sea, now within the Tel Aviv-Jaffa city boundary. This cemetery fell into disuse over the years and was forgotten. Today it is in the grounds of a large luxury hotel and a public park that plays host to homosexual encounters. Afifa Rajani was institutionalised until she died in a religious asylum for the mentally unstable in Jaffa, looked after by her maidservant Amina. There are no records with regard to their burial sites. Descendants of the Rajani family escaped from Jaffa by sea during the Palestinian Nakba of 1948 along with 75,000 other Arab residents of Jaffa. They have dispersed and live now in Europe, America, Jordan and Egypt.

Nothing is left of the elegant Rajani estate. After the 1948 war its lands were taken under Israeli control and handed over to the Tel Aviv municipality, which later became the Tel Aviv-Jaffa municipality. A metropolis grew where the estate once stood, many of its buildings in the Bauhaus style. The river next to the estate has dried up and in its place are railway tracks and a highway. The capacious house was razed during the war and the hill on which it stood remained desolate for a long period. A few years ago the land was purchased by a Jewish developer who built three towers on the ruins: one square, one triangular and one circular. They house businesses and a commercial and entertainment centre.

Arab Jaffa was conquered in 1948 by the Jews after aerial bombardment, a naval siege and the controlled blasting of neighbourhood buildings. After the fall of the old city, the Muslim districts and the Arab souks fell into disrepair, and over the years a large park was planted on their remains and is now a pleasant backdrop for young couples on their wedding day. Much of the Neve Shalom neighbourhood and that of the adjacent Arab town of Manshiyeh were destroyed and are now mostly fields and car parks. The old railway station remains standing, and after a hundred years of neglect is undergoing a restoration.

Author's Note

I wish to emphasise that in contrast to the way it was expressed in the Preface, and also in contrast to the impression that readers may have formed, *The House of Rajani* is absolutely a work of fiction and is not based on any so-called 'diaries'.

The House of Rajani is in no way or form a historical document. It is a work of fiction, and this is how I would ask my readers to treat it.

Alon Hilu
Tel Aviv, 2010

A Note On the Translator

Evan Fallenberg is a US-born writer and translator living in Israel. His novel *Light Fell* was awarded the American Library Association prize for fiction and the Edmund White Award, and his translation of Meir Shalev's *A Pigeon and a Boy* was a PEN Translation Prize finalist and winner of the National Jewish Book Award.

www.evanfallenberg.com